D1244993

SHADOWS

OVER MAIN

STREET

VOLUME THREE

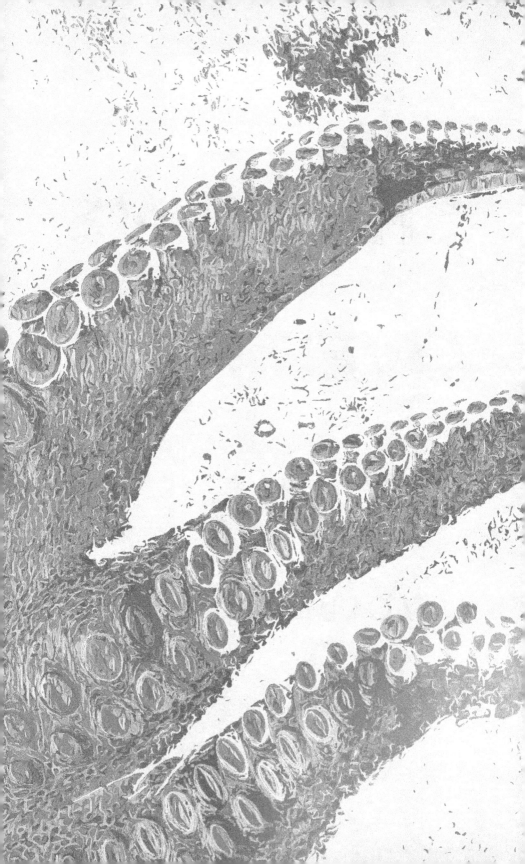

SHADOWS

OVER MAIN

STREET

VOLUME THREE

EDITED BY
DOUG MURANO & D. ALEXANDER WARD

BLEEDING
EDGE BOOKS

Shadows Over Main Street: Volume Three
Anthology copyright © 2023 by Bleeding Edge Books
Print ISBN: 979-8218242329

Anthology edited by Doug Murano & D. Alexander Ward
Cover & interior artwork by Luke Spooner | Carrion House
Cover & interior design by Todd Keisling | Dullington Design Co.

Foreword copyright © 2023 by Doug Murano & D. Alexander Ward
Individual works copyright by their individual authors, unless stated otherwise:
"Homeowner's Association of Unfathomable Horrors Beyond the Stars" previously
appeared in *Shadows Over Main Street: Volume Two*, copyright © 2017 by Jay Wilburn.

This is a work of fiction. Names, characters, businesses, places, events, and incidents
are either the products of the authors' imaginations or used in a fictitious manner. Any
resemblance to actual persons, living or dead, or actual events is purely coincidental.

No part of this publication may be reproduced, stored in a retrieval system, or transmitted
in any form or by any means, without the prior permission in writing of the publisher,
nor be otherwise circulated in any form of binding or cover than that in which it is
published and without a similar condition including this condition being imposed on the
subsequent purchaser.

Bleeding Edge Books
www.bleedingedgepub.com

For Jay Wilburn

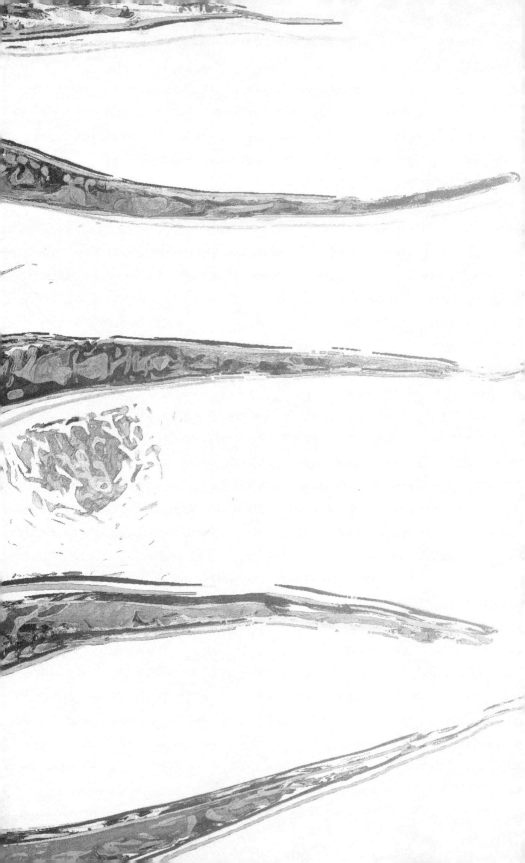

TABLE OF CONTENTS

A BRIEF HISTORY OF SHADOWS OVER MAIN STREET

BY DOUG MURANO AND D. ALEXANDER WARD

This is it. This the end.

We began this journey together about ten years ago based on a relatively goofy idea D. Alexander Ward had to take Lovecraft's Cthulhu Mythos and smash it into the world of Andy Griffith's Mayberry, and then ask writers to do something amazing with that theme.

Why? Because it sounded like a lot of fun.

It seemed like a fine idea at the time, but to say we were both wet behind the ears would be an understatement. We didn't know squat about putting together a book of stories, but we sure had read a lot of them, having both grown up on a steady diet of horror and dark fiction.

The idea also needed refining, needed a larger appeal, and so it was that the ill-fated *Shadows Over Mayberry* was transformed into *Shadows Over Main Street*—and the idea became better for it.

We shopped the themed anthology to several small presses who, for their own reasons, declined. Whatever the substance of their reasons, one thing we heard over and over again was this: *Anthologies don't sell.*

We were just green and dumb enough to kick that feedback to the curb and forge ahead. Eventually, our stubbornness paid off. *Shadows Over Main Street* was published in 2014. Among many excellent tales, each with its own unique take on the mythos, it showcased venerated authors like Gary Braunbeck, Mary SanGiovanni, Nick Mamatas, Chesya Burke, Kevin Lucia, and Brian Hodge, as well as Jay Wilburn and the first-ever published short story by Josh Malerman.

It was a lot of fun. So, we did it again.

The second volume, originally released by Cutting Block Books was, frankly, an embarrassment of riches. It featured stories from Ronald Malfi, Damien Angelica Walters, Joe R. Lansdale, Joyce Carol Oates, Max Booth, III, Jay Wilburn, Eden Royce, and that esteemed practitioner of Lovecraftian horror, William Meikle. Just as with the first volume, all of those tales mingled with the stories of other authors, some known and some new and powerful in their own right, to yield the final result of that tome of eldritch tales.

And still, we were haunted by that refrain: *Anthologies don't sell.*

In the years since, Doug and D. have been finalists for the Bram Stoker Award for their co-edited anthology, *Gutted: Beautiful Horror Stories*, and D. Alexander Ward for his anthology, *Lost Highways: Dark Fictions from the Road*. Doug is a recipient of the Bram Stoker Award for his anthology *BEHOLD: Oddities, Curiosities, and Undefinable Wonders* and he has received the Shirley Jackson Award for *The Hideous Book of Hidden Horrors*.

And to aspiring editors and publishers: Don't let anyone tell you anthologies don't sell.

Not only do carefully curated and marketed anthologies have the potential to sell, but they are the lifeblood of horror and dark fiction, propelling the genre ever forward. It is by way of anthologies that readers are exposed to new works of literature from authors with whom they are familiar as well as authors who are up-and-coming. New voices are vital. If horror and dark fiction are not constantly evolving and giving birth to new voices and ideas, they will wither and die.

Anyway, we were still having fun.

So, we decided to do it one last time.

That same spirit that drove us through the obstacles and hairpin turns of putting out the first volume runs through the inky arteries of these pages, once again populated by storytellers both familiar and new. Elder statesman of the Cthulhu Mythos, Ramsey Campbell practices his art alongside exciting newer authors like Ao-Hui Lin, Eric LaRocca, and Clay McLeod Chapman… to name just a few.

But you already know this. That is why the third and final volume of our journey rests now in your hands.

It has been our passion and our pleasure to curate these books over the years and to share the work of the authors and artists who have so graciously brought them to life.

But now the stars are right. At long last, eternal twilight has come 'round.

Take our hands, dear reader, and let us enjoy this final stroll down Main Street…together.

D. ALEXANDER WARD
Hanover, Virginia

DOUG MURANO
Brookings, South Dakota

OUR SUMMER IN THE PIT

BY CLAY MCLEOD CHAPMAN

The Pit really wasn't much of a pit, if I'm being honest. But what else were we all going to call it? The crater was ours. Nothing but a bowl-shaped cavity carved less than ten feet into the earth, about the width of a Winnebago. Not the biggest depression, I know. Not like Boxhole or Upheaval Dome or any of those other impact craters we learned about in science, but it was definitely deep enough for us kids to crawl in and nearly disappear below its lip.

Could've been a meteorite that made it. Could've just as easily been an abandoned construction site. We all had our theories, but none of us truly knew how it came about.

Who cares where it came from? The Pit was hidden behind our neighborhood so we claimed it as our own and that's all that really mattered to any of us back then.

Up until Kip got sick, that is.

There were five of us that summer. At the beginning of it, at least. August is a whole different story. Let's see, there was me. Kelly and Allison Cassidy. Jason. And—yeah, Kip.

We were all around about the same age, except for Allison. She was older than the rest of us by a year, already in sixth grade while we were still stuck in fifth, which she just loved to bring up whenever she got the opportunity, which was pretty much whenever she opened her mouth to breathe oxygen. Always huffing on about how she wasn't our babysitter:

I'm not changing your diapers, dipshits.

Not that it stopped her from tagging along. Allison didn't have any friends her own age. She was stuck with us just as much as we were stuck with her. Her fish lips. Mudskipper mouth.

Ew, stop looking at me like that.

I wasn't looking at you...

You want to kiss me or something?

No.

Yeah, you do.

Do not...

What forged our friendship? Could've been fate or the simple fact that we all lived in the same subdivision. I don't think we would've been pals if Woodmont wasn't our 'hood. I always got the sense that Jason would've preferred to've played at home alone, where there's AC, but his mom insisted the fresh air would do him good. Kip never talked about his mom or dad, so I don't know what his family's deal was. Truth is, our parents kicked us all out of our houses in the morning and told us not to come back until the street lights flickered on. Until then, they didn't give a flip where we were as long as we stayed out of trouble. We'd hop on our bikes and pedal around the neighborhood. That's it. Wasn't like there was much else to do.

There just wasn't anywhere for us to go, you know?

Where we going? Jason asked us all.

Kip was the only one to answer, our de facto leader. *How about the creek?*

Again?

Got any better ideas?

What about my house?

To do what?

I dunno...

Woodmont was landlocked. There was a cross-stich of train tracks on one side and a highway on the other. Crossing that concrete artery was never really an option. Not on our Schwinns. This was the Atari era, so *Frogger* was on all of our minds. There was this *one story* about that *one kid* from the neighborhood, years back, who tried braving all four lanes on his bike and getting pancaked by some semi before he even reached the median. That truckdriver dragged this kid's Huffy halfway to Powhatan before he even realized there was a mangled corpse caught along his semi's underside, scraping pavement for miles and miles and miles...

None of us knew this kid's name or which house he lived in, but you better believe we all believed that story. You just can't make that kind of stuff up. It had to've happened to somebody at some time, the tale getting passed down through generations of Woodmonters.

So, yeah—no hitting up the highway for us.

That left the tracks. They were certainly less of a threat. The only time an actual train trolleyed through was the butt-crack of dawn, before the sun even came up, so there was never any worry over an Amtrack barreling down on us. Mostly just freight trains chugged through, hefting these open beds piled high with eastern white pines. Trunks for lumber. New homes.

I got an idea, Kip said, hopping on his bike and pedaling off. *Come on. Let's go.*

Where?

Just follow me…

The neighborhood on the other side of the tracks was called Greenfield. I knew some kids from that subdivision, but there was this weird territorial rivalry between us and them, some real old school Sharks versus Jets junk, so we didn't mingle much with those guys. They kept on their side of the tracks and we kept on ours. A truce amongst tribes. Anyone who set foot on the other side was entering into enemy territory and would suffer the consequences.

Going outta my mind, Jason muttered. *I'm so friggin' bored. It's too hot out here.*

Quit whining.

Where we going? Kelly asked and I wish I had an answer, even if she was talking to Kip.

Just up ahead.

Where?

You'll see…

Beyond both of our neighborhoods was this patch of undeveloped land nestled into the surrounding woods. You had to wander further along the tracks to reach it. That meant dismounting our bikes and walking them over the sleepers. Didn't take all that long to get there. Less than an hour, tops. Neither neighborhood could claim it. It wasn't a part of Greenfield and it definitely wasn't Woodmont's. It wasn't anybody's, really. Just this empty stretch of flattened ground. A liminal bit of land. Looked like somebody had tried building something on it at some point, cutting down all the nearby trees and bulldozing the ground, only to call it quits.

That's where we first found The Pit.

Check it out, Kip said. *How cool is that?*

What is it? Kelly asked.

A pit.

Who said it? Wasn't me. Must've been Kip. Maybe Jason, I can't recall. Simply saying the word 'pit' was enough. The name just stuck, I guess. That's what we called it all summer.

The Pit.

What do you think caused it? Kelley asked, transfixed.

Meteor, maybe? I know how nerdy I must've sounded, suggesting some meteorite hit Virginia however many millions of years ago, making this meager depression in the ground. It certainly wouldn't have been the first. I was huge into science back then. Not like real-real science, but the kind of stuff that sort of felt scientific. Science-y. Like, did you know there's an impact crater located right at the mouth of the Chesapeake Bay? No lie. Still there. A big ol' bolide struck the eastern shore over 35 million years ago. One mile deep, over fifty miles wide.

This crater was nowhere near as big as that one, but still. It was ours.

Kip called bullshit. *Yeah, right. That's no meteor.*

Well, what do you think it is?

Kip figured it was the beginnings of somebody's basement. A home was supposed to go there. We were standing in the middle of what would've been a brand new subdivision. If I squinted hard enough, I could almost picture the houses sprouting out from the ground.

So why did they stop? I asked. *Why leave?*

Nobody really had an answer for that.

We tossed rocks into The Pit. There really wasn't much else to do with it. Some weeds sprouted out from the basin. Crab grass, I guess. I spotted a green bottle. Maybe it was blue. Could've been an empty Seven-Up or something else, half buried in the soil. Its color kept changing. Rusted beer cans settled at the bottom. The ashen remnants of a bonfire, courtesy of the Mullet Militia. That's what we called the heavy metal high schoolers who came out here at night to party. They'd drink whatever beer they pilfered from their parents, tossing the empties into The Pit. Our Pit. Sacrificing cats out here in the middle of the night. Or kids.

This is stupid, Allison said. *You dragged us out here for this?*

Yeah.

It's just a stupid hole in the ground.

But that wasn't true. Even I knew that. Felt it, somehow, even from the very first moment. Kip might've been convinced that it was manmade, but a part of me still believed—wanted to believe—that The Pit was the product of hypervelocity impact with an astronomical object. Even a meteor the size of a soccer ball could leave behind a circular depression in the earth's surface. It definitely wouldn't have been the first to hit Virginia, all those millions of years ago. What if a chunk of an asteroid had broken off and landed back here? In Woodmont?

Last one in's a rotten egg. Kip was the first to hop in. He was always the first. He pretended The Pit was a pool—*Cannonball!*—skidding down the slope on his heels. *Come on in!*

Jason was next. Then Allison, eye rolling all the way down.

Kelly and me stood at the edge, our toes poking over the pit's lip.

You going in? She asked me and I kind of just shrugged.

Don't be such a chickenshit, Allison shouted. *Come on!*

Here's the thing. I had a crush on Kelly, but Kelly had a crush on Kip. That's at least what Jason said. If Kip was going somewhere, anywhere, then so would Kelly, and if Kelly was going, then you'd better believe I was, too. That meant Allison was chaperoning her baby sister. Talk about a total dick-killer. Wasn't like the three of us boys were horndogs or whatever. Allison just didn't trust us. She knew what was up, I guess. If I was standing next to Kelly, she'd give me this look—more like a goddamn glare—that said: *Back off, asshole.* It wasn't like I was all doe-eyed around Kelly or anything. She never noticed. The only person who knew I had a crush on her was Jason, but he swore he'd never tell. I would punch him so hard, so help me God.

Who did Kip have a crush on? Good question. I'd say The Pit.

Bones!

Bullshit. Allison was the first to curse out of all of us, since she was a year older.

Look.

Kip was right. Half-buried at the bottom of the Pit, beneath the loose bedding of pebbles, were these sun-bleached teeth. *Are those fangs?* Kip took a stick and started digging around the skull, sweeping the rocks away from its domed slope like he was some kind of junior archeologist and this was our big dig. Pebbles had settled into its sockets, whatever it was.

What is it? I asked, still standing along the ledge. *A cat?*

Bigger than a cat.

A raccoon?

Kip poked his stick through one of its eyeholes in order to loosen it, try and pry it out from the dirt, but it wouldn't budge. He got down on his knees and started using his hands to pull it out. He always wore the same pair of cargo shorts every single day through that whole summer. Maybe they weren't the *exact* same pair, but they were at least the same brand, so it kind of looked like he only had one set of shorts, which was enough for Alison to mess with him.

Better be careful, she started. *Don't wanna get your crusty shorts all dirty…*

Shut up.

What? Your mom can only afford one pair?

Up yours.

Crusty shorts, crusty shorts, crust—

Kip uprooted the skull with his bare hands like a toothsome potato. *Whoa, check it out...* He held it up over his head for us all to see. He shifted his position in The Pit, doing some kind of kneeling 360, dragging his leg over the soft bedding of pebbles. *How friggin' cool is tha—*

I heard Kip hiss.

At first, I thought he was making some kind of caveman sound at Alison, baring his teeth at her. But he dropped the skull and clutched his shin with both hands. Blood immediately seeped through his fingers, not a lot, but enough for us to clench our breaths tight in our lungs.

Kip picked something out from his leg.

A piece of glass. Just a shard of green glass. Maybe it was purple. The color kind of depended on where the sun struck it. A broken bottle, that's all. The whole Pit was full of junk.

You should clean that up, Kelly said and I felt jealous.

Yeah, okay.

Here's the thing: We were always getting injured somehow. This wasn't Kip's first scrape. We were all wounded. Nothing ever needed stitches—or if it did, we never got them. We just sucked it up. Bruised knees and shallow lacerations were just part of our summer.

Which is just to say none of us—not me, at least—gave Kip's cut much thought. Even he forgot all about it. Life just moved on. We all walked our bikes along the tracks as the sun sank deeper into the surrounding trees, listening to the crickets. We never said goodbye to one another at the end of the day. We just broke off at our respective houses, simply heading in for the night, knowing we'd pick up where we left off the following morning.

That evening, at dinner, my mom asked me what we'd been up to that day.

Nothing, I said. Always said.

I never mentioned The Pit, not to Mom or anyone else, even when it was on the forefront of my mind. Always on my mind. I couldn't stop thinking about it. I dreamt of tiny meteors making their way down to Earth, gaining their cosmic velocity before hitting the ground and sending a massive shockwave all through Woodmont, the roads rippling with its impact, until it knocked every last house down in its wake. *Kabooooooom.*

We spent the summer out there.

In The Pit.

We all just gravitated towards it, I guess. Wasn't like there was some conscious decision on our part. Nobody said anything out loud. We'd simply find each other and head for the tracks.

Kip started limping not long after that. He slowed down. He wasn't running around like the rest of us anymore. He just sort of hobbled along, catching up to us. Always out of breath.

Hey, wait up…

He stopped wearing shorts. Which was stupid. Wearing pants in the middle of July?

Slow down!

Sometimes he'd beat us out there. Like he got a leg up on the rest of us, waking up early and getting to work.

Work.

Kip enlisted the rest of us to help excavate the skeletons that were embedded in the gravel bed at the bottom of The Pit. So far, we'd found the remains of a possum, a dog, and what we're pretty sure was a deer.

It's unclear how much we were mingling bones, but we laid out the remains of each animal along the surrounding ground, trying our best to piece together the puzzles of these dead creatures and see if we could figure out which bones belonged to which. Kelly was pretty good at finding the flow of bones. She'd see connections between vertebrae the rest of us just couldn't see, like it was all a jigsaw. Before long, by the middle of July, I'd say, the ground around The Pit was layered in concentric skeletal circles, each one its own animal. Like patterns. Ceramic white. Osseous heatwaves radiating out from our crater.

That's really beautiful, I said to Kelly, immediately regretting it.

You think?

Um… what's that one? I pointed to what could've been a raccoon.

She shrugged. *Skunk, maybe?*

Kip wanted to camp out there. He brought it up one day like it was no big deal. *What if we spent the night?* Allison shot it down straight away. There was no way her and Kelly's parents would ever let them go camping with a bunch of boys, so they were no-gos from the get-go. Jason was down, but he'd have to tell his mom that he was spending the night at someone's house. Me… I felt weird about it. Something was off about Kip's eagerness to come out here at night. In the dark. I didn't like it, whatever it was. I didn't want to. I made up some story about my mother not letting me, which wasn't true. I didn't even bring it up to my parents.

I'm not going to say I was afraid of The Pit, but there was definitely a part of me that wondered what was up with it. Up with Kip. He was looking pretty worse for wear by then. Paler, I guess. Blue. Most of us were getting sunburns from our time outside, while he seemed to be losing his tan. All the colors were sucked out from his skin the longer he was here.

You okay? I asked. *You look kinda sick.*

I'm fine.

Are you sure you don't wanna—

I'm fine.

By late July, there sure seemed to be a lot more bones lining the surrounding ground. You know how Saturn has all those rings of debris wrapped around it? Our Pit had skeletal rings. Skulls and ribs and femurs belonging to all kinds of unknown animals now circled around our hole in the ground. Kelly was making all kinds of patterns by then. A single skeleton could stretch out three or four feet, each bone laid out a few inches from its neighbor. After a while, the bones tended to blend together. Kelly was less concerned about piecing them back the way they were when these animals were still alive, and more—I don't know—just finding a flow for the bones. Letting the skeletons take on their own shape. Their own rhythms. It looked less like a bunch of different dead animals and more like some weird morse code written out in bones.

Can you hear them? Kelly asked me once, staring out at all the patterns. I didn't really know what she meant by it, so I just sort of acted like I hadn't heard her.

We all just kept going out there. Day after day. Wasn't like anyone suggested it. Nobody said anything like, *Hey, who wants to go to The Pit?* Or, *How about we take a ride to The Pit?*

We just went.

If we didn't bike out together, we'd all meet up there.

I was pretty positive Kip was coming out to The Pit without the rest of us. He was always the first on site and the last to leave. When it was time to go home for the day, he'd make up some stupid excuse about staying behind. *I'll catch up,* but he never did. I noticed a sleeping bag rolled up and tucked behind a palette of bricks. Fresh candy bar wrappers littered the grass.

I tried bringing this all up to Kelly one day while we were walking our bikes out to The Pit. *Do you think Kip's okay? Do you think he's acting a little, I dunno... weird?*

What's the matter? Allison piped in before Kelly could. *Worried about your boyfriend?*

Shut up.

When we reached The Pit, I didn't see Kip. I thought we'd actually beaten him out there. First time for everything, I guess.

Ow ow ow...

...Kip?

Ow ow ow...

Kip? We could all hear him, even if we couldn't see him.

Ow ow ow...

He was in The Pit. Rolling on his back. Rutting like a pig.

It was so weird. We all circled around the edge and just looked at him for a while. Watching him grovel. It was hard to tell if he was in pain or enjoying himself. I don't know how long we all stood there, just gawking at him. Felt like forever. I skidded down the slope and grabbed his arm to help him up, but he hissed through his teeth at me, batting my hand away.

Ow ow oowwww...

What's wrong?

Ow ow ow...

His left pants leg was soaked through. It wasn't blood, or not only blood. It was orange. Rusty colored fluid oozed through. I tugged his pants just to see what was going on under there.

Branches of amethyst laced his legs, the veins a deep purple. Blisters speckled his skin. Angry red welts. One of them had popped and I swore I thought it was blinking back at me.

It was.

This gasping aperture budged from the crater of skin.

A mouth.

I could make out the jaws opening and closing.

A worm.

I picked up a bone. A rib or something super-thin. Maybe it was a raccoon penis bone or whatever. I don't know why I did it, I just wanted something in my hand. To poke the worm with. I brought the tip closer to Kip's blister and the worm or whatever actually reached out for it. Budded up less than inch and gripped onto the stick. That worm tugged, so I tugged back.

Ow ow ow. Kip winced and hissed when I pulled too tight.

That is so gross, Allison said. *I'm gonna be sick…*

Be careful, Kelly said to me. *Don't break it.*

Break it?

Go slow, she said. *Wind it up.* I remembered something our science teacher had told us last year and I knew exactly what Kelly was getting at.

Ever seen the symbol for medicine? It's got Asclepius? The god of medicine? He's always got his rod with the serpent all twisted around it. Some people believe it's not a snake at all.

Some say it's a tapeworm.

A guinea worm. The old-fashioned way of removing the parasite was to take a stick and wrap one end around and slowly twist and twist until you tugged the worm all the way out. Guinea worms get so long, sometimes as long as ten feet, living under their host's skin, that it takes months and months to uproot them. You just got to keep twisting and twisting and…

So, we did.

I don't know how long we worked at it. Could've been there for hours. All day for I know. Allison kept complaining how queasy she was feeling, so we got Jason and her to ride their bikes back to Woodmont to go tell somebody's parents. Anybody's parents. Get help.

What about you? Allison had asked her baby sister. *You can't stay here…*

I'll be fine. Just go.

Me and Kelly took turns slowly twisting the rib, winding that worm out from Kip's wound. Whenever one of our wrists got too sore to continue, we'd trade off. That worm had wrapped itself around the entire length of bone. I didn't think a worm could grow that long.

It had to be—what? Two feet? Three? It just kept going and going and still there was more of it, spooling around the bone like pulsating fishing line. There's no telling how far it went.

Me and Kelly never left Kip's side. Never left The Pit. Kip kept moaning. Sweated all the way through his clothes. He had bitten down on his bottom lip so hard, he'd drawn blood.

I'm tired, I said. *Can you take a turn?*

Sure, Kelly said.

When I handed her the bone, our fingers touched. Just for a second. It was more like a graze, skin brushing against skin, but it was enough to send a ripple through me. A shockwave.

Kelly must've felt it, too, 'cause she looked up at me. Felt like the first time we'd ever been alone. Like, truly alone. Just the two of us. We'd spent so much time together, the whole summer, and yet, through it all, through everything, we'd never actually had any time by ourselves before. I mean, even now Kip was there, on the ground, but it still felt like it was just us two.

I'd never noticed how green Kelly's eyes were before.

Or were they purple?

The sun was starting to sink behind the surrounding tree line and I didn't think we were even close to getting the whole tapeworm out.

Kelly must've tugged too hard because the tendril snapped. *Oh, shit!* She almost lost the other half, watching the tapeworm reel itself back into Kip's skin like the draw-string on a doll. But instead of saying something stupid like, *Hi, my name is Polly!,* it was just Kip hissing *ow ow oooooww...*

I caught the tapeworm in time. I pinched the flickering bit between my fingers and gently held on long enough for Kelly to wrap it back around the bone. *That was a close one...* We were running out of sunlight by the breath. I really didn't feel like staying out here at night.

Where were our parents? Where was Jason? Allison?

What do we do now?

Just keep going, I guess.

After a while a winding on the worm in silence, Kelly finally asked, *So how come you never kissed me?*

You knew?

Yeah. I was so embarrassed, so I didn't say anything. For once I was thankful the sun was going down, so she couldn't see how much I was blushing.

Kelly filled up the silence. *Guess I was waiting for you to say something. Why didn't you?*

I was too afraid, I guess.

Of what?

The Pit, I thought. I don't know why. It was the first thing that popped into my mind.

The Pit. Always The Pit. We were pulled back here, into this very same hole, day after day, for months now, rutting through the bones of others, digging deeper. Searching.

It's not too late, Kelly said. *Summer isn't over yet…*

I didn't know what she meant by that.

Kelly closed her eyes first. Her lips parted just enough that I could barely make out her tongue nestled behind her teeth.

She breathed in and held it. Tilted her head to one shoulder. I was supposed to do something, wasn't I? Follow her lead and mirror her movements? Lean in and meet her lips?

I'd never done this before. I didn't know what I was supposed to do with myself. My hands. My whole body felt awkward, overheated. I was still holding onto the tapeworm.

All I could do was close my eyes and ram my face into Kelly's, ram it in so forcefully, with such cosmic velocity that it ruptured the surface of her face, embedding my bones deep into her own and creating an impact crater in her skull that would last millions of years. Molten strands of amethyst fuse our bodies together, her flesh melting into steaming rivulets, while I just force my way in deeper, *deeper,* burrowing as far as my bones will go, *deeper,* my skull a geode that's crawled across the cosmos and now it's cracked open and leaking its lavender passengers into the fertile soil. The type of kiss that would linger long after we're gone.

God, I was never forgetting this summer.

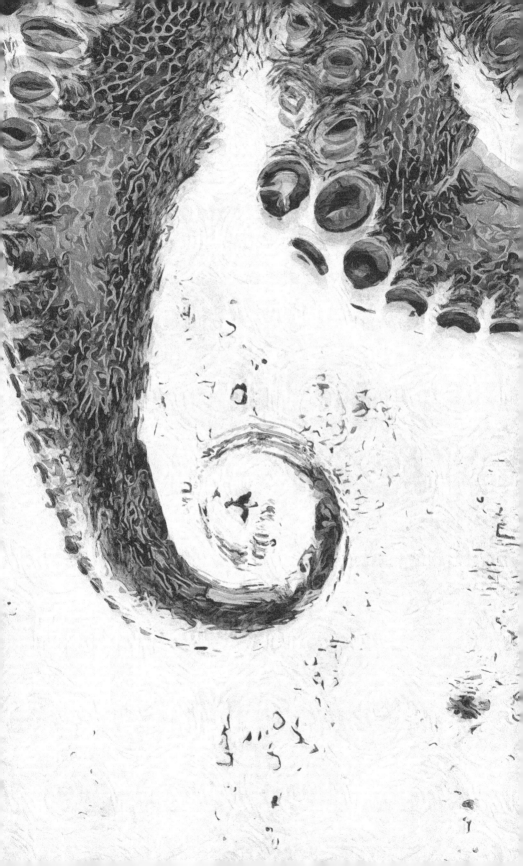

POSTCARDS FROM SAGUAROLAND

BY PEDRO INIGUEZ

1.

Like television static in the middle of the night, visions of aberrant shapes flickered in and out of Gustavo's mind as he dreamed. He stood alone on an expanse of barren land baring only gnarled, dead roots and dry shrubs bristling in a breeze. Something pulled his gaze toward the night sky. Akin to rustling behind a black curtain there were forms—or the hints of forms—skulking in the darkness between the stars. He wanted desperately to look away.

Before he could turn, a hail of meteorites plunged to Earth, the cosmic scattershot strangely inaudible as it decimated the desert landscape. Curious, he took two paces forward. A throng of squirming monstrosities burst from beneath charred, glassy craters. Under the faint glow of moonlight, he could discern only the vaguest of features. Their shapes were amorphous, their extremities gelatinous and pallid and covered in oozing polyps. They scurried forth, thin stalks sprouting from their bodies upon which countless obsidian eyes blinked in tandem. Though they bore no mouths, he knew they were coming to feast upon his flesh.

Gustavo opened his eyes, woken by the cold sting at the small of his back. His eyes adjusted and the dark, vast desert greeted him. Only the world was upside down. Nearby, a cluster of saguaros stood watch, their long limbs menacing in the shadows.

His brain slogged through a haze; he couldn't remember what had happened or how he'd gotten here.

Something punctured his skin before it sheared through the length of his spine, stopping just shy of his shoulder blades. He screamed, the pain flaring throughout his body like a sweeping fire. Instinctively, he tried to flail his arms but a quick glance proved his wrists were bound below his head, his fingers wriggling not more than four feet from a patch of dry desert scrub.

Like syrup, something warm and wet ran along his bare back and past his neck, finally soaking into the tangle of disheveled hair. He tilted his head so that his chin pressed against his chest. Above, thick strands of rope bound his ankles to a shoddy-looking gibbet.

A swell of blood rushed to his head, thrumming to the beat of his heart before cold perspiration trickled down his temples. He had come to know this torture device from his time in another country. When he had been a different person and under the employ of questionable men. Only, he had been on the opposite end of the scaffolding then.

Cold fingers clutched his hamstring and turned him slowly around. Emily Brentwood stood over him, a large blood-stained hunting knife in her hand. A warm smile had been etched across her pale face. Beside her, Dillan Jacob held a torch, the flames illuminating his expressionless face in a raging red light. There were a dozen others he didn't recognize. Gringos like them.

Behind them, a small mob regarded his swaying body like children watching a magician pull a string of cards from his mouth. They were garbed in braids and colorful dresses; in cowboy hats, tight blue jeans, and leather boots. Gustavo recognized their tanned faces from town. The *abuela* with braids. The stone-faced man behind the wheel of the pickup truck. The little girls from the alley. They were his *compatriotas*. His countrymen. Only something was off.

It was then he thought he saw movement, something shifting on their faces. *Under* their faces. He narrowed his eyes; small eyeholes appeared to be cut out of their heads like Halloween masks. Behind the cavities, black, beady pinholes rolled about, staring back, the skin underneath them pale, glistening, writhing.

He gazed across the desert, looking for someone, anyone that could help. Not more than a few hundred feet behind the mob, the amber lights of the warehouse parking lot flickered like fireflies. He licked his lips and tried calling out for help. No words came. A powerful gust blew in. The air nipped at his skin, cooling the blood at his back and turning the hairs on his body prickly like cactus needles. The saguaro themselves swayed delicately side-to-side. But those looked peculiar, too. Under the faint glow of the torch's fire he thought he glimpsed the impressions of flayed, strung-up corpses.

Emily stepped behind him and slid the knife up his back again, the incision ending at the base of his skull. He shrieked and watched a trail of vapor fade into the night sky where the stars didn't flicker, like unblinking eyes.

"They came from the darkness between the galaxies," she said softly into his ear while laying a gentle, frigid hand upon his cheek. "Not by choice, but here we are."

Gustavo felt control over his limbs slip away as they shivered uncontrollably. He knew he was going into shock.

"Their flesh was not meant for the harshness of our sun."

Though his back was starting to numb, he thought he felt, briefly, a scorching sensation radiate along his back. His mind tried to make sense of what he'd been feeling and his imagination drifted into abysmal places. He pictured her nailed fingers plunging into his spine and pulling the skin from his tissue.

"They have asked us to provide them with tinted skins so that they may know the pleasures of walking uninhibited among our world."

"Tinted s-skins?" Gustavo stammered through chattering teeth. He coughed; his every breath more labored than the last. He thought about people that looked like him. Hundreds trekked into border towns like this every day. He thought about his boys, their brown, ashy skin being peeled away.

The postcard. What had he done? His eyes welled with tears, obscuring the world around him.

"More are already on their way. Can you hear them? The song of the Pallid Ones grows louder."

Gustavo heard only the shuffling of feet dragging over gravel in the distance. Slowly, the scraping grew louder, jarring in the silence of the desert. He craned his neck. Something vile approached. It was the color of a cold, dead cadaver, its skin gleaming with something slick and moist.

As the distorted thing neared the light of the torch, the flesh on Gustavo's back tingled. *No.* He shook his head and shut his eyes so hard they hurt. It was all he could do.

He wept. This couldn't be real. Things like this only happened in dreams.

2.

Gustavo woke abruptly inside the sedan, simultaneously bracing his left hand against the driver's side window while slamming his foot on the brake pedal. Once he'd realized that the car had been parked, he eased up and sighed. *Idiot.*

The dream had been terrifying, he knew that much, though the details had already evaporated into the ether. He was only certain that his head was pounding. He rubbed his temples and glared at the empty tequila bottle on the mat. For a moment he had forgotten where he had been. Everything came back as soon as he peered out the smudged window. It was the same dull border town, the buildings still small and unimposing, the tinted windows from local shops etched with the scrawl of old graffiti. The paint on most buildings had faded, washed out by the light of an oppressive sun. The foundations appeared to be sinking into the Sonoran Desert, soon to be swallowed whole and forgotten like every outpost he'd driven through. It was the kind of cookie cutter oasis found along the highways of the American Southwest. Except this place had been different. This place really was a refuge.

Gustavo got out and stretched. The sun began its descent over some low-lying hills on the western horizon, its fading light casting long blue shadows across the boulevard. He looked at his watch. There was still time.

He ambled up Main Street for half a block until he came upon a phone booth. He dug out some change and dropped a dollar's worth of quarters through the slot.

As far as children went, Carlitos and Hector were two of the loveliest boys a father could've been gifted. Though, he wasn't sure they thought so highly of him. Not anymore. And Sandra. Well, he knew what his wife thought of him. He tried to convince them, and himself, that leaving was for the best. Things had gotten too dangerous for him to stay. Besides, there would be good jobs on the other side and he could wire them money. But sometimes plans had a way of dying premature deaths.

How long had it been since he had heard their voices? He had stopped counting the days for some time. Since the money dried up. Gustavo cradled the phone between his face and shoulder. His hands trembled as his finger hovered over the grimy keypad. He had rehearsed the speech dozens of times during those long, lonely drives though empty stretches of highway. He knew he'd say that he loved them. That he was really going to straighten up his act this time. But now he had found a town that offered decent work and welcomed people that looked like them. Soon, their troubles would be over and he would be able to send for them across the border. No more begging gringos for change at the crossing line. No more watered-down charro bean dinners. He punched in his old phone number.

The line was dead.

His heart sank into his belly and he swallowed a hard lump that may as well have been a stone. Seldom existed worse tortures in this life than broken promises.

He hung up and shoved two fingers into the coin release slot. It was empty.

A pickup truck ambled down the street, its driver, a sullen-looking Mexican man in a cowboy hat, eyed him suspiciously from the dark of the cab. Gustavo broke eye contact and kept on.

On the walk back to the car he stopped to gaze at his reflection on a tinted window. He was looking gaunt, thinner than he remembered. Even his skin had tanned considerably from those long days driving through the desert. He ran a hand through his greasy black hair, doing his best to part it neatly in the middle. Then he wiped the crust from his bloodshot eyes. He looked like shit but it was the best he was going to look for a while. At least until he could find a place of his own with a shower. He looked at the signage above. *Jacob Drugstore.*

Gustavo peered through the open door. A small spinning rack atop the counter contained a collection of postcards.

Inside, a young blonde cashier no older than eighteen flashed a smile that beckoned him forth. Gustavo shuffled inside.

"Hey, amigo" the cashier said. "Name's Dillan Jacob. I'm covering for my Pop so let me know if you need any help."

Gustavo nodded. "Just going to take a quick look," he said. He spun the rack, gazing at everything from ephemeral collages to postcards with local Southwest-themed artwork.

He plucked one that caught his eye: A colorful abstract oil painting of the open desert, majestic saguaros seemingly waving their arms in welcome. *Greetings from Saguaroland.*

"I'll take this one and enough postage to send this to Mexico," Gustavo said, sliding the man his last twenty.

"Of course," Dillan said, ringing him up and handing him his change. "Great pick."

"Do you have a pen?"

Dillan smiled again, handing him a blue ballpoint.

Gustavo printed his old address on the back of the card. *Please, God, tell me they still live there.* He scribbled a quick note: *If you can make it here, find me. Sending my love. Gustavo Luna.*

It's all he could do now.

"I can mail that for you," Dillan said eagerly. "Mailman comes this way in about half an hour."

Gustavo looked up at him, considered his offer for a moment, and nodded. "Thank you, my friend."

"My pleasure, amigo. We're all here to help."

Outside, the sun had vanished behind inky hills. He made his way back to the car and opened the atlas. The location of the warehouse had been marked in red ink, just beyond the old train tracks on the southern edge of town.

He started the car. The streets gave way to dirt roads as the town faded in his rearview mirror. The wash of light pollution gradually receded and the desert grew darker and wider. On either side of road, the silhouettes of saguaros reached out for him like desperate marionettes. He wasn't sure if they were pleading for help or to trying to swallow him whole like voracious monsters.

The car rumbled past the tracks. Ahead, the warehouse loomed behind a barbed wire fence, its corrugated exterior depressing and stark under the light of the stars. Tonight, he would start a new chapter. He wouldn't mess this up. Not for anything in the world. He pulled into the warm amber glow of the parking lot.

3.

The morning sun beat down on Gustavo Luna's face as he stepped out of the car, its light especially cruel and blinding. He shielded his eyes with both hands and surveyed his new surroundings.

As far as he could tell it was a small town dotted with liquor stores, gas stations, mobile homes, and janky watering holes. On either side of town, the Sonoran Desert stretched into the horizon. Nothing but crumbling highway billboards, towering saguaros, dry scrub, and dirt. Heaps and heaps of dirt. It had probably all been unincorporated land nestled along the Mexican border as far as he could tell.

Gustavo had come across countless places like this, though some had been affixed to prairies or snow-covered valleys. In his experience, they were all the same. Each town had its share of drunkards, dullards, or unwelcoming bigots. There were always the kind ones too, but those were getting rarer these days. There hadn't been much on the jobs front in any of them, either. Not for someone like him. He supposed there were always big cities but those posed the biggest danger. Too many people. Too many eyes. He wasn't about to be shipped back to a country that chewed you up and spat you out a killer or poorer than when you first went in. He wondered how his boys were doing and bit his lip. Wherever they were he hoped they knew that he was trying his best.

He leaned over the atlas on the hood of the car and traced his finger along the last route he had taken. Where had he gotten lost? He shook his head. Maybe he'd dozed off, taken a wrong turn somewhere. Wherever he was, it wasn't on the map. He covered his mouth to stifle a yawn. His eyes felt heavy and dry. It felt like he had been driving for ages. A dark journey of never-ending blacktop. He folded up the atlas and tried to gather his bearings. He stood near the corner of Main Street and Rawlins, which appeared to be the town's main hub; all thrift shops, convenient stores, and tax service centers. It would be as good a place as any to start.

A terrible scent wafted on a warm current of air. He covered his mouth and fought the urge to wretch right there on the street. Flies hovered ravenously over something lodged in a storm drain just beside the car. The anomaly was opaque, its flesh cancerous, like a dead jellyfish swathed in small, burbling cysts. He prodded the thing with his shoe and the flies scattered. Nothing but a plastic bag crawling with maggots, its insides filled with something moist and rotten. He decided he didn't want to know.

His car's engine ticked as it struggled to cool in the sunlight and he thought he could use some cooling off too. He hopped up on the sidewalk and took refuge under the shade of an awning.

Next, he would do the usual and go door-to-door inquiring about jobs until it was time to pack it in and leave. He'd likely be told the same thing: *Sorry, amigo. No trabajo. No work here.*

An old brown woman in braids glared at him behind a barred window in her home across the street before drawing the curtains shut. She reminded him of his abuela and better days.

He sauntered down the street, eyeing the local shops and businesses for any Help Wanted signs but everything was bust. Halfway down the street a pair of dark-skinned girls in matching pink shirts gawked at him from the maw of a darkened alley. He waved. They turned and scampered into the shadows. So, his *jente* were here. A welcome sight. But the odd stares. They were likely wary of strangers like he was. Always on guard. He didn't blame them. You never knew who was going to turn you over to the *migra*. There was nothing promised about the Promised Land. Any day could be your last here.

Something caught his attention just a-ways down the block. The large signage painted on the front of an unassuming building at the end of the street was hard to miss: *Saguaroland Staffing Agency*.

He half-jogged there and wiped the sweat from his brow with the back of his hand. It was a dusty beige building with cracking walls and dented venetian blinds, not too unlike the rest of the town's aesthetic. Inside, the cool conditioned air was a welcome relief on his warm skin. A pale, blonde woman behind a desk smiled through ruby lips and waved him over.

"Welcome, amigo," she said. "How can I help you?"

Gustavo cleared his throat. "I saw your sign. I am looking for work."

"Well, come on in," she said sweeping her hand over a chair in front of her desk. "My name's Emily Brentwood, by the way."

"Gustavo Luna," he said, sitting down. Besides Emily, the office was empty. A muted television set mounted on a corner wall played a news segment about the alarming rise of missing people in the state. Which state? He wasn't exactly sure where he was just yet.

"A pleasure." She reached into a drawer and retrieved a few forms.

"I don't have papers," he interrupted. He looked at his mud-caked shoes, his fingers tapping anxiously on the table.

Emily placed her hands over his. They were cold but soft. Sincere. Gustavo blushed, suddenly self-conscious of the missing pinky on his left hand and the tattooed knuckles on his right. He peered up. Her eyes had already settled where he didn't want them to and he pulled away. They were scars from another life. Like an itch, he wanted to shed his old skin and molt into another. Had it been possible to be two different people in a single lifespan?

He hoped she didn't ask about the markings.

She didn't.

"You have very strong hands, Gustavo. There's an opening for an overnight position at a warehouse just outside of town. They could use a guy like you."

"But-"

"All under the table." She winked. "We get lots of undocumented laborers around these parts. We consider ourselves something of a sanctuary town."

Gustavo eased back into the chair and smiled. It had been the first time in ages.

"Now, the job is minimum wage but you can expect quarterly raises if they decide to keep you. Can you start tonight?"

"Yes, of course!" Moisture started to pool under his eyes. He couldn't believe a word of it. He wanted to call his children and share the news. In time, the nightmare would be over. The terrors of poverty, the cartels, of lives unfulfilled began to look more and more like an obstacle that could be surmounted with time and care and patience.

"Please don't cry," she said smiling once more through bleached teeth. "Everything will be ok. I promise."

Gustavo wiped the tears from his eyes and nodded.

Emily scribbled an address on the back of a business card and slid it across the table.

"It's just over the train tracks," she said. "They're going to love you."

He wanted to hug her. The world suddenly looked a little brighter. This truly was a land of opportunity. Of redemption.

He smiled again. This couldn't be real. Things like this only happened in dreams.

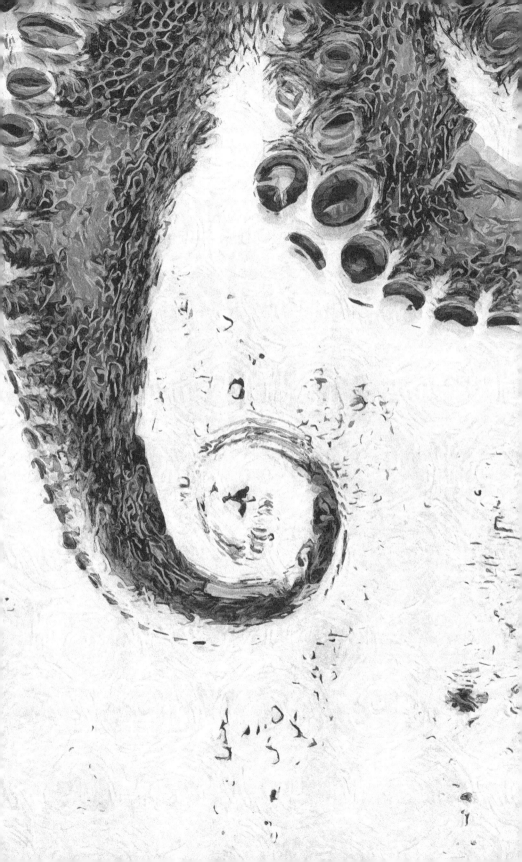

A PART OF
SOMEONE ELSE'S DREAM

BY T.T. MADDEN

I sit on the park bench and listen to the sounds of children playing, of birds flitting all around me, of bugs chirping in the bushes. A voice that sounds like me but can't be me says I'm safe now. That I no longer need to worry. But that voice can't be me because I feel inherently unsafe. Almost every day. It is simply a part of my being in this world.

And yet I think that maybe I am not in this world; the voice that sounds like me but cannot be me speaks with the pleasantness of a dream. Is that where I am? A dreamland? It certainly moves like a dream. I read somewhere that we can never remember the beginnings of dreams, that we're just in them. That makes sense, because I cannot remember the beginning of this moment.

But what is it called when you know you're dreaming and you can't wake up?

The voice that sounds like me says this place is paradise, and here is another reason I know this voice cannot be me; this place is not paradise. Something in my palms itches. If this is paradise, then why don't I see anyone I know?

And why don't I see anyone who looks like me?

The park is filled with alabaster faces. Mothers and children, largely. No men. A few young women who could be nannies or perhaps older sisters. There's something strange about them, the way they're dressed. The way they speak, the way they move. It all feels out of time; floral print and polka dots, dresses and skirts, high heels even on playground sand. All curves and hourglass shapes and bright colors. The children, too, wear clothes befitting their gender, and I wonder not just where I am, but when I am. The nannies or older sisters or whoever they are speak to the children in transatlantic accents, and everyone moves strangely, like I'm watching them as a film and some of their frames have been removed, making them stutter and hitch.

There is only one other dark-skinned face at the park; an old man with heavy, seen-it-all-before eyes. Sitting on a bench and feeding pigeons. He spots me immediately, the shock I feel on my own face absent on his. Only a slow expectation. Shoulders slumped. A resignation. I make to move to him, half-rise, but he holds up a hand, palm out.

Stop.

He lifts a finger to his lips.

Shh.

I sit back down, suddenly aware that we face a danger just by being here. By daring to exist in this place. We face a danger, but I do not know what it is.

Not here, the old man's look tells me. *Not now.*

And then he lifts a finger, points upward. That's when I see it.

There is something wrong with the sky. Whatever it is that makes the sky blue is for some reason gone and I can see into the vast bleakness of space beyond. But it doesn't look like I think it should. Not dark and dotted with pretty little stars. No, it's the color of an old bruise; purples and blues and jaundiced yellows on the edges. And I can see *things* in it. Galaxy-big tentacles and star-sweeping bat-wings and eyes with black hole pupils. Shapes too big and alien for me to even properly fathom.

And as soon as I register all the dark things in the space beyond, they're gone, the sky returned to blue. Like it's an error the world doesn't want me to see. It's back to normal, but I can still feel it, still know it's there. Hiding just behind that sheet of robin's-egg.

I look back for the old man, who holds a finger over his lips.

If there is a transition, I do not notice it. There are no transitions in dreams, we are simply in the next place. And so I've come to assume that there are none here in these Dreamlands either. I am simply in a dining room. I am not eating, and I think *of course*. Here, I am the one who serves. It is a vocation for which I have not been trained, and yet I have done it, am doing it, because it is what this place demands of me.

The old man from the park is here. We are both standing against opposite walls while the group who I somehow know, with that dream knowledge, to be the family of the house and the next-door neighbors sit and chat, wine glasses in hand. They are all dressed like the people in the park; from a time gone by. A time I've been told was perfect. Something itches at the back of my mind; the knowledge that that cannot possibly be true, that perfect time. I cannot articulate why or even how I know it. I slowly, carefully, rub my palms against my sides to quell that itching, but it does not work.

The old man must have noticed, because when my glance passes over him he tenses, straightens his back, and I know he is silently telling me to do the same. I do, aware of being in sudden mortal danger if I do not.

I stand completely silent, completely still, and try to think, to focus on what it is, where that sense of danger is coming from, but I cannot pinpoint that unsettling feeling. It feels like it's all around. Like it's in the walls of this place, the very air. I look without moving my head, see the wallpaper ripple in what I know is not just a trick of the light. Something moves behind those yellow flowers, like a shark below the waves, but infinitely more dangerous.

The people at the table are completely oblivious to the old man and I, the only dark-skinned faces in the room. The men talk about their perfect, quiet neighborhood, with its absence of undesirables, and the women gossip over the sudden and fiery fate of one Arthur Jermyn, who apparently set himself aflame the other day. Good riddance, they say, considering what he discovered. They wouldn't want that kind of element contaminating the rest of their perfect neighborhood.

I do not remember learning who this man is, I only know I know of him, that he was an *example*. An example of what, I think, but I cannot *wonder*. Something will not allow my mind to go that far. There is something inside my head. Smothering it. Keeping my brain confined within these four walls. Keeping it in its place.

The thing inside the wallpaper ripples, and it feels like the walls are coming inward. The surface of the wall stretches, fluid, and I can see the impression of scales pressed against the other side. Rising, then sinking below the wall-wave. And yet all I can do is stand completely still, knowing a horrid, indescribable fate awaits me if I break my statuesque resolve.

When called upon, I remove plates. I bring dessert. I refill glass after glass of wine. Each time those at the table avoid eye contact with me just as I do with them. For them, it is because they believe me beneath them. But for me, it is out of confusion just as much as it is fear. I see the way they look not at me, only *towards* me, without seeing me. Only glancing out of the corners of their eyes. The husbands whose eyes narrow with simultaneous hatred and disgust at my proximity, the wives whose eyes widen with simultaneous fear and lechery at my physique.

Images flash before my eyes that I cannot identify as imagined fears, memories, or nightmares. The men at the table surrounding me menacingly and knowing there is no escape just as they cower before me and my exotic power. I see the women fleeing from me, just as they come closer at the same time. Each time a saucer, a glass, or bottle shakes in my hand as I pull away. With each dream sliding into the next, I wonder which, if any, are real, and think that, somehow, they all are, all at once, only that some are real in other places.

I remember the transition this time. I don't remember doing it, don't remember being in the moment, but I at least remember it happening. We are outside now, and the sun is setting. Outside, why? It's something we must do every night. Tradition demands it, though I cannot recall why. I don't suppose anyone can. Such is the way of tradition.

As I try to figure it out, I feel a hand on my elbow pulling me away, down the front walk and into the street. I'm too distracted by the big, bright houses, by the perfectly-trimmed lawns, by the immaculate whiteness of the fences shining even in the night. It's only after a moment I realize it's the old man who has me.

"Not with them. The hell you thinkin'?"

I look over my shoulder and notice he's pulling me into the street, away from the family we served at the dinner table. He takes us to the middle of the street, where we stand with the only other familiar-looking people I've seen in this whole neighborhood. Black and brown skin, but they're all dressed like the old man and I. Like cooks. Like gardeners. No one is dressed like they actually own one of the houses. Because of course they don't. Not in this Dreamland, I realize.

"Look," the old man says, and I follow his gaze to the sunset. To what I thought at first was a sunset.

There's a perpetual fire on the horizon, the flames not orange, but dream-blue, sea-green, wound-purple. A city is silhouetted against the endless blaze, buildings that never burn or crumble no matter how long the flames lick at them. I can only look at the sight for a few moments at a time. It does something to me, like staring at the sun too long. But whatever is happening to me is inside my mind, not in my eyes. I can only glance at the fire before looking away. Look back again for just a moment. Look away. Back again.

But not the homeowners, not the people gathered on their perfect lawns with their perfect families in front of their perfect houses. All around us, they turn towards the perpetual destruction like flowers to the sun, drinking it in. Somewhere inside I know that the fire I'm seeing is the real world, but as it exists now through their eyes, and we in the street were only brought along to this place to be part of someone else's dream.

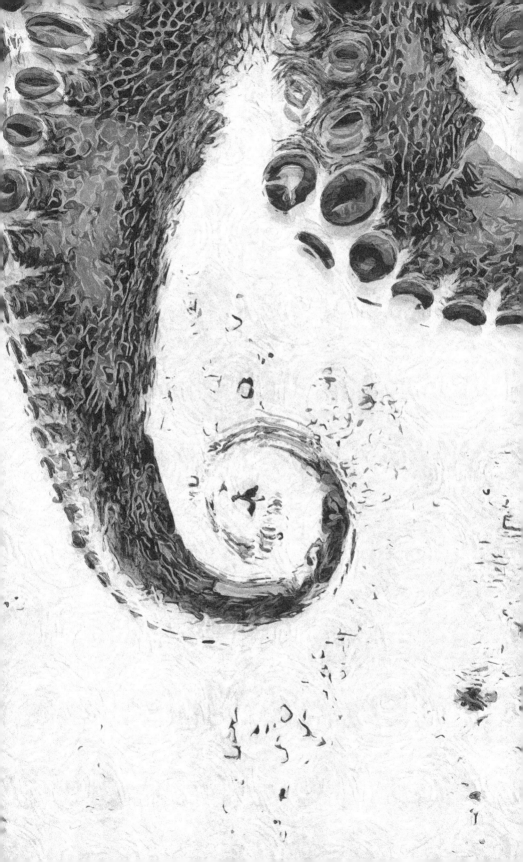

WHAT BELONGS TO YOU WILL NEVER BE YOURS

BY ERIC LAROCCA

PART ONE

For the first time in my life, I peer into the toilet bowl after I've relieved myself and I gaze at the dark brown spiral of shit I've created.

Usually, I don't tend to look at the waste I've deposited in the small basin.

I never have before. I've been told not to, in fact. *Why should I start now?*

Instead, I'll typically go about my business and once I'm satisfied with the results, I'll snatch some nearby tissue paper and clean myself. Sometimes it hurts when I wipe, and I can sense my eyes watering at the roughness of the pressure even though I know better to be gentle.

But today, for some inexplicable reason, I decide to gaze at the waste I had left there—my pittance of an offering for all the fish and rats scouring the thin canals of sewage sprawling beneath my apartment building.

It was a difficult labor to endure. Perhaps that's why I looked in the first place. It had been arduous to relieve myself and the excrement felt sharp, pointed almost.

I had expected that I might feel empty when I first looked at my cord of shit. I had told myself to be prepared to feel disgust or shame followed by a hollowness that usually accompanies the sight of something so unimaginative, something so crude.

But I don't feel any those things.

I'm surprised to discover that I feel an intense longing instead—a blissful and rapturous yearning to crawl inside the bowl and slip beneath the toilet water until I sink to the bottom of the basin where I've made my nightly contribution.

I wonder why I haven't looked at my waste after I've relieved myself before.

Of course, the answer is obvious: when I was very little, my mother used to slide sewing needles underneath the rims of my fingernails whenever I would tell her I needed to go to the bathroom. It wasn't until later I learned that it was her unusual method of preventing her only daughter from indulging in the sacrilege of self-pleasure. Regardless, cleanliness was also at the forefront of my poor mother's mind.

"There's nothing natural with relieving yourself," she'd tell me. *"It's shameful. An abomination."*

That word:

Abomination.

Is that what I've created?

I knew she believed in all sincerity everything she told me. Sometimes I'd press my ear against the washroom door, and I'd listen to her pray while she sat on the toilet, begging God to forgive her for such disgrace, such inexcusable vulgarity.

But I don't feel that same dishonor as I gaze upon the rope of excrement I've created, watching it as it bobs on the surface before sinking to the bottom of the bowl. There's nothing inherently vile about its appearance.

In fact, it looks like the bits of wet clay I've been molding at my art class every Thursday evening.

I cannot possibly begin to understand why I feel the need to lean closer toward the rim of the toilet bowl and gaze upon my shit with scrupulous inspection. *What do I expect to find there, after all? The answer to a question I had forgotten about? A fragment of my identity?*

It's then I feel an indescribable urge to speak to the excrement as I watch it laze underneath the water's surface that's been dyed a light shade of yellow from my urine.

Why should I feel the need to speak to the waste I've created? Why should I even address it? After all, it's a non-living thing. It has no identity, no logic, no creeds of which to speak. I know for certain that the only reasonable thing to do would be to pull the toilet's handle and send the pile of shit on a waterslide to the sewers.

But I cannot.

For some peculiar reason, I cannot bear to press the toilet handle and dispose of the waste I've created—the organic thing I've brought into this world without force, without coercion.

It's a thing that simply wanted to be.

What could I possibly say to my waste? It probably already knows the more intimate aspects of my character, my being. After all, it was once inside me—desperately yearning for life, frantically yearning to be.

Or does it?

I can't help but wonder to myself if it actually knows me the way I think it knows me. After all, do children inherently know everything about their mothers at birth? Absolutely not. Those things are learned and taught over time as the child slowly inherits the weight of becoming a fully realized person.

It most likely doesn't know my name, I think to myself.

That's what I'll tell it. I'll tell my waste what my name is. Just so that it knows.

However, just as I'm about to speak—just as I'm about to open my mouth—I realize that my name has been vacuumed from my mind. It feels as though someone—something—had screwed tight the leaky faucet where my name drips from inside my brain.

Why can't I remember my name? I wonder to myself. *Surely, I must be able to think of it, remember it. How could I possibly forget something so important, so vital to the essence of my being.*

I reach deep inside my thoughts, manhandling my recollections and attempting to beat them into submission. I demand them to tell me what my name is, but they won't.

There's nothing I can do to force the memory of the name I've been called.

It feels as if my name has never existed. It feels as if my being, my essence had been brought into this world cold, nameless, and shaking.

Perhaps I was. Perhaps all of us are.

Realizing I have papers with my name written across them, I dash from the washroom and make my way into the kitchenette. I snatch my purse from the counter and root around inside until I locate my wallet. I slide out my driver's license and study the name printed there: *Abigail.*

It feels strange to confess, but I'm disappointed in the discovery. I don't care for the name too much and I can't help but resent my parents for cursing me with a name so benign, so thoughtless.

Regardless, that's my name. The very name I had forgotten.

I decide to slip my driver's license into my pocket so that I can pull it out on a moment's notice. Just in case I'm asked and forget again.

Of course, I don't anticipate that will happen; however, there's something—a shapeless presence—lingering in the air that seems to whisper to me and tell me that more is to come, more is to be misplaced and lost.

I return to the washroom and gaze once more inside the toilet bowl at the waste I've created.

It stares back at me even though it doesn't have eyes or the thinking capacity to try to inspect me.

I get down on my knees and whisper my name into the toilet bowl:

Abigail

Abigail

Abigail

The sound of my voice echoes a little inside the basin and my name eventually wafts back to me like smoke from a distant fire.

I can't tell if I'm more excited to tell the pile of shit what my name is, or if I'm more desperate to make certain I don't forget again.

PART TWO

It's nearly two-thirty in the afternoon when one of my friends, Claire, rings my doorbell and asks if she can come inside to chat. I can tell she's been fighting with her girlfriend again and needs someone to talk to. Her eyes are puffy from crying.

She and I have fucked before and even briefly considered a scenario in which we'd belong to one another. But ultimately, we decided against it, and it wasn't long after that Claire met her current girlfriend, Lydia.

I don't necessarily care for Lydia.

I don't like how she often pulls her hair back in a high ponytail. I become nauseated when she refers to Claire affectionately as "Claire Bear." I find her completely insufferable, but I'll never divulge any of this to my friend.

Claire and I sit at the kitchen table drinking the tea I've prepared. She doesn't say much to me at first, almost as if the words she wants to tell me have been bottled up and she can't bear to part with them.

Eventually, the chamomile tea works like a laxative and starts softening the conversation between us. She tells me how Lydia has been uncharacteristically distant lately—how she hasn't been getting enough sleep at night because she's up all hours working on her doctoral dissertation.

Of course, I tell her that's to be expected and that things will change once Lydia secures her final degree.

But Claire doesn't seem too convinced.

In fact, I can't blame her. After all, my thoughts aren't present at the kitchen table. Instead, my mind is tirelessly working in the nearby bathroom—door shut, fan running, wondering about the excrement I've left in the toilet bowl. I couldn't bear to flush it. I had to leave it there—to see what it might become.

It feels foolish to think that my pile of shit inside the toilet bowl will grow and become something else entirely—something wondrous, something truly beautiful.

Why should I think such things? It's not as if it's given me any expectation that it will thrive if I don't flush it to the sewers.

Claire asks me if I'm feeling okay and that I look apprehensive, scared even.

I tell her that I'm fine. But then part of me wonders if I should tell her what happened earlier when I had forgotten my name.

I worry what she'll think of me if I divulge something so ludicrous, so absurd to her.

I decide against it.

We chat for another hour or so and eventually she tells me how she needs to go to the market to pick up some vegetables for the stir fry she's planning to cook for Lydia tonight.

I roll my eyes when she's not looking at me.

After Claire kisses me on the cheek and says goodbye, I lock my apartment door and sprint back to the washroom. I lift the toilet lid and gaze at the excrement lying there once more.

I'm going to add to you, I tell it.

I'm going to build upon you until you are infinite and as ageless as the universe.

I feel stupid thinking something so silly. But at least nobody is around to witness my indiscretion.

I pull down my underwear and sit on the toilet seat, loosening and eventually releasing more of myself—more bits of my essence, my soul—into the basin.

When I'm finished, I pull myself off the toilet and turn around to gaze down at more of the waste I've deposited there. The water is murky and dark brown like the water's surface in a Floridian swamp. Bits of excrement bob along the surface like clay.

I continue to inspect the creation I've made and, for once, I feel a sense of pride. I feel as though I've created something. I feel as though I've fashioned something truly unique.

I'm a creator.

Once again, I feel an indescribable urge to tell the waste swirling in the toilet bowl more about me. I feel as though that's the very least I owe what I've created.

After all, it's so easy to create something and then walk away from what you've brought into this world. That's exactly what my mother and father had done, after all.

What could I possibly tell this toilet bowl full of shit about me that it doesn't already know? I wonder to myself. *What could I say? Everything seems so inconsequential, so unimportant now.*

It's then I realize that I could perhaps tell the excrement how old I am.

But as soon as I search my thoughts for my age, I realize that the number is absent from my mind. It's as if the number had been unspooled, digit by digit, and sent hurtling away from its place of honor where it had once been glued inside my brain.

How can this be? I think to myself. *How could I forget my name? Then my age?*

It's then I realize that once again I've forgotten my name. Not only my age, but my name as well.

Both things are seemingly absent from my mind and make no promises of returning anytime soon.

I swipe my driver's license from my pocket and inspect the name again: *Abigail.*

I then glance at my birthdate.

I'm thirty-six years old.

Is that true? I wonder. *Surely, that can't be true.*

I don't feel thirty-six years old. I don't recall turning thirty-six. I don't even recall turning thirty-five. If that's the case, how can I possibly be thirty-six?

But why would my driver's license be incorrect? Why would the documentation lie to me? Is it possible that the driver's license is incorrect and the answer to my age and name is now residing inside the toilet bowl?

That's very possible, I think to myself as I stare into the basin.

Then I see something that surprises me, that prickles the hairs on the nape of my neck, that drains the warmth from my face:

I notice something squirming beneath the surface of the brown toilet water,

something insisting to be recognized,

something demanding to be released,

anything.

PART THREE

Later that night, I feel the need to relieve myself. But I'm frightened.

It seems every time I excuse myself to the washroom and use the toilet, more of my identity slips away from me.

I understand less of myself each time I create waste.

I try to hold it as best as possible. I try to cross my legs as if I were fastening a hose to shut off. But it's been nearly impossible to deprive myself of shitting ever since I had my gallbladder removed two years ago. Everything I consume seems to run right through me as if there were a tiny river built inside me.

I tiptoe from my bedroom into the washroom and, once again, I peer inside the toilet bowl where I've allowed the waste to remain for the night. I've toyed with the idea of flushing everything—disposing of my precious excrement and starting over again.

But something prevents me each time I make the effort to consider such a thing, almost as if someone were pulling strings inside my mind and commanding me to not think about certain things.

The shit inside the toilet bowl looks peaceful, almost as if it were dozing.

I can bear it no longer.

I need to relieve myself once more.

I squat over the toilet and go about my business. It feels like it goes on forever, as if my very guts were being dragged out from my asshole.

Finally, when I sense the last remaining bits dislodge from myself, I rise from my seat and peer back down at the basin where I've added to my glorious creation.

What I see surprises me: the excrement, now black and viscous looking, has begun to poke through the surface of urine and it resembles the skeletal remnants of a hand—an animal-like claw reaching out for anyone who might be willing to grab hold of it.

Is that person me? I think to myself. *Is my shit begging me to help it? To save it from where I've let it rest?*

But I can't begin to answer those questions now.

Something else is knocking at the front door of my thoughts. Something begging to be answered. Something demanding to be addressed.

Where am I? I wonder. *What am I doing here? To whom do I belong? More importantly, why am I here?*

All these thoughts come crashing into my mind like a flood conjured by the apocalypse.

I have none of the answers. That truly scares me.

Quickly thinking, I snatch my driver's license from my pocket once more and start to go over the details written on the card. But I'm much too careless and the license slips from my sweaty hands, plunking into the toilet bowl and vanishing beneath the oily black surface.

All the answers—suddenly gone. Disappeared.

But that can't be, I think. *I need that card. I need to hold onto it. I need those answers.*

It's then I hear the imprecise murmur of a voice—certainly not my own—churning on the periphery of my thoughts. The voice coils inside me like a thread of metal working its way into place inside some sort of machinery, desperately searching for where it fits.

The voice beckons me to come closer.

I do.

No. Come closer, it orders me in a frighteningly insisting tone. *Closer.*

My face is now hovering mere centimeters above the toilet water's surface. I sense my nostrils twitch as they fill with the pungent odor, the awful scent.

You're not close enough, the voice in my mind whispers to me.

Before I can resist, I find myself being pulled beneath the toilet water and sliding deep inside the shit-filled basin that's already grown in size to accommodate the largeness of my body.

I thought I would be scared. I thought I would resist more and beg to be released. But I don't. Whether the fear is nonexistent or whether it's been sponged from my mind, I cannot be certain.

I sense shit-slimed tentacles braiding themselves around my hands and feet—binding me there in some perverted act of bondage that it seems to enjoy a little too much.

It's glad that I'm here. I know that full well.

My empty mind begins to cool and soften as I plunge further into the ancient constellations swirling all around me. Threads of shit begin to coil inside my every open hole. From my ears to my mouth to my vagina. I am completely and utterly filled.

I'm pulled deeper and deeper until I'm face to face with a giant eyeball, its wizened pupil dilating as it searches me for a semblance of recognition, a modicum of familiarity.

I wonder if it will cast me aside, if it will abandon me as I had once thought to abandon it.

But it doesn't.

It surprisingly doesn't.

Instead, it pulls me closer into a seemingly infinite closet of starshine and dust from universes now long since extinct.

I try to comprehend what I'm seeing, but I cannot. Perhaps I don't want to. Perhaps I'm better off not knowing. Just like I'm happier not knowing my name, my age or where I am, why I'm truly here.

Unfortunately, those horrible questions are answered by the poor loved ones who eventually find me slouched beside the toilet, clutching onto the rim with both hands, and shit smearing my mouth and between my thighs.

They feel pity for me and how I was taken from this world.

Robbed of my youth. Far too young.

A closed casket will be the only appropriate course of action for my body.

But sadly, they don't know the ancient wisdom I was temporarily granted before I expired—the deity I had created from my very bowels

and the God that I had consumed

before I, in turn,

was devoured

by starlight

as black

as smoke.

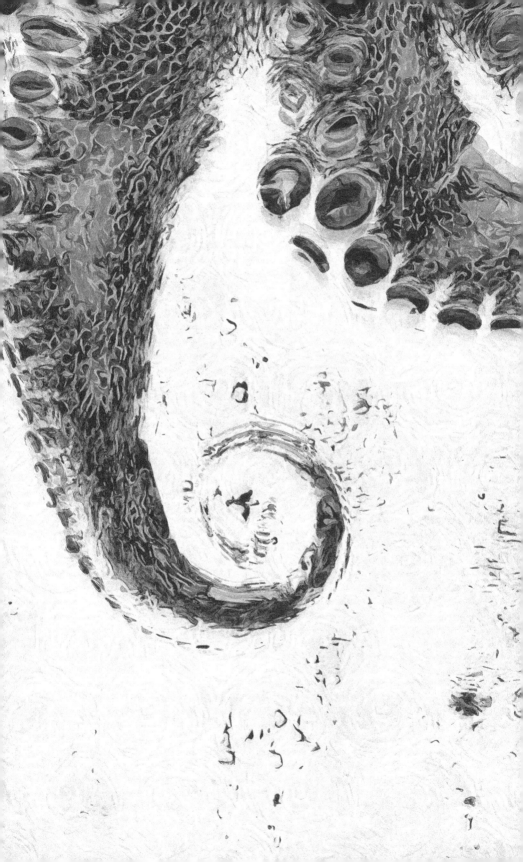

CLOSING DAY

BY RAMSEY CAMPBELL

When the navigator directed Green to turn around in the one-way street he thought the layout of Youtheven had baffled the device as much as him. Might the sound of hammering denote the business he was growing desperate to find? As he swung the car into a parking space alongside a row of small neat shops he saw where the noise was coming from. GAME, the window promised, and the butcher—a brawny man whose ruddiness competed with much of the meat on display—was pounding a piece of beef with a tenderiser. Before Green could move off, the butcher strode to the doorway at a speed that dismissed his bulk. "Are you here for tomorrow?" he called.

Green eased his window down. "I'm looking for a funeral director."

"Leslie Burbane will be dealing with you."

"That's the chap, but how—"

"He's the only one we've got. You can leave yourself there. He's just up the next lane."

The search had bewildered Green enough to make him wonder "Won't I need to go to him?"

"I'm telling you to leave your car." The butcher used his reddened implement to indicate the route. "We'll see you at the dance," he said.

Green doubted this, whatever it referred to, but all that mattered just now was the route. The cobbled alley led between a bakery displaying cakes iced in kindergarten colours and a toddlers' shop where plastic infants modelled dinky outfits. It ended at another of the crescents of which Youtheven appeared mostly to consist, along with circular roads linked by narrow lanes, by no means all of which admitted traffic. He felt as if he'd escaped a maze if not a web when he saw Youtheven Funerals beyond the lane.

Beneath the gilded name the window enshrined a pair of marble headstones apparently awaiting inscriptions. The door set off a subdued bell in the foyer, where armchairs flanked low tables spread with glossy brochures depicting elderly couples rendered carefree by their posthumous prospects. The discreet note summoned a middle-aged man in a suit the colour of fog, who paced into the foyer like a mime of consolation. "Mr Bernard Green?" he barely asked.

Green recognised the voice, which was as smooth as the pale oval face. "Mr Burbane. We spoke on the phone."

"You'll be here to view."

Green could have thought the large moist sympathetic eyes were doing this to him, but of course Burbane meant Green's uncle. "I should," Green said. "It's been years since I've seen him."

"He was taken from us too soon."

This sounded so personal it prompted Green to ask "Did you know him?"

"The town did."

"I understand," Green said, having concluded the regret had been professional. "Who's your oldest person now?"

"That needn't concern us for the present, Mr Green."

"I think Uncle Terence was proud of his age. I got the impression your town made him feel special."

"Indeed he was and would have been. You kept in touch, then."

"Just by phone, but that was nearly till the end."

The undertaker glanced back from leading Green into an inner corridor. "Did he mention our plan for him?"

"I didn't even know you were involved till you rang. I'm grateful you'd made the arrangements. You did say everything was covered."

"I believe everything is as it should be. I'll invite you to see for yourself."

The corridor felt stuffed with silence soft as plush, and Green did his best to keep his footsteps as muted as the undertaker's. An open coffin stood on trestles in a room at the far end. Politely indirect lighting showed Green his uncle's supine form. While the old man was attired in the kind of formal outfit he'd worn when lecturing at Brichester, bow tie and all, he looked shrunken to fit into the suit, reduced to a husk of himself. The face had grown anonymously placid, and the hands lay on the chest as if they'd tired of the expressive gestures they used to bring to even the most trivial conversation. "You've made him look peaceful," Green felt he should remark.

"He would have been."

Green lingered for an interval he hoped was decent, and didn't speak again until they returned to the foyer. "I'd better see if anything needs doing at the house. You said you had a key for me."

"Did you have any trouble finding us?"

"Quite a lot, to be honest. Who on earth designed your town?"

"You might say it designed itself. It will save time if I show you where you have to go."

"Or you could give me directions. I don't want to take you away from your job."

"I'd be falling short if I didn't make sure you were settled." Louder than Green would have expected, Burbane called along the corridor "I'm just delivering our visitor, Rhoda. If there's any business I leave it in your expert hands." Outside he blinked about as people in the street rather more than glanced at Green. "Did you not travel by car?" Burbane said.

"It's down by the butchers."

"Ah, our game man. Another asset to the town."

Presumably this meant other than Green's uncle. From the alley Green heard the thumping of the tenderiser. "When I was looking for you," he admitted, "I thought that was somebody fixing a lid."

"He deals with our meat." Burbane greeted the butcher by raising both hands with the thumb and forefinger curved into a circle and the rest of the fingers stretched high. "We'll be seeing you, Arnold," he shouted.

"Whenever I'm called for," the butcher responded and dealt a raw item on the marble slab a preparatory thump.

"Head for the centre," Burbane told Green. "There, up Century Lane. Ignore the signs. There won't be any trouble."

Green needed convincing, not just because a No Entry sign guarded the route but once he saw how narrow the lane was. He wouldn't be able to open his door, not that there should be any need. He tried to feel privileged, a visitor granted the freedom of the town, but as the car nosed into the next street a woman on the pavement scowled at him. When she noticed his passenger, her lips shaped an O that Green took to denote recognition and acceptance. "How do people manage to drive round here?" Green wondered aloud.

"They mostly don't," Burbane said. "That wasn't what the town was built for."

"I don't suppose there were cars back then, but doesn't anybody want to make it friendlier?"

"I hope you'll encounter all the friendliness you require."

Green wasn't sure if he'd offended the undertaker, who said "Now take Old Way."

This alley left the last of the shops behind. The inmost section of Youtheven must be the original village, where lanes connected street after diminishing circular street of limestone cottages as pale as the late April sky. Burbane sent the car along a lane and then another, and Green had to assume they'd somehow gone astray. Temple Vantage encircled a park, and he'd scarcely set off around the perimeter when the undertaker said "Stop here."

Green did, but only to protest "This isn't where my uncle lived."

"Not merely lived, I'm afraid."

"You're saying he was visiting here when he died."

"I mean this was his house."

"But he lived on Baker's Crescent. When did he move?"

"Some little time ago. Were you in touch except by phone?" When Green shook his head, which failed to dislodge a dull lump of guilt, Burbane said "Then you may assume he saw no reason to bring it up."

"Why wouldn't he have mentioned it?"

"Perhaps he had more pressing issues to concern him."

As Burbane released his seatbelt Green felt bound to ask "Would you like me to drive you back now I know the way?"

"Please don't trouble," Burbane said and left the car. "I need to keep myself fit for tomorrow."

"Is that for the dance your butcher seems to think I should be at?"

71

"There has always been a celebration."

"For the oldest person, would that be?"

"We only wish your uncle could have participated as he should." Burbane produced a key as he sauntered up the shrill gravel path between a pair of minimally planted flowerbeds, and then he hesitated at the oaken door of the small cottage. "How will you sleep, Mr Green?"

"I've brought a bag. I thought using his bed would be a bit much."

"You feel it's too soon to take his place."

"I've no plans for that. I just thought he could have died in the bed."

"He did, most unexpectedly." Burbane slipped the key into the lock, then held it with a thumb and forefinger. "You're bound to be here to inherit," he said.

"I'll come back if I need to, but I don't even know if there's a will."

"We have one."

"You're telling me my uncle left it with you? Isn't that unusual?"

"It would be." Burbane's smile was too faint to be clear. "The town," he said, "has a will."

If this was a pleasantry, it fell short of Green. "I expect he didn't need to make one," he said. "There isn't anybody else."

"Apart from yourself."

"Or for me either."

"There's the town."

Green had no idea what reassurance this was intended to convey. Burbane turned the key at last, withdrawing it as he edged the door inwards. "I shouldn't think you'll have much use for this," he said.

"I'll be going out for dinner for a start."

"I promise you will find you've been provided for."

"I'll see about that when I've settled in," Green said, thrusting out a hand. "I may go for a walk later," he was annoyed to have to explain.

"No harm in that." Just the same, Burbane appeared to need to consider the possibility before passing Green the key. "Expect to be welcomed," he said.

Green stood in the doorway to watch him out of sight, and then he fetched his suitcase and the sleeping-bag before he explored the cottage. The accommodation felt as temporary as the undertaker's viewing room. The suite that faced a television in the lounge brought to mind a display in a furniture store, while the utensils in the stony kitchen were so clean they looked unused. The bed in which someone must have found his uncle retained no sense of its last occupant. The bathroom was devoid of toiletries, and a speck of toothpaste on the mirror was the solitary sign of life. He couldn't help feeling relieved as he saw the final room, which his uncle had made into as much of a study as he could.

For lack of shelves, philosophical treatises were piled against every wall. Someone had installed a heavy desk at the window and added a pivoting chair. The desk was strewn with scribbled sheets of paper, on one of which an uncapped fountain pen pointed its inky nib at the end of a phrase or sentence. As Green advanced to read it he could just distinguish through a mass of trees a building, possibly a bandstand, in the middle of the park. There must be a pond or lake beyond the trees as well, the source of a large liquid plop that put him in mind of a fish mouthing at water, though the cause had to be considerably bigger than a fish—a rock somebody had shied in, perhaps. Green perched on the perilously rakish chair and peered at the words that led to the abandoned fountain pen, where a full stop had swelled into a blue amoebic blotch under the nib.

He hoped just his uncle's handwriting had degenerated at the end, but he feared the old man's brain might have since they'd last spoken. The shaky longhand that sprawled across the page was barely recognisable as his, and close to illegible. Green took quite a time to conclude that the sentence asserted *This is my house now.* Had his uncle grown so uncertain of it that he needed to reassure himself? One page played with the name of the town: Youtheven, Youtheaven, Youtheaving, Youthieving, Youthaven… Another simply declared in enormous spavined capitals NO WILL—a declaration of intent or a statement of the situation? A sentence longer than most on the desk required a good deal of decoding, but at last Green decided it said *Much that is ancient has yet to be borne into the world.* Or was that *born,* rounded off by a blotch where the nib had loitered or faltered? He assumed the sentence was a philosophical observation his uncle had found no time to develop. He was leafing through more pages and despairing of their illegibility when the doorbell shrilled.

Whoever was there must have hushed their approach. Green raised the rumbling sash to catch an all but hairless youth in the act of leaving a capacious plastic box on the doorstep. "Hello?" Green called.

The youth scarcely bothered glancing back or up as he retreated down the gnashing path. "Delivery for Green."

"Hang on. I'm not the man you want."

"You are now."

"No, you're thinking of my uncle. He was your oldest person."

"Right, they always live there."

This was bewildering enough to delay Green's response. "Wait," he called louder. "What have you brought me?"

"Mr Arnold said to feed you up."

"But I haven't ordered anything."

"Didn't have to." The youth visibly resented needing to turn at the gate to explain "All paid for like it always is."

"You aren't saying my uncle never paid."

"He wouldn't have tonight when there's tomorrow," the youth said and climbed into a van named **ARNOLD'S GAME.**

By the time Green hurried to the front door the van had gone. He hefted the unexpectedly heavy cold box and unloaded it on the kitchen table. A meat and potato pie, an equally circular plump pink sausage, a substantial pair of pork pies, a brace of thick beefburgers just as round, a carton of onion rings, a container of chips shaped like coins... How many meals was all this designed to comprise? Had his uncle been expected to make a selection and send the rest back? At least the butcher hadn't included any game, which Green wouldn't have had the patience to cook. Having consigned most of the produce to the refrigerator, he microwaved the meat and potato pie and ate it from its tinfoil dish with a fork he found in a drawer that offered just enough utensils for a single user. The dinner was so filling he felt dutiful well before he finished it, but gratitude seemed to require him to complete the task. He crumpled the dish into the bin and washed the fork, and then he went out for a stroll around the park.

The entrance was halfway along the perimeter, opposite a hall belonging to the church of St Nicholas, a spiny structure as white as the headstones that glimmered around it in the dusk. Ivy elaborated the ironwork of the park gates, which were padlocked. Beyond the lethally pointed railings the trees massed so close together that Green remained uncertain what the building at the centre was: some kind of folly devised to resemble a temple? He couldn't locate the body of water that emitted the odd liquid plop reminiscent of the smacking of moist lips. He was delayed by people emerging from their cottages to exhort him to have a good night, so sympathetically that he assumed they knew why he was in Youtheven. By the time the circuit brought him back to his uncle's cottage the repetitions had begun to feel ritualistic, and he was ready for bed.

The sofa opposite the television offered just enough room for the sleeping-bag and the pillow Green had brought with him. The day had exhausted him, and he slept until a baby's complaints wakened him. The harsh hungry cries seemed to have set off a number of dogs whose snarling howls merged with the wails, so that Green could have fancied he was hearing a single massive voice. How many people were hushing the infant? Now they were crooning a lullaby, a repetition of a solitary sound. If this was a word, was it "Soon"? The cries subsided, taking the animal noises with them, and the lullaby or else the respite from the plaint worked for Green as well.

His phone roused him, and daylight through his eyelids made him worry he was late for work. No, the summer term didn't start until next week, and in any case he wasn't at home, all of which reassured him until he saw the sun was high above the park. He fumbled to cut off the trilling. "Bernard Green."

"Leslie Burbane, Mr Green. Just to advise you'll be collected."

Green struggled to sit up in the bag. "I wasn't meaning to sleep this late."

"No urgency, Mr Green. You've still almost an hour, so please do make all the use you can of the provisions. You've a full day ahead."

Green felt addressed like someone of his uncle's years, not that he would have taken such a tone himself. He used the shower, a cramped glass cabinet that made him think of a casket stood on end. He microwaved the burgers and a handful of the chips, a meal that turned out to be even more substantial than it looked. As he squirted a last gasping gurgle of soap from a collapsed plastic bottle at the plate and utensils in the sink, the doorbell rang. Burbane was on the step, and letting his suit express sombreness. "I just need to wash up," Green said.

"You look immaculate, Mr Green. Everything we would hope for."

"Wash up the breakfast things," Green said with as much of a laugh as he thought the misunderstanding warranted. "Or lunch or whatever it was."

"So long as you're sated, and please don't trouble to clear up after yourself."

"I nearly have. I won't be a moment." Green hurried to scrub the items with a plastic brush before rinsing them and tugging out the plug. The round hole emitted a soapy plop that called to mind the noises he'd heard in the park. As he dried his hands on a tattered dwarfish towel, Burbane took hold of both sides of the kitchen doorframe. "I'm on my way right now," Green felt prompted to assure him.

When he followed the undertaker he found the man had brought no car. "Shall I drive?" Green said.

"Stride out, Mr Green. Use your legs while you can."

From the garden path Green glimpsed the building encircled by trees. "Is that a folly in the park?"

"We have no folly here."

Had Green inadvertently offended him? The angle of the sunlight let Green see how all the trees in sight leaned towards the middle of the park, a spectacle that put him in mind of a carnivorous plant, although the trees closest to the central building looked withered if not dead. As Green lingered in a bid to establish their condition Burbane said "You'll be able to see what's there later."

He led the way along the nearest lane and then the alley opposite.

It soon became clear that there was a direct route between the cottage and the undertakers, for pedestrians at any rate. On the inmost shopping street Green saw CLOSED signs all around him. "This will be your early closing day, then," he said.

"Say rather it's our civic spirit, Mr Green."

"Is this about my uncle again?"

"It has to be." With a renewal of yesterday's sympathy Burbane said "But you mustn't feel left out."

Green wondered why this even needed saying. The next lane took them to the undertakers, outside which a hearse and a pair of limousines were parked. The coffin was already in the hearse. "If you'll take your place," Burbane said, "we can begin."

He joined a quartet of pallbearers in the limousine behind the hearse while the driver of the last vehicle held the door wide for Green. As the cars crept along the street, every shop let out its staff, who stepped forward to augment the procession. "This is all for my uncle," Green was moved to remark.

The driver eyed him for a moment in the mirror. "It would have been."

The widest lanes led directly to the church opposite the park. By the time the parade arrived Green could have thought it involved the entire populace. As Burbane raised the tailgate of the hearse, Green said "Let me help. It's the least I ought to do."

The pallbearers glanced at one another. "You have much to contribute, Mr Green," Burbane said.

"Then that can be some of it."

"These gentlemen will take the weight." Once this had been established Burbane murmured "Please take the head."

Green made for the front of the coffin, only to be sent to the back. The pallbearers must indeed be shouldering most of the burden, since he could have fancied he was helping them carry an empty box. By the time they marched in slow motion through the porch, every pew inside the church was full except for the left-hand front bench, which Green took to be reserved exclusively for him. He stepped back while the pallbearers lowered the coffin onto a trestle in front of the altar, beyond which a great stained-glass disc portrayed a ring of haloed saints extending their hands to a circular illumination, presumably holier than a mere sun. As he sat across the aisle from the butcher and his family the priest, a portly fellow whose freckled face looked eager to share its contentment, climbed into the pulpit. "We are here today to give thanks for a dedicated life…"

Green supposed his uncle's had been, though the priest delayed naming him. "I know Terence Green would have offered his ceremony to our town…" The service consisted largely of readings and hymns, one of which reiterated "Take my life, it's all for thee." Wasn't this hymn supposed to be associated with a birth? The priest kept his eyes on Green throughout the many repetitions of the line, and Green could only assume this was meant to prepare him for delivering the eulogy. From the pulpit he summarised his uncle's life, not least the philosophy on which it was founded: that continuity was the core of existence, how insignificant its absence would render life, how he'd regarded himself as a contributor to the world to come. The response heartened Green, though he was surprised to hear applause in church.

Had the hymn about taking a life been a favourite of his uncle's? He couldn't think of any other reason to repeat it as the pallbearers converged on the coffin. When he joined them he was thrown by the weight his shoulder had to take, as if the men had recalled that the casket was meant to be burdensome. He could have felt it was leading him to the open grave behind the church, where the pallbearers mimed the labour of lowering the coffin into the earth. The priest blessed the grave and kept his eyes downcast while he declared with some force that they were burying the body of their brother. Green scattered a handful of soil on the lid, which responded with a hollow resonance, and a few of the crowd that had gathered in the churchyard copied him, apparently out of politeness. "Let me show you to the celebration," Burbane said and ushered him into the church hall.

The long room was as pale as a mausoleum. One stretch of wall was decorated with children's paintings Green took to represent sunsets surrounded by rays of light. Some resembled pits ringed by scrawny trees, except why would a pit be so red? No doubt these betrayed enthusiastic childish inexperience, particularly since the colour had leaked beyond each outline. At the far end of the crowded hall a buffet occupied a table that spanned the room. "Tuck in whenever you're ready," Arnold strode over to urge him.

"I've not long eaten. There's still plenty of food at the house. Am I supposed to take it home?"

"You have."

"No, I mean when I leave."

"No need to think of leaving us just yet. Come and try the wife's home brew," the butcher said and grasped Green's arm to steer him.

The butcher's wife, a jovial muscular woman who looked capable of besting him at wrestling, filled a plastic tumbler to the brim with nettle wine. "Drink up, Mr Green," she bellowed. "To the one who brought you here."

Green took a sip before risking a mouthful. On further acquaintance he didn't find the citric tang too sharp. "To my uncle," he declared, elevating the tumbler.

"To Mr Green," Arnold called, and Green heard everybody in

the hall echo him. He was trying to decide whether the tribute had been shouted outside too when the crowd parted to let a wiry oldster wheel her chair to him. "Thank you for coming to us, Mr Green," she exerted herself to pronounce.

"Elsie is our oldest now," Mrs Arnold said.

"She's saying it's nearly my time. Thank you for giving me an extra bit of life."

Green wondered how he could have and then thought he understood. "What I said in church, you mean."

"What you brought us," Elsie apparently agreed and used both tremulous hands to lift the tumbler Mrs Arnold gave her. The old woman's gesture looked oddly religious. "To Mr Green," she quavered.

"Uncle Terence," Green said, but the crowd drowned his voice. Elsie's words prompted any number of people to approach and thank him. Since they each raised a tumbler, he did too, and Mrs Arnold wasn't slow in keeping his replenished. He yielded to her exhortations and her husband's to sample the buffet, if only because he was growing really quite intoxicated. No doubt other people were, and perhaps someone's behaviour had grown inappropriate; otherwise they would hardly need reminding it was a wake. As Green tried to locate them and their conduct, Burbane accosted him. "You were wanting to see our park."

"Maze swell." Green's speech was no longer up to much of a job. "Less Eden," he prompted.

The crowd outside the hall made way for him, and so did the multitude in the road. "Or foreign," he assumed aloud and strove to reshape the syllables. "All for him."

"That's us," someone said, and Green heard other mutters as Burbane guided him across the road, gripping his upper arm. "Will he do?" "We can try." "He's the closest." The park gates were wide open, and a narrow path snaked between the trees so deviously that he remained unable to make out the central edifice, however hard he struggled to focus his eyes. He was distracted by a massive liquid plop beyond the trees that consolidated the night, followed by a splintering crunch. "Wast hat?" he demanded.

"Tree's gone by four." Burbane was steering from behind with both hands on Green's arms, which must be why Green had misheard. The butcher could hardly have said "He's gone before" either, and Green was trying to reconceive the syllables when he heard voices through the trees. "Wasn't enough," Arnold said.

"Must have to be live," said his wife.

They and ten people just as burly stood in front of a tarnished central dome held high by rusty pillars. Beneath the withered trees that bowed towards the edifice, a ragged bed of nettles fringed the circular floor, which was so dark that Green could have taken it for exposed earth. As he squinted at it, the round rim seemed to grow restless. Before he could judge whether this was the fault of his unfocused vision or a low breeze enlivening the nettles, Arnold said "Time for the tender dance."

The Arnolds and their companions tramped forwards as Burbane brought his charge to them. Burbane and the butcher each took one of Green's hands with an outstretched arm and led him across the nettles. The domed building had no floor, he saw now—just gaping darkness. Was some exhalation from within it shifting the nettles? He could have thought the rim itself was stirring. He had no chance to confirm this before everyone around him joined hands and began to circle the pit below the dome. Soon the anticlockwise dance gained such a speed that his breath could barely keep up, not least because his arms were tugged to their fullest length, constricting his chest.

"What's this for?" he made a gasping effort to articulate. "It doesn't feel so tender."

"You will," someone said—perhaps the butcher, if not a member of the multitude Green glimpsed filling the entire perimeter road. He would have demanded an explanation except for the noise that deafened him: not the howl of a child or the baying of dogs, but an inhuman sound he'd misheard as a mixture of both. It rose out of the blackness around which he was helplessly whirling. "What is it?" he pleaded with the meagre voice he had.

"It's hardly born yet," Burbane murmured. "It still lets us choose." He danced back from the unstable rim, so that Green was able to hope the ceremony was finished. No, the circle of dancers had parted in order to regroup. They gathered around him, pressing so close and twirling him so fast he felt he was being squeezed and reeled out of himself. He had a fearful sense that the dance was living up to its name, softening him strengthless. "Let me go," he begged, and at once they did. He spun away from them like a child's top, only to teeter on the lively yielding brink of a blackness that greeted him with a huge raw breath. He flung himself clear, although in a direction his whirligig of a brain couldn't judge. He was throwing out his hands to break his fall when the unnaturally extended lips closed on them for a taste, and then the gelatinous slab of a tongue sank to await him in the noisome dark while the vast mouth welcomed him with every row of teeth.

SUN DOWN

BY LAIRD BARRON

"Great Aunt" Amrutha kicked in a glorious fireball that took off the top of a Seattle retirement home. According to her estate lawyer, she'd left us a note, thirty grand in a safe deposit box with a bundle of stone sacrificial knives, and a piece of property all the way across the continent in New York State. Alas, not the ritzy ancestral Hunsucker manse. Instead, a forgotten shack tucked away in the Catskills outside of a hamlet named Sundown. She'd referred to it as her special hideout. A woman has secrets and that had been the least of hers. The deed said, *Satan's Den.* Seemed appropriate, based upon my hazy recollection.

"Woohoo, E," I said to my "wife" upon hanging up with the lawyer. "They finally nailed the bitch."

"Which one?" Erinyes wrung her bloody apron in the sink.

"The main pain."

"Glory hallelujah. Wait, are we certain?"

"Dead certain," I said with the intonation of a voiceover artist.

That very week, I signed the papers and loaded the "family" into our trusty 1976 Fleetwood station wagon for the drive from Central California. Escaped just in time to beat the yearly immolation. Not that I was taking a poll: Sid, the battle-scarred "tabby," gave nary a shit. Our "dog," Stalker, was quite sanguine about rolling in dead things somewhere new. However, the "kids" weren't enthused at the prospect of uprooting.

"Screw this noise. Wake me when we land." Gertrude slipped on earphones. The last we heard from her for the entire trip.

Stein sighed and opened a ratty copy of *The Flowers of Evil.* I'd tried fruitlessly to convince him that moldering French poets were passé in the digital age. Hyper-violent, hyper-sexual manga was a more appropriate cover for an adolescent. Perhaps some tasteful tentacle erotica. He lit an unfiltered Gauloises (the old brand you can't find anymore) and ignored me, as usual.

In honor of our destination, I cranked Gordon Lightfoot on the eight-track player the whole way.

I'd last visited the Catskill Mountains during childhood and didn't recognize much. Forest is forest wherever you go—dark, foreboding, and full of blinking red eyes. Sundown proper lay within the larger town of Denning, forty minutes southwest of Kingston. One ill-paved street and a handful of businesses. Tourist attractions? Catskill Preserve, Sundown Wild Forest, the Vernooy Kill Falls, and Peter Paul's Bait Shack on Main. North, Big Indian Forest and the town of Phoenicia. South—the Rondout Reservoir, Napanoch, Kerhonkson, and Ellenville. West, the mountains kept on going, green and mysterious. Essentially, the outskirts of Bumfuck, USA.

A rutted dirt lane brought us home to Satan's Den. The decrepit house was embedded in a patch of swampy backwoods. Late afternoon and the overgrown yard was already smoky with blue shade. Windows were boarded; peaked tar paper roof and a collapsed front porch. Antlers over the door and 666 done in spray-paint. Deer skulls nailed to cottonwood trees. Social media memes such as, *would you stay in this place overnight for a million dollars?* featured haunted houses that looked nicer and more welcoming.

"We're *here* because we wore out our welcome *there*," E said to forestall the inevitable griping. This was true. Even if Amrutha hadn't died, we were slated to exit the Golden State, one way or another. "Your father will acquire necessary supplies and establish contact with the locals. Stalker and Sid, you'll conduct reconnaissance. The rest of us are on infrastructure detail. Let's try to get HQ operational within the week. Stay on guard. Your aunt may have planted boobytraps." She stared at the "kids" in the rearview as she spoke. "If you're good, we'll have a celebration. Ice cream cake!"

Ice cream cake was a greater incentive than one might suppose.

Ants and mice scattered before our footfalls. Bats nested in the attic. Doors, rooms, and passages were narrow in the American gothic tradition. A warren that provided the illusion of greater size. I got turned around a few times. Holes in the hardwood planks revealed the cellar, which was more akin to a partially excavated cave. Mushroom beds festooned the bank of a chortling stream.

"There's a creek in the basement." Stein stroked the goatee he'd painstakingly cultivated the past year or two.

"I hope that's not a complaint," E said.

"By Imdugud's scaly feathers, nay! This hovel might lack electricity, but we've running water, at least."

"Fuck yeah." Gertrude leaned over, spat a gob of phlegm, and watched it fall.

That first night, I risked a fire in the hearth to toast the varmints Stalker had caught. Groundhog and racoon surprise. Unlike the nasty stray cats and dogs haunting our previous suburban digs, critters in this neighborhood proved fat, juicy, and unwary.

Despite E's optimism, it required a month of intensive labor in the summer heat to restore the house to even a condemnable status, get the power and phone hooked up, and to purge the most invasive creatures occupying its myriad nooks and crannies. Stalker and Sid discovered the cellar brook vanished into a deeper cavern system. The duo also excitedly reported that a prehistoric dolmen shrine squatted on a hill in a grove behind the house. They'd fled at the marrow-freezing chill of a gathering presence, presumably awakened by their intrusion. Stein, our inhouse chronicler, recorded every detail in the ledger.

Contrary to our justifiable paranoia, "Aunt" Amrutha hadn't installed any traps. Still, the house and environs possessed several, shall we say, eccentric qualities. For example, the bat colony in the attic was led by a belligerent and dangerous individual named Deadwing who refused to relocate. Due to his cunning and prodigious size, I agreed to share our accommodations in exchange for several mild concessions. No sucking our blood in the night; don't eat the "cat," and whatnot. He warned me of less-than-obvious hazards associated with the property.

Thus, I established rules on a slate in the kitchen:

Do not respond to knocks at front door after dark.

Solicitors are off-limits unless otherwise directed.

Travel in pairs, always go armed.

The phone must be answered no sooner than the third ring, no later than the fourth.

Anyone caught with a witchboard loses a hand.

Mirrors must be hung only in specified locations.
Avoid the attic door between midnight and 3 A.M.
Remember: Imdugud saves.
Stein asked why in regard to the penultimate item.
"Because it doesn't lead to the stupid attic," Gertrude said.
"Not every time," I said. Ceiling timbers shifted.

We settled in and gradually established a routine. I plotted, E delegated, and the others executed. As the head of a "family," my priorities radically deviated from Amrutha's. She'd used the house as a retreat, interacting with the community by strict necessity. Our role was more active, along the lines of agent provocateurs. No telling how long we'd stay; the nature of our existence ensures unpredictable deviation between the sedentary and nomadic. Peasants brandishing torches and pitchforks and so forth are often the inciting element of an abrupt change of scenery, an exploration of new hunting grounds. Other times, we're summoned or dispatched on expeditions by the dark powers that hold us in thrall.

Tradition ruled: whatever came, the Hunsuckers would kill it, eat it, or endure it.

"Where's the damned cat?" E said upon noticing Sid had taken a fortnight's powder. This wasn't unusual. He patrolled the grounds and astral wastes alike. "Feline" time is not congruent with the experiences of lesser beings.

"He's around." I declined to mention I'd spotted him the previous evening across the creek through a notch in the cottonwoods. He'd loomed, massive as the Great Sphinx, cracking the bones and sinew of a bear in his fangs, licking gore from the dirt. I tiptoed the opposite direction.

F olks in the Big Apple might be aloof, but Sundown luminaries welcomed our arrival with open arms. During various sorties into town, the Reverend, Fire Chief, Boy Scout Den Mother, Head Knitter of the knitting circle, Pet Shop Owner, friendly neighborhood State Trooper, and the like, pumped my hand and/or clapped my shoulder. Realtor and self-appointed Mayor of Sundown, Ronald Terwilliger, braced me at the hardware store as I loaded bags of quick lime onto a cart. He and his wife were the subjects of "Aunt" Amrutha's death note. He greased the skids with a bit of mind-numbing chitchat, then proffered an invitation to the annual town barbeque.

"You're at the old Hunsucker place. What's that, thirteen acres? Man alive…nobody's lived there since the '90s. Except drifters and such. Hell of a reconstruction project, eh? Yeah, yeah. I've brokered a few deals in that area. Tried to buy it off your aunt. She wouldn't take my calls. Condolences for your loss. Hey, we're almost on top of a little yearly shindig…"

"The rats never left and now they're back," I said when he paused for breath.

He went blank until I smiled.

So it was that we Hunsuckers put in an appearance at Meadowlark Memorial Park on a blisteringly hot afternoon in August. A small crowd (three quarters of the town population, no doubt) had gathered to spread picnic blankets on the yellow grass, fry hamburgers, toss horseshoes in the sand pit, and sip booze while a quartet of retirees played big band and classic pop.

Ten seconds after meeting the Terwilligers in their natural environment (the center of attention of collected buffoons), I knew Amrutha had estimated the situation correctly. They were goners. My impression of Mr. Terwilliger was of a big chin and pointy elbows. A real grinner. He wore a natty blazer despite the baking heat. Ed Gorey or Gahan Wilson could've drawn the fellow and his wife, Beatrice, who bore him a vaguely fraternal resemblance.

He handed us party cups of lemonade and vodka. Needed way more vodka. "Ah, Mr. and Mrs. Hunsucker. A pleasure."

Oh, sure it is, buddy. More handshakes, more lies.

A heavyset wearer of polo shirts strolled over; Trooper Gosvenor, half in the bag and restraining his savage impulses behind an affable façade. "Howdy, neighbors. You met Patrick Bruss of beautiful Monticello? Pat reads your letters." He tapped a reedy fellow's arm and turned him from the grill to face us.

Postmaster Pat laughed, swooping his spatula like Zorro's rapier. "Howdy doo. Rare, medium, or charcoal?" I told him he was fortunate to live in Monticello. He didn't get the joke because I was quite serious. We had no business there for the moment.

That was basically that except for mingling with expressions of pained geniality, fondling our drinks, and politely laughing at the Monticello Postmaster's corny repartee. Trooper Gosvenor occasionally tried to sneak a peek down E's dress. Probably got an eyeful as she wasn't keen on bras. For a while, I thought the most interesting development would be the fact the "kids" were making friends. Gertrude compared headphones with a blonde girl in a punk hairdo and tracksuit while Stein hung out in the company of several boys near an ice chest full of canned soda.

"Rad 'stache'," a teen dressed for skateboarding said to Stein who nodded, pleased, unconsciously stroking his goatee as he was increasingly wont to do.

Then, Mrs. Terwilliger, drunk and voluble, pushed her breasts into my personal space and blinked at me with the cagey malice unique to besotted villainesses. "Hello, you're a weaselly little guy, aren't ya? I mean that in a fun way. What kinda name is Hunsucker? Is that American? Don't sound American."

"It's Swiss," I said, which sounded more or less correct. "An *American* name would be Sacagawea. Or Pontiac, or Seattle…" My gentle taunt didn't sting; rather the smugness of her expression intensified as if some barely perceptible accent of mine confirmed her suspicions. I'd left my favorite flint dagger in the nightstand drawer. Good thing, too.

"Swiss," she said. Her blotchy complexion made for an interesting complement to her flower print dress. "Your breath is cold."

"Honey—" Mr. Terwilliger said, grinning frantically.

"I'm not too polite to say it." Mrs. Terwilliger held her cup of wine at a perilous angle. Her perfume nearly crossed my eyes. "Amrutha Hunsucker lived here, years ago. My parents knew her. She died in that explosion in Seattle. Blasted an apartment building…"

"That's the one," I said. E stood behind me. I felt her unholy gaze boring into my spine. I shook my head, thinking, *those aren't nail extensions, you fools!*

"Weird, huh?" Mrs. Terwilliger turned her head like a German shepherd trying to solve a puzzle. "I mean, they're saying she spent a lot of time in the Middle East—"

"Sweetie pie, honeybunch—" Mr. Terwilliger's hand settled on her shoulder and she closed her mouth and turned away. I led E toward the band for a dance. Required some muscle on my part. Two gangs retreating after a clash.

"Aren't those two a kick in the pants?" my "wife" said through gritted teeth as we swayed to Sinatra. "Been a while since anyone recognized us."

"Amrutha was on to something." Her note had read, *Loose ends, darlings. Eradicate any Terwilliger you happen to meet in Sundown. See you in hell, AA.* Even dead and reduced to scribbles on parchment, I shivered to recall her voice, the dire acts of which she'd been capable.

E said, "How is it possible? Doth a crisis point approach?" She tended to lisp archaic when her canines thickened with excitement.

"I don't know."

"Are they opposition? Did they blow Amrutha to smithereens?"

"Unlikely. They're a different problem, else she would've written *Vengeance.* "Auntie" loved vengeance."

"We'd better do something. Fast."

"They're gonna be smoke," I said as the Terwilligers argued beyond earshot. Mrs. Terwilliger had her dander up. Oh, she'd definitely seen through our façade.

"Sometimes it's a pleasure."

"Who are you kidding? It's *always* a pleasure."

She squeezed my ass in warning.

Weird what the subconscious mind fixates upon. With so many horrors catalogued to choose among, I often beheld Stein's "rad 'stache" in my dreams. Dripping black from charnel feasting.

"**S**id? Do me a favor will you?" I reclined upon the front porch rocker, enjoying the mosquitos and humidity. He curled upon my knee, snoozing. "Zip over to the Terwilligers' house and murder them for me."

Sid yawned. His claws flexed and retracted. *No thanks.*

"Why not?"

Fuck you, is why not.

I chucked him yowling into a thornbush and went inside to counsel with my true-blue friend, Stalker. The "dog" vowed to ride or die.

Tracksuit Girl brought Gertrude home after an errand. Cute little pickup truck (her dad's as I learned). Our guest was instantly enamored of Sid and Stalker, which outweighed her wide-eyed appraisal of our rustic home: dirt and leaves, hanging pelts, stains, and rancid odors galore; an ambience better suited to a colonial hunting lodge.

The myth that pets and owners eventually resemble one another was a fact in the case of our "animals." The unearthly forces that tenanted their mortal forms had subtly reshaped "kitty" and "doggo" into vaguely humanoid physiognomies. They passed a cursory glance; closer inspection was to embark upon a deeply repellant trip into the uncanny valley. Sometimes, I heard the former dispossessed versions of them meowing and whining in phantom complaint. Same might hold true for the ostensibly human members of our pack.

Stalker snuffled the girl's ankles, then retreated into the murky shadows that covered everything in the house (day or night) between lonely pools of lamplight. Fluffy and black, he virtually melded into the background. Sid curled in front of the TV, raptly watching a VHS recording of babies chewing on binkies, crawling around, et cetera.

"OMG!" Tracksuit Girl actually said it that way--Oh-Em-Gee. "Can I pet that adorable floof? Pleeeeease? I'm gonna pet him." She bent to pat the "cat's" head. Never a good idea. He gave her a nip and emitted convincing feline hisses. The girl sucked blood from her thumb. "Is Sid short for Sid Vicious?"

Stein said, "No, it's an acronym—"

Gertrude gave her "brother" a sidelong glance. "Come on. I'll show you the back yard." She grabbed the blonde's hand and exited stage left.

"You'll stay for supper?" E said to the air.

"You bet!" Tracksuit Girl called back with the bright enthusiasm of a cheerleader hurrahing for her losing squad.

E raised a brow at me. I sighed, set aside the paper, and dressed in long pants and Wellingtons. I waded into the creek (the same one which traveled under our home's foundation) and caught a beaver by the tail as he submarined for his den. We wrestled and thrashed and splashed. My grip was iron, as was my resolve. Flat on the bank, he squealed for his miserable life; I unlimbered my dagger. E dressed the carcass and served it in a roasting pan, tail on, apple stuffed in its mouth. Tracksuit Girl became emotional as the lid was lifted. She didn't shut the front door as she fled. Her rig careened along the driveway. I didn't have a chance to question her regarding the ol' Jesus-fish bumper sticker or her evident parental issues.

Stein scooped baked brain from the cavity onto his plate. "Was there some kind of point to this exhibition?" he said to Gertrude through a dripping mouthful.

Gertrude slowly raised her head to beam a wide, radiantly evil smile. "No big. I only needed a lock of hair and her middle name, anyway." Bravado, or maybe not. Reliably cruel in matters of the heart, she was also an enigma. Days later, after Tracksuit Girl's disappearance, Gertrude wore the tracksuit.

Nobody said anything.

Trooper Gosvenor dropped by unannounced, Stratton campaign hat in hand. In the wake of her disappearance, Trackgirl's parents had grudgingly reported her as a missing person, although they figured she'd run away due to unspecified conflicts at home. A concerned citizen anonymously suggested "searching the Hunsucker residence." Nutty as that might sound, Trooper Gosvenor was obligated to investigate every lead, no matter how far-fetched.

He said, "These, er, this concerned individual is persistent, lemme tell you what. Sooner I perform due diligence, sooner I can get them off my case. Ten minutes, tops, and I'll skedaddle."

E poured iced tea and served petite fours she'd acquired from the general store's surprisingly well-stocked pastry section. I contemplated murdering the cop where he sat, bluff and hale, in that enormous wingback parlor chair. Tempting as the fantasy of his agonizing demise was, it wouldn't solve the larger problem. Doubtless, the Terwilligers were behind this surprise visit. Per E's theory, they'd somehow pierced the veil that cloaks our activities. The gift of true awareness is rare among humanity, and a real pain in the neck for those of us who count on the stolid ignorance of cattle.

"Shall we commence the tour?" I said.

He wiped his sheepish lips and dusted crumbs from his ridiculous handlebar mustache. "Lead on, Macduff!"

"Lay on."

"What?"

"This way, my friend." And away we went to peep into every dark corner of the house. Thankfully, he lacked the gift and didn't see a goddamned thing I didn't want him to.

"Might regret letting John Law go," E said as we waved adieu to the trooper's departing cruiser.

"He'll be the first domino," I said.

Stein had drawn meticulously annotated maps of our estate and the broader region. Of special interest was as the nearby dolmen and its inimical occupants.

"Our presence will wake them soon," Stein said. We'd hiked to where the dense woods thinned into a clearing. Nine crooked megaliths crowned a hill and formed the maw of a misshapen skull. The blooded sunset drained into the wilderness and each henge glimmered then darkened in turn.

"*They* were awake when Amrutha lived here," I said of the inhabitants of the hill. "She chose this homestead for a reason."

"You understand the danger."

"There is danger either way. Perform the calculations. I'll handle the rest."

He removed a bone scroll case from his coat. His ink and quill penmanship was cramped and voluminous, yet immaculate. "Ahead of you, "dad.""

"Thanks, "son.""

Time passed. The kaleidoscope of stars turned the necessary fraction.

By the dark of the moon, I strung warding charms in branches; dug a shallow depression in the back yard, laid some stones, and piled dead branches high. Built a medieval fire of Shakespearean majesty. Stalker crouched loyally at my side, whining.

I trilled and capered. I painted dread symbols of Slaughin, Anzû, and Old Leech upon my flesh in crimson ochre. At last, I said unto my furry companion, "All right, doggo. Let us get down to brass tacks."

Dad—His voice grated for he seldom spoke the tongue of men.

"Herd the foul presence into the yard. I'll handle the rest."

Bad smell thing. Scared, da-ad—

"Enough. Obey me."

Unwise, Stalker whimpered. *Unwiseunwiseunwise--*

"Quiet, slave, or it's the lash." I snapped my fingers. "Now, fetch."

He skulked into the night-shrouded trees. Soon came mournful howls as if the Hound of the Baskervilles himself had crawled from the bowels of hell. Awakened birds shrieked in terror.

"So fucking melodramatic," I said to mask a momentary pang of guilt.

In due course, Stalker returned to cower underfoot, reeking of his own piss-drench. Brush whipped. A slither of Limbless Ones approached, intertwined in a loathsome mound that thankfully shuddered to a halt beyond the rim of firelight. The abomination's torpidness suggested it had long slumbered in a sunless crevice favored by its ilk.

I cried, "Welcome to this steading, O servitors of the undulant gods!"

Its answer traveled into my bleeding ear as a whisper pregnant with static. *We are the interlocuter. Speak. We shall hear you.*

"I crave a boon."

Naturally. Speak. We shall determine the merits of your request.

"On behalf of those who dwell in the desecrated manse, I seek to reaffirm the accord you shared with its previous occupants. May we reaffirm an oath of nonaggression and cooperation." I laced my fingers together. "A compact of mutual succor."

After a silence that dragged on longer than I liked, the entity said, *What provender is offered?*

I cast Trooper Gosvenor's badge toward my visitor. Easily purloined, I'd idly wondered how the trooper accounted for its disappearance. "Mortal flesh and blood. 1212 Gollancz Drive. The back door is open." Gosvenor's residence—a doublewide trailer with all the amenities. Divorced and dogless. He spent the wasteland hours in a beer binge stupor on the couch before a widescreen TV. Possibly, he was entertaining the barracks secretary, who'd played a significant role in his ruined marriage. A twofer, then.

So be it. The compact is renewed. The entity unceremoniously sloughed into the underbrush.

"Flawless victory," I said to Stalker. Cold sweat obliterated my lovely runes. The "dog" had already made himself scarce.

Trooper Gosvenor suffered the vague, intuitively gruesome fate one might expect. Authorities declined to provide details of the robbery-homicide at 1212 Gollancz Drive. Scant fuss resulted. The hamlet sort of blinked, then moved on quickly.

Truth be told, I would've happily sicced our friends under the hill on other pesky humans. Sadly, the Terwilliger property, coincidentally or not, occupied land replete with crystal deposits—anathema to things that slithered in the earth—nor were the slimy devils equipped to track and pursue moving prey. Best to handle it ourselves. So, we surveilled the couple, nailing down their habits and routines. Mr. Terwilliger eventually went to the city on business; the perfect night to strike! I'll eschew the tedious details of how E lured Mrs. Terwilliger to Meadowlark Park via a phony text message and cut to the literal chase.

Mrs. Terwilliger proved agile and fleet of foot for a middle-aged woman in jeggings and flats. She almost made it back to her car. Stalker, the MVP of any foot pursuit, vaulted over shrubbery. He hamstrung her with a snap of his jaws. She fell, then rolled over and fire bloomed in her hands and Stalker yelped and collapsed.

"Oh, Beatrice, you miserable crosspatch." I bent, accelerating into a leap; a leopard knifing into a deer. Eat your heart out, Carl Lewis.

Mrs. Terwilliger must've been flying on pure adrenaline, what with the tendons sticking out of her leg. That level of stress tends to unsteady one's aim. Nonetheless, her snub revolver cracked thrice more and she put all three slugs through my chest. Less painful than some injuries I've experienced. Painful enough. I lost my composure and ripped her arm free of its socket before regaining control. Stood there holding hands while she gushed and bubbled and ceased.

Woozy, I sat beside the "dog" where he lay panting. A shadow crossed the face of the moon. Erinyes stood, hands on her hips, evaluating the mess.

"Wasn't the plan to interrogate the wench? Never mind, don't answer." She knelt and ministered to Stalker who wagged his tail in fear or gratitude. A day or two on the porch, he'd be fine. If a weapon isn't consecrated or imbued with sorcerous power, it merely represents an inconvenience to a Hunsucker.

I plucked the bullets from my breastbone and dropped them into my pocket. "Well, that surprised me, I'll admit."

"Every hick west of Rosendale is packing heat," E said. "Surely you knew."

I did now.

Time passed. We licked our wounds.

"Aha, there's a simple explanation for our problems." Stein triumphantly presented a memo pad. He chain-smoked while I methodically perused page after page of notes.

His exhaustive research into various musty internet alcoves and genealogy services ultimately revealed that Mrs. Terwilliger was distantly related to a branch of the Miller bloodline. The Millers were anti-occultists. Witchfinders, demonologists, exorcists, and (generally) unwitting tools of powers far greater than themselves. Their cloddish meddling predated the Dark Ages—went back to the day some bobble headed tart promised her firstborn in exchange for the secrets of alchemy and a comfortable marriage.

Poor Beatrice had likely obeyed gut instinct, unaware of the context of her antipathy for E and myself. Mr. Terwilliger, being a generic fellow of no particular account, undoubtedly knew less than nothing. Alas, alack, I'm not a merciful creature. What had Amrutha written? Oh, yes—loose ends.

M r. Terwilliger reported his wife missing. The cops didn't act quickly enough to suit him, so he made the fatal mistake of sneaking into our house. Who knows what was in his mind? I shushed a growling Stalker and let our visitor stumble around, terrorizing himself as he encountered objects and clues that the residents were inhuman ghouls. E grew bored of the game. She drifted off a high rafter and battened upon him. Large and strong as he might've been, a rabbit can't escape the clutches of a hawk. We dragged him upstairs for the coup de grâce.

"Who are you people?" Mr. Terwilliger said as E's extra-long, extra-sharp thumbnail pricked his jugular. "*What* are you?"

"The ghosts of four human beings, one cat, and one dog," I said over my "wife's" shoulder. This description wasn't accurate; served its purpose, however. His expression changed, altered by profound misunderstanding. I continued, "We're so lonely. You've no idea."

E pushed her thumb in and a good deal of his lubricants gushed forth.

The hallway lamp was dead so the door stood as a black henge in the sickly moonglow. The icy knob oozed faint vapors. I covered my hand with my sleeve, turned the knob, pulled, and gazed into an abyss beneath an interstellar vista of dripping Van Gogh stars. One step past the precipice, a tornado blazed and whirled. Tendrils of purple radioactive fire snapped across light years. Muffled voices chanted and screamed in anguish. Angels, demons, and damned souls chorused in an orchestra. Smaller, more distant vortexes, danced and danced here and there; sparks in the blackness.

I grasped Mr. Terwilliger's arms. E got his ankles. On the count of three, we heaved him into the pit of pits, the abscess in the tenderloin of Creation. Trailing a stream of oozy bubbles, he regained consciousness mid-plummet. You'd think his shrieks would've ceased sooner than they did. Acoustics are funny in the Great Dark. His shoe had come off. I pitched it into the depths.

Following this blip, our existence steadied again into a welcome humdrum. For the immediate future, our position in the hamlet was secure. Each of us retired to their own corner to dream and devise pet stratagems. We hunted (carefully and judiciously) and watched VHS tapes of our favorite moldy-oldy shows.

I wasn't overly concerned that the police might put two-and-two together regarding the spike of local missing persons. Should some enterprising sleuth actually put in the legwork, it wouldn't endanger us anyway. Our "family's" secret weapon is that of a specific and potent variation of the Mandela effect. A power granted by the forces of night. To reference that occult detective from the golden era of pulp: we cloud the minds of men. People simply forget the incriminating details of our most heinous trespasses. Or misattribute those trespasses as we desire.

There are limits, certain thresholds, if you will. Plausible deniability is the name of the game. Eventually, the magic wears thin. Wreak enough havoc, pile up enough corpses, or disappear them, even jaded 21st Century denizens catch on to the reality that they are provender of the hideously ineffable. That lightbulb moment is always our cue to mosey while the moseying is good.

Life *does* provide surprises.

The owner of the hardware store rang up my nails, barbed wire, and pickaxe. Had I heard? The police conducted a raid of an apocalypse cult in Ohio and rescued twenty underaged youths, including Tracksuit Girl. One of those "shed your worldly possessions and submit to the order" deals. She was due to return any day. At the house, I asked Gertrude for an explanation and learned the girl had confided plans to abscond on her eighteenth birthday. Gertrude, in a wholly uncharacteristic gesture, bought her a ticket and wished her bon voyage.

"Why assist, um, what's her name…?" I said.

"Mercy. Her name is Mercy. Geez, dad. Why'd she bail? Lots of family drama. Might even say a household schism. The Terwilligers made a stink, else her parents wouldn't care. Had to save face. It's a small town."

"How very altruistic, dear. Unless you wanted to see her exploited by a cult. Fiendishly brilliant in that case."

"No. I assumed she'd catch wise to their scams. She's a survivor." My favorite little murderess stared into the distance, pondering. "Her aura is strange. Fate doesn't know what to make of her and neither do I. A psychic thundercloud hangs over her head. Or that's all bullshit. Maybe I'm playing the long con. She trusts me. Imagine her sense of compounded horror when she realizes what I am, ten, fifteen years on…Delicious, delicious betrayal. What if we're destined to be archnemeses? Exciting, right?"

"Sure is!" I said gamely.

Did more loose ends dangle for the snipping?

Tracksuit Girl dressed in a hoodie, jeans, and tennis shoes when she climbed off the bus near midnight. The stop was at the entrance of town, about a mile from her house.

I started the wagon where it sat hidden behind a hedge. I idled alongside her as she trudged. Rolled down the window and said, "Hi, Mercy. Need a lift?"

She seemed different; harder, wiser by the shine of the car's running lights. The set of her jaw and the steel in her eyes gave an impression of a young woman who could survive a wilderness plane crash or be the last sister standing in the wake of a sorority house massacre.

She said, "I'm good, Mr. Hunsucker. Got to rehearse my lines one more time before I walk through the door. Tail tucked, contrite. Y'know?"

"Understood. Can I ask one question?"

"Fire."

"Did you heed the call of that, er, prophet, or were you interested in pissing off your folks?"

"Only thing I've ever wanted was to get away, Mr. Hunsucker. G'night."

"Okay. Come see Gertrude. She's happy you're back."

"Better not be happy," Mercy said. Hunched forward and kept trucking.

I laughed and let her go. For the moment.

The lone blinking stoplight painted cold shopfronts bloody.

Yes, Sundown was the epitome of bucolic tranquility. Stuck in a yesteryear when doctors made house calls, pies cooled on window sills, and streets rolled up at dusk. One could smell pine needles and curing hay. Beyond Main Street spread trees and hills, all lumpish in the dark…and other hamlets were scattered in the gods' green finery. Nobody locked their doors around here. Not yet.

We weren't leaving anytime soon.

I smiled wide. Strained the cords of my neck. Then I turned onto the secondary road that led to the house. Through the trees, a flickering, unearthly purple glow in the attic window guided me home.

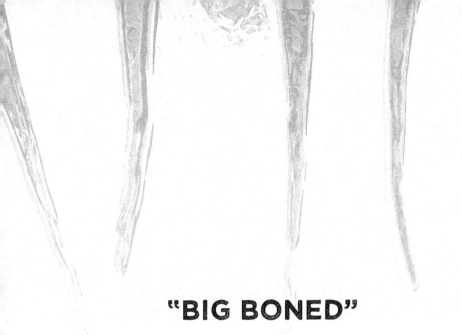

"BIG BONED"

BY KRISTI DEMEESTER

A crown wasn't a requirement for starving, but most of us adopted it as a rule. We imagined the crystals as diamonds, the metal as silver, the weight of the circlet resting atop our hairsprayed updos the triumph we'd been chasing all seventeen years of our lives. Sequins and glitter look better against exposed hip and collarbones and stomachs that have started eating themselves because there's nothing else to consume.

There were other rules, of course. Spray tans were on Thursdays. Teeth whitening strips during the nightly forty-five minutes of Pilates. No cheat meals during pageant season prep. Brittany Leigh's mom would sell you the Fen-Phen she could still get in Mexico for five hundred or a Fenti bag if the Pilates wasn't working. Pedicures once a week. A full set of acrylics too. Square tips. Not too long. French only. Wax every other week. Brows. Legs. Underarms. Forearms. Bikini. Facials at least once a month with full extractions. Doctor's notes for the flu when you missed two or three weeks of school to recover from a nose job.

And the meetings. The last Sunday morning of each month, we'd meet in Amanda Thompson's house to worship at the sanctified altar of her guest house with its private bathroom. Our tongues wrapped around the holy vomit that came after binging, and we'd hold each other's hands and hair and give thanks for the glory that were our sanctified bodies.

We were a coven of beauty queens, and we moved through the world like Furies. Had we not had sashes, we would have gone looking for nooses to wrap about our necks. In our world, there were only the hot, glaring lights of a runway stage; the corseting of the ribcage so not even our breath would expand our bellies; the balancing on our Lucite heels as we savored the taste of perfume and hairspray on our tongues. We'd been anointed as the blessed few, and every pageant felt like an act of creation. A slippery birth.

So, when Brianna Palmer announced she wasn't going to do the Miss Brunswick High Pageant, we called an emergency meeting.

"She said it's sexist. That it's demeaning to parade around onstage like that, and that it promotes body image problems," Hanna Brinkley said and wiped the back of her hand across her mouth before checking her teeth in her compact mirror.

"I mean…she's not *wrong*, but it's like, we all know the game, right? Who gives a shit if it means you get a crown at the end of it," Trina Jacobson said, and the group collectively nodded.

"She never came to meetings anyway. Said it was gross," Ashlynn McGee said.

"Plus, she never even made top ten," Tansy Vaughn said. "And her talent was that creepy puppet thing."

"Ventriloquism," I said, and we all rolled our eyes.

Jessica Evans didn't say anything—she'd lost a bit too much blood—but we all knew what she thought. We were a singular unit—an entity born of a thirst that only few things could quench. There was no need to punish Brianna for her betrayal. She'd never known the truth of such transcendence. We could let her vanish back into the nothingness of high school and never suffer any sort of retribution. She'd only been set on the path. She hadn't truly *known*.

"Whatever. Fuck her," I said, and we all nodded. Even Jessica Evans managed to shake her brunette curls one time before letting herself droop onto Kayla Taylor's shoulder.

Amanda Thompson placed the dagger back in its velvet wrap— it was her house, and she deserved such an honor—and we drifted back to our own homes, our lives that existed outside of the magic we'd created in that basement room. We did our Pilates, pushed our meals around on our plates before our parents were distracted enough not to notice us scraping them into the garbage, and we came together and apart each Sunday to consume what we needed— each of us offering up small parts of herself so that the group might be sustained. It was so little to ask when it meant we might know what it meant to have a crown placed on our heads. To know what it meant to be deemed the best. To be *perfect*.

We'd begun the descent into the final weeks before Miss Brunswick High, when Tansy Vaughn came to school minus at least five pounds. Her hair shone against cheekbones gone sharper, and her collarbone traced an elegant line above the cleavage that came courtesy of the boob job her father had paid for when she turned eighteen.

The rest of us had not lost any weight. We maintained. We toned. But we were no thinner than we were before our last meeting.

We cornered her at lunch, the table spread with our requisite La Croixs and Diet Cokes.

"How?" we said.

Tansy Vaughn shrugged her shoulders, but she was looking anywhere but at us, and we knew. She'd taken more than her share. We had sworn, in the beginning, that we would offer what we could, and in return, would not glut ourselves. To do so would upset the delicate balance of our group. It wouldn't be *fair*.

That afternoon, we met without Tansy Vaughn, but not at Amanda Thompson's house because she would guess that's where we'd gone and show up anyway.

"Who gave it to her?" Kayla Taylor asked, and we all stared at each other in silence. It didn't need to be said. We all knew it hadn't been one of us. We would have all felt it.

"She couldn't have taken it from anyone else. It wouldn't work the same way. Not if they aren't one of us," Hanna Brinkley said.

"Brianna Palmer?" Trina Jacobson asked, but it wouldn't be her. She'd never taken part in the meetings. If she'd known, she would have stayed.

"No," Ashlynn McGee said, and every head turned. "She's taking it from herself." She stared down at her hands, and we all felt how much she wanted to tear at her cuticles, to taste the sharp tang of blood, because we wanted it, too. More than that, of course, but still, our mouths watered.

"I know because I did it, too. For the Miss Glow pageant. Just the tiniest bit. But I lost two pounds," Ashlyn McGee said, and we fell into a stunned silence.

"How could we not have known?" I asked. We all leaned forward, our nostrils flared, our mouths still damp with want.

"Maybe because it was so small. But I never did it again. I swear it. I barely made top five anyway, so it didn't even matter," Ashlynn McGee said.

"Anyone else have anything they'd like to confess, since the rules apparently don't fucking matter?" I asked, and only Ashlynn McGee shook her head. The rest of us had gone still, still, still while we listened to the hunger raging in our bellies.

We had been so good. Such good girls. Didn't we deserve a treat? Didn't we deserve a reward? Ever since that night, the night Maribel Harrington won Miss Teen Peach even though she'd never trained, not like *we* had; the night we cut our palms, scarlet drops against fake diamonds and silk, and sworn fealty to whatever would hear us if only we would be the ones to cry mascara tears, the rose's thorns pricking our arms as we accepted the bouquet and the crown, since that night, the scales had dropped away from our eyes. We'd learned that the ritual for calling forth an entity doesn't matter as long as there is need.

Whatever ancient creature we had woken thirsted in the same ways we did, but we were the ones with the teeth.

Once, she'd been a goddess. Worshiped. Feared. Had slept to the sound of screams like music, a river of blood flowing at her feet. She did not appear before us, but we felt her move through us and take root. She saw how we were worthy. How we moved through the world in the same ways she once had. How ravenous we were. And she showed us what we needed to know. How to rip and tear and eat so we might become what had remained hidden inside us—those last vestigial pieces filed away until we resembled marble. Without flaw. Without imperfection. Those worthy of the crown of both the living and the dead. We would take our places beside her, listening as the screams became sighs, and everything we'd ever desired would belong to us. Only to us.

For so long, we'd taken so little. Tiny slices stolen from our inner thighs, the lower parts of our stomachs that remained hidden under the waistband of our bikini-cut underwear, the insides of our arms. The meat of us then split into smaller and then smaller pieces until they were practically wafer thin. A communion to melt on our tongues as we invoked our holy goddess who'd granted us perfection. But first we would purge the unholy matter that was food. After, we ate of each other's flesh, and it was good.

After that first time, we'd all placed. Four of us won crowns. We were golden daughters—shining totems of what it meant to have everything women were supposed to want. When the noises started—our heads filled with the delicate sounds of screaming—it didn't matter. We were beauty queens. It had never mattered what was in our heads, after all, and we were grateful for our blessing.

So, yes. We deserved a treat.

Ashlynn McGee moved first, but Trina Jacobson was behind her and grabbed her arm, those French tips digging into the tender meat.

"Don't," Ashlynn McGee said, but we were already on her in a snarl of arms and legs and teeth. There was no need for the knife.

But we weren't monsters. We didn't kill her, and ate from the places no one would see. When she screamed, the sound joined the screams we carried in our heads, and *oh,* it was better than our fingers between our legs, better than heads turning when we walked down the hallways at school. Better than anything except the crown.

When we were finally finished, we all knew she wouldn't compete again. Not in anything that had a swimsuit category. Or in a dress with a slit any higher than her knee.

We licked our lips clean while she sobbed.

"Don't get any blood on the carpet. My mom will kill me," Kayla Taylor said and tossed a roll of paper towels at Ashlynn McGee. She blotted at the reddish smears, and Kayla Taylor tore off another paper towel and wiped at her own mouth.

"You have *got* to learn how to cry pretty," she said, and we all nodded. It was another rule. Crying was a requisite part of wearing a crown, but it should always be lovely.

"I will. I promise," Ashlynn McGee said, and we all hugged her and licked the tears from her cheeks. She was still one of us.

We went home, and we all dreamed of roses, of crowns, of an audience with no mouths even though the air was filled with the sound of their screaming. We all woke with the sensation of meat caught between our teeth. We all woke thinner than we'd been the day before.

Tansy Vaughn didn't wake up at all.

Her parents told the police she'd kissed them goodnight at 10 p.m. They'd heard music coming from her room for about thirty minutes, and then quiet. They'd gone to bed themselves around midnight, after finishing a second bottle of Pinot Grigio. Yes, they'd slept solidly. No, they'd not heard anything strange in the night. Tansy was well-liked. Popular. Pretty. A beauty queen. There had never been any strange incidents. No drug use. Never. Not their Tansy. No secret boyfriends. Only her pageant friends, and they loved Tansy. Loved her so much. They'd been friends since they were little girls. Everyone loved Tansy.

They searched the house and the woods behind the house, but they never did find Tansy. Told her parents it was likely she'd run away. So many teen girls did that. Met some guy on the Internet and took off to meet him. She'd either come home or she wouldn't, but there was no evidence of foul play. Nothing they could do except pray. And wait.

But the next night, after the police had made their rounds to question all of us, Ashlyn McGee called and asked us to come to her house.

We settled into a circle on her cream rug, her porcelain dolls watching from above, her dress tossed carelessly on the duvet, as she stood in the center in bra and underwear. Her stomach, her thighs were completely smooth. The jagged indentations we'd marked her with had vanished.

"We ate her, didn't we?" Ashlyn McGee asked, and the screaming in our heads became a satisfied hum.

"We were all asleep by that point. How the fuck could we have eaten her?" Jessica Evans said, but we all knew. We all remembered that slick, full feeling we'd woken to the morning Tansy Vaughn went missing. We'd all been there when Jake Mollien's neck had practically broken when we walked into school right before the first period bell rang.

"How the fuck am I just magically healed then?" Ashlyn McGee asked.

"Maybe it was from before," Kayla Taylor said.

"Put your clothes back on. We've all seen your tits," I said, and Ashlyn McGee pulled her dress back over her head.

"Shouldn't you be, oh, I dunno, grateful to be back to normal?" Amanda Thompson asked.

"I never said I wasn't."

"Then shut the hell up and enjoy it."

"How long will it last? Now that we've... you know," Kayla Taylor said.

"Miss Brunswick High is in eleven days. It'll be long enough," I said.

"You can't know that," Ashlyn McGee said, but Amanda Thompson had brought the dagger, and she held it out to us.

"We give back. Pledge ourselves again," Amanda Thompson said.

"Exactly. She heard us the first time. It's only right that we thank her for everything she's given us," I said and took the dagger from Amanda Thompson. Slashed a thin line across my palm. In the evening shadows, the blood glittered.

"I drink of you, my sisters. I drink of the screaming inside you. Of the sighs they will become. I drink of the crown. Both the living and the dead," I said, and the words were a part of me I had never known. A part that had woken only recently, and I wanted it all. The voice, the screams that would become sighs. I wanted all of it.

One by one we opened ourselves—a living altar sanctified by blood—and we had never been more beautiful. If the judges could have seen us, they would have fallen to their knees and sobbed. We were an impossible decision.

None of us ate during those final eleven days. We would do nothing to taint our purification. Nothing to keep us from the sighs. From the crown.

We rose on the morning of Miss Brunswick High, our skin flawless, our bodies angular and sharp, our teeth like pearls, and together, we began. Hair appointments. Makeup appointments. Those middle-aged women fluttering around us, cooing over how pretty we were. We could hear them screaming inside their heads, and we sighed with the pleasure of it.

When we descended on the auditorium—our gowns in their clear, plastic coverings—we were legion.

They'd set up a picture of Tansy Vaughn beside the stage. *In loving memory*, it read.

"I told her she should have gotten her head shot airbrushed," Kayla Taylor said when we passed it. "Her nose looks crooked."

The few other girls who'd made the foolish decision to participate stared at us as we changed into our casual wear. They, too, bared their teeth into something that resembled smiles, but they'd not hallowed themselves. They knew nothing about screaming that would become sighs. Of the crown that was both the living and the dead. Our goddess would have looked upon them in fury for how little they could offer.

Backstage, we joined hands. Anyone who saw us would have thought we were praying. I suppose we were, in our way. But we were listening, the taste of blood and perfume on our tongues, as the screams built and built into an unholy shrieking.

"I drink of the crown," we whispered, and then we were giggling, everyone hugging each other and dropping air kisses near cheeks as the emcee stepped onstage.

The applause ran through us like water, and we shivered as the lights hit our skin, as the audience gasped each time we stepped on stage. Every category was somehow better than the last, and when we stepped onto the stage in our evening wear, the screaming started. The clapping and shouts of appreciation a cacophony of sound that dropped over the auditorium like a dome, and us at the center of it, our feet placed perfectly as we executed our turns.

"Lovely. Just lovely. Aren't they lovely, folks?" the emcee asked, and the crowd roared their appreciation, and we drank it in. Like blood. Like flesh. Like a scream become a sigh. Like an end become a beginning—the entrance of a goddess into a world that had long forgotten what it meant to wear a crown.

They had no need to announce the top ten, but they did it anyway. Of course, we were called forth, our hands clasped together as we smiled down. There were others among us, but they were inconsequential. They were detritus.

We answered our interview questions: what to do about lesser education in lower socioeconomic areas, how to address issues related to cyber bullying, what the role of natural preservation should be in our advancing world. The audience breathed as one as they listened—a collective sigh.

When the emcee announced the top five, we had not expected one of the others to remain. She should not have. Even the audience knew. When the emcee called her name, they went silent. No screams. No sighs. She tried to clasp our hands, but we were too tightly bound, and she was not part of us. She was an abomination. An obscenity. She was not for the crown.

It had been so long since we'd eaten anything, and she smelled of an optimism she did not deserve. We couldn't help ourselves. We drooled.

Then finally, blessedly, the top three. Kayla Taylor, Amanda Thompson, and me. The other girl was banished back from whatever suburban cul-de-sac she'd crawled out of. We forgave her. It wasn't her fault, after all.

But the judges…they had not screamed. Had not sighed. They were unworthy of their roles, but they held the crowns, and we would obey for as long as we needed to.

Amanda Thompson was second runner up, and she took her sash, her flowers, her smaller crown and blew kisses at the audience, and then it was only Kayla Taylor and I onstage, our arms wrapped around each other as we waited. So patient. So composed even as our stomachs screamed into the audience's silence.

And then it was Kayla Taylor's name called, not mine, and the audience rose to their feet as I stepped forward to accept the final crown, tears glittering prettily. We rushed together, our lips staining each other's cheeks before whispering how *hungry. How hungry.*

We had pledged ourselves to a goddess, and hadn't we always been building to an end? Hadn't we always known that once we took the crown, she would also be able to step forward and reclaim what had been taken from her so long ago?

We descended and went among them. Those who would worship us, and those who would not. We'd denied ourselves for so long, but no more. The judges looked upon us in awe. In horror.

"You are not worthy," we said in one voice, and then unhinged our jaws.

Screams and sighs, and it was an ascension into the beautiful chaos our goddess had promised. The crown of the living and the dead.

We were so hungry, and finally, *finally,* we would feed. And at the very end, the world would tremble at our feet.

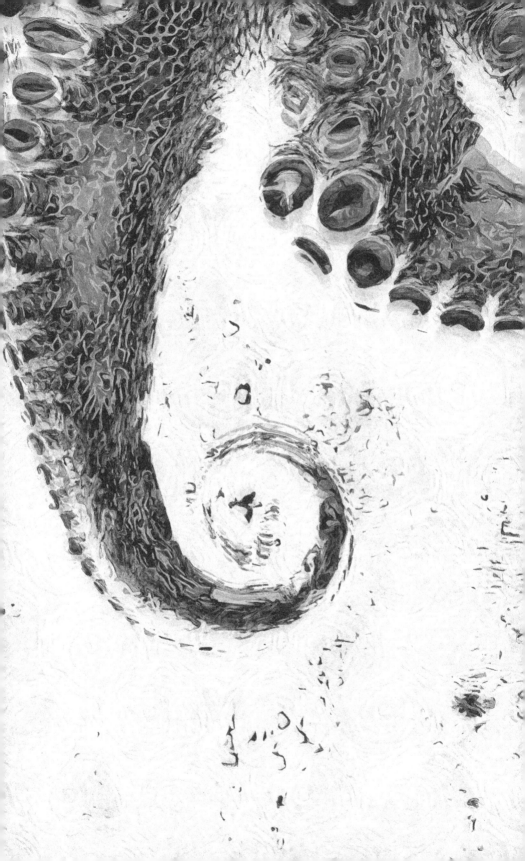

THE HOLIDAY BOOK AND BAKE SALE

BY ROB E. BOLEY

Matthew might as well have been riding his beach cruiser bike through the apocalypse. The town of Beatrice Beach, Delaware in December was as cold and still as a corpse. The streets were deserted. Most of the homes sat empty.

A hand-lettered sign outside of the Beatrice Beach Church of Eternal Bliss proclaimed that the Holiday Book and Bake Sale would today run from 9 a.m. to 1 p.m. He walked his bike through the gravel lot and leaned it against a brick garden planter full of dirt. The church's chocolate-colored clapboard siding made the one-story building look like a long, rich cake. His stomach growled. Wasn't there a fairy tale about a candy house with a witch inside? Closing his eyes, he thought perhaps he could hear the ocean, which was only a block away. He could certainly smell it, that salty spice in the air that was at once fresh and stagnant, newborn and ancient.

He'd only been to Beatrice Beach once before, with his partner

Melanie's family for a summer vacation. Then, the town had been bustling and crowded with families and couples. Cars everywhere. Music. Laughter. At nights, they took Ubers to clubs in neighboring coastal cities. They danced and drank late into the night. It was at the end of one of those nights that he and Melanie had screwed in the outdoor shower at her parents' summer house, not bothering to use a condom.

Now, gravel crunched behind him, and Melanie wheeled her cruiser next to his. Her belly swelled with the unplanned result of that fateful decision.

"Should we lock them together?" he asked.

She kissed his cheek. "Here? Nah."

His hand slid over her bulging belly. "How's our little button? Everything okay?"

"Relax. The button enjoyed the ride. You worry too much."

She wasn't wrong. Yesterday, when they'd spotted the flyers in town for the church's Holiday Book and Bake Sale, Melanie got that glowing smile that lit up more than her face. They still had the summer house to themselves for four more days before her family showed up for a Christmas getaway, and she was aching for a good read. She checked on her phone's map app the distance between her parents' summer house and the church, saw it was only a little over a mile, and suggested they take the bikes. He'd spent an hour last night in bed reading about the dangers of biking while pregnant, but she'd silenced him with, "I want to be as active as possible before I turn into a grumpy beach ball. My feet hurt too much to walk. We are biking. Now put that phone away and pleasure me."

Hard to argue with that.

Now he took a final look up and down the street—cold, deserted, and contemplative, comparing it with his memories from last summer—warm, bustling, and vibrant. He couldn't help feeling like this was some metaphor for his social life before and after parenthood. Well so be it.

They walked arm-in-arm up the church's ramp. An elderly man in a tie-dyed hoodie exited the building carrying two canvas bags stuffed to the handles with books. His big fluffy beard made him look like Santa's illegitimate brother.

"Shit," Melanie said. "We should've brought bags."

Matthew squeezed her hand. "We probably shouldn't say *shit* in the church."

She giggled. "Gawd, this building looks like a giant hunk of chocolate. I'm famished. This mom-to-be is about to murder some cookies."

Tie-Dyed Santa stood with his back to the door, propping it open for them. They hurried inside, and Matthew thanked the man. As they passed, he noticed a sandwich bag full of cookies resting precariously on top of each bag of books.

They entered a fluorescent-lit room with five long rows of folding tables, each filled with neat rows of books resting spines-up. All but the far row held hardbacks, only a quarter each. The last row had paperbacks at a dime apiece. The baked goods were arranged on a set of tables set up along the far wall. *Frosty the Snowman* played at low volume. Dozens of customers shuffled down the aisles, many holding stacks of books.

"Everyone left in town must be here," Matthew said.

"Oh, Matt." Melanie clutched his arm. "This is everything I wanted."

He kissed her cheek. "Go getcha some."

She waded into the first aisle while he helped himself to a complimentary cup of coffee. The non-fiction section was small—

only two tables, but he found a book on parenting and another on the French and Indian War. For the next hour, Melanie perused the books. Volunteers with hand-written name tags were constantly restocking, so she made multiple laps. He sat on a folding chair off to the side, watching the people, flipping through his books, and studying the room. A variety of artwork hung upon the walls—much of it surprisingly rooted in almost psychedelic fantasy. Glowing angels rising from ocean waves. Serene mer-creatures swimming in blue waters. Mostly naked people frolicking in a lush garden. A billboard proclaimed, "The path to Eternal Bliss is marked by Sacrifice." Another offered, "The Lord opens the Gate for the truly Innocent."

He ventured into the sluggish fray every few minutes to retrieve Melanie's current stack of books. When he took her third stack, he said, "You know, you only have about three more months. How many books can you possibly read before the button's born?"

"Well, what about after?"

"After, we'll be too busy with dirty diapers and breastmilk to read."

"Hush your mouth."

She dismissed him with a playful wave of her hand. On the way back to his plastic perch, he passed an older woman with a braided ponytail restocking the tables from a milk crate full of hardbacks. Her name tag read "Emilie." She called to one of the others. "Where's George? This is supposed to be his job."

Across the room, someone replied, "Last I saw, he was sneaking off this morning with a bag of cookies."

"That rat."

Matthew chuckled under his breath. Once seated, he flipped through Melanie's latest finds. A mystery. A thriller. Horror.

Romance. Her tastes were all over the place. Each of the book had the letters "C.C." neatly printed in blue ink on the upper outside corner of the first page. He wondered if that stood for something. Church copy? Cookie crowd? Come consign? Chocolate church?

By the time she was done, Melanie had amassed twenty-three dollars and forty cents worth of books. The two elderly women staffing the book cashier table seemed quite pleased. The plump one with dancing eyes and gray hair wore a nametag on her Rudolph the Red-nosed Reindeer sweater identifying her as "Lois" with a smiley face "o" and a tiny red heart dotting the "i." The thinner one with short, peppery hair and a pointy chin wore a red and green flannel with a long red cardigan. Her name tag was in all caps: "CONNIE."

"How much longer do you have?" Lois asked Melanie with a buttery smile, after collecting cash from Matthew. For a beat the question seemed terribly ominous.

"Probably not long enough to read most of these," Melanie said.

"Babies are a pure blessing," Connie said. "Truly innocent."

Lois nodded. "So delicate. So precious." She counted out the change and pressed it into Matthew's palm. Her hands were soft and scarred. She kept her eyes on Melanie. "Are you a fast reader, dear? Connie here reads at the speed of light. She sprints through the margins but I like to wander between the lines. What about you?"

"I guess I'm more of a wanderer, too."

Connie was stuffing all the books into two oversized shopping bags. "Once I start a good tale, I simply must find out how it ends. I go through a book a day in the off-season."

Lois grinned. "She's read most every book in this room, I wager."

"I write my initials on the first page so I can remember which ones I've read. Otherwise, people donate them back and I read them all over again with this vague sense of déjà vu."

Melanie laughed at that. All through this exchange, Matthew watched the women's eyes to see if they noticed his and Melanie's lack of wedding rings. If they did, he could detect no judgment. If anything, these two radiated a kind of giddy joy that was almost contagious. He made a mental note to see if the Church of Eternal Bliss had a website. They'd considered going to church once the button was old enough, and this seemed like a happy place. Maybe they had a location back in Pittsburgh. He looked around for a restroom. The coffee had run right through him and was anxious to escape.

"Have you visited the bake sale?" Connie asked, and his bladder groaned.

"That's our next stop," Matthew said.

"Well, you simply must try the sugar cookies," Lois said. "They were my great grandmother Gigi's recipe, and they've won no less than eleven blue ribbons."

Melanie bit her lip the way she sometimes did in bed when he did something just right with his fingers. "We'll definitely get some."

"You won't regret it," Connie told them.

"They're the ones wrapped in plastic," Lois said. "Otherwise, they might crumble. They're so delicate. So precious."

The cookie tables were filled with all manner of cookies—no-bakes, chocolate chip, oatmeal, rum balls, and pin-wheel. White-gloved volunteers loaded customers' cookies into white boxes which were then weighed on an electric scale.

Melanie pointed at a plate of M&M cookies. "Matt, they have our cookies!"

That was them. Matthew and Melanie. Matt and Mel. M&M.

Elvis crooned out *White Christmas* while the pressure in Matthew's bladder grew. Melanie selected one of everything, plus several of

Gigi's bagged sugar cookies. He wasn't sure they had room in the bikes' baskets for all these cookies, much less the books.

As they checked out, he spotted a sign for the restrooms pointing at a closed door. They followed the sign into a long hallway, the restrooms at the far end.

"Shockingly, I don't have to pee." Melanie sat in a plastic chair, the cookies on her lap. "Go ahead. I'll wait here with the books."

He grinned. "And the cookies. Save me a couple, would you?"

"Hurry up. And remember, if you shake it more than twice, you're playing with it."

"I'll keep that in mind."

After leaning the towering bags of books against each other beside her chair, he hustled down the hall. He shoved open the men's room door. Blackness. A light blinked on as he sprinted to the urinal and fumbled with his pants. He only barely cleared the zipper in time. The first spray of urine hit the front of the urinal before he managed to aim inside the bowl. Soon, sweet relief. He leaned forward, forehead pressed to the wall over the urinal, and let out a low moan.

He took a step back from the urinal and it automatically flushed. That's when he saw the shoe protruding from under the stall.

His cheeks blushed. Crap. Someone heard him moan. How loud had he been?

Except... the bathroom had been dark when he entered.

Someone would've had to be in the bathroom for quite a while—and very still—for the lights to have shut down. He swallowed hard.

For the longest time, he stared at the shoe. A black Nike. Maybe it was just a shoe? But no, when he stepped back and crouched, he saw an ankle. And bunched-down pants.

He shifted upright, considered.

"Are you, uh, okay in there?" he asked, his voice barely a croak. Nothing.

The silence was sharp and heavy, the edge of a cleaver pressing upon tender flesh. He realized he was still exposed, and he tucked himself away, zipped up.

The urinal automatically flushed.

He nearly screamed.

Okay, screw this. He stepped onto the urinal's lip so that he could see over the stall. He stared down at a middle-aged man sprawled lifeless upon the toilet. His green Christmas sweater showed a station wagon carrying a large Christmas tree. It read: "BEND OVER. I'LL SHOW YOU." His nametag identified him as George.

His eyes were rolled back as if staring at the wall behind him. Mouth agape. His beard was stained with cookie crumbs and pink froth. In his lap, one hand clenched a plastic bag full of crumbs.

Oh shit. The cookies! Melanie!

Matthew pivoted to step down, except his foot slipped on the urinal bowl—still wet from his pee. He spilled sideways, striking his head.

The urinal flushed again, gargling downward a stream of liquid but also of consciousness. The moment faded to gray, then blackness.

Emptiness.

He woke in darkness, confused.

When he sat up, the overhead lights blinked on. His head pounded. How long had he been out? The black Nikes still rested on the floor in the stall. The cookies …

He scrabbled to his feet. The room arced sideways. He clutched the metal divider between the urinal and the sink, waited for the room to stop swaying. When it didn't stop, he staggered forward anyway, yanking open the door and spilling into the hall.

Silence. Stillness. He stared down the hall, hoping he'd see Melanie but knowing that he wouldn't.

Dread scurried down his spine and pooled in his stomach. He ran down the hall, footsteps squeaking on the shiny floor. Their bags of books still sat beside the chair. Melanie and the cookies were gone. His heart quickened. His head throbbed. He pushed open the door that lead to the Holiday Book and Bake Sale.

Books still filled the tables. A few cookies were left, too, but no one was there. He checked his phone. No calls. No texts. It was 1:45. He'd been unconscious for at least an hour.

Outside, their bikes still leaned together where they'd left them.

The streets were deserted. He fumbled out his cell and tried calling Melanie but the call went straight to voicemail. Still clutching his phone in one sweaty hand, he walked toward the road. Gravel crunched beneath his shoes. Down the street toward the ocean, a pick-up truck idled. He jogged toward it, ready to ask the driver if he'd seen Melanie.

He slowed his pace as he approached the man slumped over the wheel. Something pink was splattered on the side window, which was barely cracked. Inside, the Muppets sang *Jingle Bell Rock.* The driver wore a tie-dyed hoodie. A half empty bag of cookies sat next to him on the seat.

Matthew backed away from the truck, shaking his head. He tried calling Melanie again. Voicemail. He tried 911. It kept ringing but no one answered.

In the distance, waves churned. From that same direction came a cacophony of wailing and cawing unlike anything he'd ever heard. He followed the noise. The street dead-ended at an empty parking lot which had a wood ramp that led up and over the slight dune buffering the neighborhood from the ocean. He ran to the ramp, which was covered in crumbs. Bread crumbs? No, he knelt and picked up one of the morsels. The bit of cookie crumbled in his fingers, leaving a smear of creamy sugar. *So delicate. So precious.*

He followed the trail of cookie crumbs up the ramp to the crest of the dune.

When he saw the beach, he froze.

Bodies littered the sands. Hundreds of them. Men. Women. Children. Some were arranged in interconnected circles. Others lay sprawled at the end of individual trails of staggering footprints. Nearly all of them wore red or green. Thousands of seagulls swarmed in the air. At first, he thought the birds were pecking at the dead bodies, but no, they were nibbling at the cookie crumbs interspersed amongst the corpses—plucking bits from dead hands or bulging pockets or even slack mouths. Many of the birds already rested dead or dying in the sand, beaks stained pink and wings flapping a lazy finale. The birds in the sky squawked and chirped. Those flopping in the sand croaked and wailed.

He called out, "Melanie!"

Only the mindless birds answered. Winds ruffled the hair and clothing of the deceased. The ocean clawed at the shore, dragging corpses out to sea. Already several bodies floated among the foamy waves. Matthew teetered down the ramp onto the beach. The birds scattered at his approach, filling the air with the flutter of wings though many plopped dying back onto the sands. He recognized many of the dead from the Holiday Book and Bake Sale. In the center of one of the macabre circles, he found Connie and Lois clasped together, their gaping mouths stained with pink foam.

The churning water grew louder, claiming more and more festively dressed bodies. The waves crashed and jostled together as if dancing. As if this was a celebration—a moment of revelry prefacing a culmination. A conception. He recalled that night in the outside shower, he and Melanie—M&M—fumbling together drunk and ravenous for each other. Unknowingly conjuring life out of chaos. Pairing chromosomes. Connecting flesh. Knitting bones. The salty waters clapped together and sprayed droplets into the chilled air. Praying. Praising. Preying. Prying.

He jogged along the shore, looking for his lover among the dead and drifting. The ocean roared triumphant.

COMMUNITY GARDEN

BY JOHN LANGAN

Turn off the news and build a garden. —Lukas Nelson

1. 1979. We had the dream in lilac season, not so much a season as a couple of weeks in mid-spring when the lilac bushes in the front yards and around the sides of our houses bloomed, threading the air with their sweet, heady scent. School almost at its end, teachers showing movies or enlisting classes to clean their rooms, keeping the kids busy until the required number of instructional days had been completed. The tail end of June and then July and August looming, huge empty chambers full of sunlight and heat and wandering the neighborhood, riding our bikes up the hill to the VFW past the old and almost-old men trudging inside, pedaling to the other side of the dirt and gravel parking lot to where a slender path cut through the sugar maples, dogwood, and redbud to the grounds of the psychiatric center. Pretty much all parents in the neighborhood and (several adjacent) were employed at the sprawling red brick hospital and its surrounding buildings. They

worked as nurses and nurses' assistants, as clerks and janitors, as cooks and security guards. They ran the laundry, the motor pool, and the small movie theater. They maintained the grounds. None were doctors: the doctors lived either in one of three large Victorian houses near the movie theater or in even bigger residences in the city of Poughkeepsie, immediately to the south, or the town of Hyde Park, to the north. The psychiatric center's sprawling grounds were not entirely unfamiliar to the children of its employees. There was a holiday show held in the movie theater the Sunday before Christmas, which included a screening of *Scrooge* and wrapped Christmas presents distributed according to age and gender by a moderately convincing Santa (leading a number of the kids to ask if he was a resident of the hospital, too), and a Fourth of July picnic with evening fireworks on the great lawn in front of the main building. As a rule, though, the hospital grounds were off-limits to anyone not visiting a patient there.

2. Needless to say, this stopped none of us from stealing onto the campus.

3. There were six to ten of us at the core of our group, all in sixth grade, though John Faranda had been held back a year and had a scar beside his left eye. Brian Smith had lost one of his front teeth in first grade when he had crawled under Eddie Eisner's desk and Eddie pulled his chair in quickly, knocking out Brian's tooth. Brian wouldn't say what he had been doing under Eddie's desk in the first place, and while the evicted tooth wasn't a permanent one, its replacement took a long time to arrive, with the result that Brian never opened his mouth more than he had to. (Eddie had left in third grade after his father, an administrator at the psychiatric center, accepted a position at a similar facility in Phoenix, Arizona.) Joey Kavaki liked to pretend his ten-speed

was a motorcycle and was forever on the verge of convincing his parents to buy him a dirt bike. (Or so he said.) John Beyer loved football and movies about the Vietnam war, in which his uncle, who lived with John and his family, had spent eighteen months. This service had earned Uncle Lou the right to drink a watery beer at the VFW. Roch Lochyer's family were Irish-from-Ireland. He had been born in Dublin, but moved to the US as a baby, in plenty of time to shed the accent that shaped his parents' speech. Matthew Galleta was taller than kids two grades ahead of him. He shared John Beyer's love of football, and they passed much of their time arguing the merits of the Dallas Cowboys (John's team) and the Pittsburgh Steelers (Matt's team). Already, Matt had outgrown the bike he'd received last Christmas, but his parents refused to buy him a new one so soon after the last, which left him riding his too-small Huffy with his knees up past his elbows. Steven Mikula's hair was so blond it was practically white. He had a knack for annoying John Faranda, who was forever threatening to kick his ass, a threat he occasionally made good on. Don Calabrese spent most weekends fishing or hunting with his dad, who was some indeterminate amount older than the rest of our parents. Kara Mulligan and Yvonne Ruperti were the two girls who hung around with the boys the most. Kara was tall and took riding lessons at a stable up in Rhinebeck. Yvonne was quiet and kind and lived with her mother and younger sister.

4. As far as we were concerned, Birch Drive, the paved loop off Route 9 our raised ranches bordered, was possibly (even probably) the most boring place on earth. The exceptions to this state of affairs were the times we were able to slip onto the psychiatric center's grounds to explore the institution's margins; as well as the trio of occasions one of the psychiatric center's inmates slipped

the notice of their caretakers and wandered all the way to our neighborhood. These events happened within three weeks of one another, during the late fall of 1978, the time before Halloween. In those pre-cell-phone days, word of a patient on the loose still went out pretty quickly, through regular phones and people hurrying to houses whose numbers they didn't have. Any child outside was swiftly summoned and ordered inside. (The escapes occurred when we were near our homes, riding our bikes in lazy circles at the ends of our driveways.) From the picture windows in our living rooms, we scanned the street, our collective eyes open for the most fascinating of creatures, a patient. All our parents, and our friends' parents, besides, had warned us what to do should we encounter a woman or man dressed in a baby blue tunic and pants, the uniform of the residents of Ward 9, the high-security wing of the psychiatric center. Should we glimpse one of these patients at a distance, we were to turn the other way immediately and walk or run to the nearest house, where we were to report what we had seen to whichever adult answered the door, and they would contact the hospital. (Secretly, we wondered if all the neighborhood adults were privy to this plan, but none of us asked, not even Joey Kavaki, who was famous for posing to his parents the questions none of the rest of us dared.) Should we come face-to-face with a man or woman in baby blue, we were to remain calm, to do nothing to provoke or antagonize them, and to exit the situation with all due speed, our destination once again the closest residence. If, God forbid and touch wood, the patient were to threaten us, to put their hands on us (this last possibility half-whispered), then we were to yell as loud as we could, scream our lungs out, and punch and kick, scratch and claw, do everything in our power to make as much noise as possible while we resisted our would-be assailant. What if this didn't work? the most anxious and most obnoxious of us asked. What if our shouting and struggling were not enough to force the patient to release us? Our parents responded as you would have expected, with assurances this would not happen, with demands not to be a smart aleck, but their expressions belied whatever platitudes or remonstrances they uttered, and in their faces, we saw reflected the horrors awaiting us at the hands of the women and men in baby blue.

5. None of us knew exactly what led to someone being confined in Ward 9. Our parents brushed away our questions with either condescension or irritation, as did any older neighbor we might ask after completing a chore such as mowing the lawn for them. John Beyer said there must be information in old newspapers, but none of our families kept *The Poughkeepsie Journal* more than a day or two, and while John said Adriance Memorial Library, in the city of Poughkeepsie, had old issues of the paper on microfilm, the library was too far a ride into unknown territory for us to bike it. Instead, we invented reasons a person might be imprisoned in a psychiatric hospital. It would have to be for something serious, this we agreed upon. What fell into such a category was the subject of considerably more debate. Our speculations alternately amused and horrified us. Roch Lochyer's suggestion of loosening someone's eyeballs from the sockets then chewing them while they were still attached to the victim was the source of a round of nightmares whose cause none of us admitted to the parents who came running up the hall in answer to our midnight shrieks.

6. When the escaped patients finally shuffled into view, those weeks leading up to Halloween, they were wearing the white formless shirts and dark blue jeans of the psychiatric center's regular patients, who, while in need of supervision and care, were not generally deemed a threat. Nothing in their pharmaceutically softened

movements indicated danger, and though we watched eagerly for any hint these two men and one woman might be faking, their slack jaws and vacant stares disguises for more sinister intentions, all three went peacefully with the men who soon appeared to retrieve them. The minute we were allowed outside again, we spent the time remaining until dinner discussing and analyzing what we had observed, sharing our mutual disappointment at the anti-climactic resolution to each scene. Later, doing homework in the privacy of our rooms or under our parents' watchful eyes at the kitchen table, we felt lingering regret shot through with another emotion, something in the vicinity of relief. But we never shared this information with one another.

7. One patient escaped Ward 9 and walked to our neighborhood, though almost none of us saw him. This was during March of 1979, when the piles of plowed winter snow had shrunk to dirty white heaps peppered with gravel. The man's name was Gore Asturias, and after subduing the pair of orderlies who brought him outside for a half hour of sun (one of whom was John Beyer's Uncle Lou) he walked with some haste off the grounds of the psychiatric center, along the path to the VFW (whose patrons failed to notice him), down the long driveway to Birch Drive, and up to the top of Birch, to Roch Lochyer's house. There, he circled to the backyard, to the screened-in porch whose door he found unlatched. He crossed the porch to the back door to the house, also unsecured. He turned the handle and stepped into the kitchen, where Mrs. Lochyer was standing at the sink, washing dishes. Roch, who like the rest of us had been ordered inside the second word of Asturias's flight reached us from a parent on duty at the psychiatric center, was sitting at the kitchen table, a glass of milk and a pair of oatmeal raisin cookies in front of him.

8. Mrs. Lochyer was tall, enough so to have played center for her high school basketball team in Ireland. Heavyset, she was remarkably strong, much more so than Mr. Lochyer, who worked in the bakery section at Shop Rite. Her curly hair was gray, and she kept it cut short. Her features seemed too small for her face, her dark eyes peering out at the world from deep sockets, her expressions unreadable. Alone of all the parents in the neighborhood, she worked in Ward 9, the overnight shift. She was not friendly; neither was she unfriendly; rather, she exhibited a stolid blankness which was no doubt useful in the care of her particular patients. At neighborhood events—say, the Galletas' Memorial Day cookout and pool party—she would trade gossip about the other employees at the psychiatric center, especially the doctors, but she refused to say anything about Ward 9. This annoyed not a few of the parents, who were only too happy to share the most intimate details of the facility's residents. If their pique bothered Mrs. Lochyer, she gave no sign of it.

9. Roch would not discuss what happened in the ten minutes preceding the arrival of the town of Poughkeepsie police, who had been phoned by the psychiatric center as soon as another nurse saw Gore Asturias striding away from the men he had beaten with no little brutality. How the cops had known to go to the Lochyer residence was unclear, as she herself had not summoned them. Our assumption was, Mrs. Lochyer was the nearest employee who worked in Ward 9, so it was logical to check her house first. (This in turn begged the more important question of how Gore Asturias had known the Lochyers' address in the first place, which would not be answered at all, let alone, satisfactorily.) Not long after the police rushed in the front door, an ambulance arrived, lights flashing and siren crying.

Our parents forbade us running up the street to Roch's house, so we remained seated at our picture windows, watching the dim rectangle into which the paramedics had vanished carrying their overstuffed bags. A second ambulance obscured the view of the door and a fire engine blocked it entirely. A tan sedan parked in the street at the edge of the Lochyers' yard and disgorged four men in tan suits who made their way behind the fire truck and (we assumed) up the front stairs. Brian Smith said his mother identified one of them as a bigwig at the psychiatric center. Roch didn't know—or wouldn't say. The next day at school, then after school, he refused to answer any questions about the prior afternoon and evening, no matter who was asking or how many times they repeated themselves. All our inquiries, he met with silence and downcast eyes, his expression one none of us could read. (Many, many years later, watching footage of the survivors of a terrible disaster on the evening news, their faces streaked with blood and ash, we flashed back to the stunned look Roch Lochyer wore and thought that this was what we had seen, all those years before.) For the ensuing two or three days, on our own and in groups of various sizes, we kept after Roch for details of whatever had occurred in his house. Then Friday came and he wasn't in school. We assumed he was home sick, which was odd, because his mother followed the practice of nurses the world over when it came to her own child, refusing to allow him to stay off sick for anything less than a raging fever and projectile vomiting/explosive diarrhea. Saturday morning, the Lochyer house was empty, the family gone. Neither kids nor parents had seen them leave. The next week, there was a report Mrs. Lochyer was working in Atlanta, where Roch was supposedly being treated for an undisclosed illness our parents assumed was a form of cancer, most likely leukemia. This was the last semi-official news we received concerning our friend, whose cheeks were dense with freckles and who wore his brown hair in a bowl cut. When we asked our parents if they had heard any updates about his condition, they averted their eyes and said they had not. Gradually, Roch receded in our thoughts; though the question of his fate would return during the quiet space from which we entered sleep.

10. There is no official record of Gore Asturias. As the internet has allowed us increased access to all manner of official records, we have searched for traces of the man who entered the Lochyers' kitchen. We have found none.

11. This has become more urgent to us now, four decades and change later, as the headaches which have plagued us for years have worsened to the point even the most reluctant and skeptical of us has sought medical attention. To a one, what began in a bland waiting room has led to the throat of an MRI, head clamped in place by a rigid plastic frame, ears covered by headphones that only reduce the machine's grinding vocalizations to a bearable level. All our diagnoses have been the same: atypical pituitary adenomas, tumors of the pituitary gland whose configurations are like nothing the radiologists and oncologists have encountered. We have sat in front of our computers, staring at the images our doctors have shared with us, at the cross-sections of our brains, at the white starbursts exploding up through the gray clouds floating within our skulls. Unresponsive to conventional treatment, the tumors have brought with them strange defects in our visual fields, flashing lights within which we glimpse creases and folds, as if the real rides a surface of fractures and cracks. Our ears have been assaulted by sudden clanging shouts, as if great metal doors are being heaved open. At unexpected moments,

the sweet, heady scent of lilac floods our nostrils. On the smell, we float into memories of the dream we had the spring after Roch Lochyer and his family left our neighborhood in the deep dark hours of a Saturday morning. More and more, it seems as if we are not remembering the dream as much as we are stepping back into it, as if, after all this time, the dream has not stopped happening, is still happening.

12. We are in the Lochyers' kitchen. We must be standing in the northeast corner of the room, where the plastic garbage pail whose lid is never properly fitted stands. To our right, Mrs. Lochyer is pivoting from her position at the sink, her hands covered in white suds. She is dressed in faded jeans and a pink sweatshirt whose sleeves are pushed up past her elbows, exposing her considerable forearms. Directly in front of us, a man is stepping through the door to the pack porch. Dressed in a tunic and pants the light blue of a baby's nursery, the man is painfully thin, his skull and neck and arms skin wrapped around bone. His Adam's apple protrudes from his throat like a beak. Head tiled back, black eyes rolling like a panicked horse's, he moves his jaw from side to side, chewing the words he forces from his lips. "They took them, Shannon," he is saying. "My organs. They took my organs." Seated between the man (who must be Gore Asturias) and his mother, but closer to the intruder, Roch hunches down into his chair, trying to shrink himself, make himself small enough not to be noticed. Gore Asturias, whose head is completely shaved, no hair or eyebrows, hauls up the front of his tunic, exposing a chest similarly hairless, its cadaverous surface traversed by long incisions held shut by thick surgical staples. "Shannon," he says through his tunic as he pulls it over his head. "What am I supposed to do without my organs?" He drops the tunic at his feet. His stapled-together torso

is covered in writing, in characters and symbols familiar and not. We recognize Greek letters, runes, what appear to be hieroglyphs. We see the crescent moon, Saturn, a circle broken at the bottom. Gore Asturias moves his fingers to the terrible wounds on his breast. "How am I supposed to live without my organs?" he says, his nails worrying at the staples sealing the longest incision, the one running right up the middle of him. Clear liquid seeps from his flesh as he digs under the staples. "I'm just a head," he says, apparently feeling no pain when a staple pulls loose and falls to the linoleum with a faint metallic ping. Despite himself, Roch cannot help staring while Gore Asturias sends more staples to join the first in a tinny rain. Something is visible through the gap his fingers, shining with clear liquid, are opening in his chest.

13. What is it we see after the final staple has torn free of Gore Asturias and the schism in his breast bulges wide? What comes into view? What wakes us screaming during that long-ago lilac season, and now in our bedrooms across the country?

14. There was something inside him, pushing to get out. It was slicked with an oily film on whose surface light broke in iridescent waves. Behind the sheen, it moved with a lazy, circular motion. Half a dozen large warts, each the diameter of a silver dollar, studded its surface. "Where did they put my organs?" Gore Asturias said. The warts split, opening into eyes, their pupils contracting in the light. Whatever was inside Gore Asturias rotated clockwise then counter-clockwise, as if in an effort to swivel its complement of eyes into better position.

15. A couple of us were ejected from sleep by the eyes staring out from the break in Gore Asturias's chest. Even those who remained in the dream experienced the absolute certainty those eyes were

looking directly at us. Roch opened his mouth for a scream he couldn't make, a shuddering inhalation which drew the thing's attention to him. Gore Asturias's body turned in Roch's direction, then convulsed as if he had stepped on a live electrical wire. Arms and legs rigid, he stumbled to his right, a cloud of white steam hissing from his chest. Mrs. Lochyer stepped forward, a gallon jug of ammonia pressed between her powerful hands, shooting a stream of ammonia across the distance between her and Gore Asturias, the liquid striking the thing within him. He crashed against the table and bent forward, the thing already halfway out of his chest, a glistening, gelid mass from which steam continued to pour as Mrs. Lochyer finished expelling the remainder of the ammonia onto it. The eyes covering it bulged. Gore Asturias was saying, "They want me to bloom." Mrs. Lochyer reached one of her long arms behind her and grabbed another gallon jug from the counter, this one of bleach. "Roch!" she shouted. "Go!" Galvanized by her command, Roch shoved his chair away from the table and half-ran, half-fell toward the front door. There was the musical sound of crumpling plastic as Mrs. Lochyer crushed the bottle's sides, spraying bleach onto the steaming thing. A fresh cloud lifted from the thing, which attempted to climb back into the safety of Gore Asturias's evacuated chest, only to surrender the effort and drop onto the table, its eyes weeping gold tears threaded with crimson. Arm held over her face Dracula-style, Mrs. Lochyer fled after Roch.

16. This was our dream, which we shared first not at all, then completely, compulsively. (Don Calabrese started.) We argued over it for days and days. Some believed it entirely; others were hesitant. Though even John Faranda, most dismissive of us all, had to concede the strangeness of our sharing the same dream. As we advanced toward and into summer, we discussed the dream

and its relation to Roch and his family less and less, but we never stopped, entirely.

17. Now, we return to our dream of Gore Asturias as the moment the images on our collective MRIs began their decades-long germination. Could an image in our unconscious minds give birth to an image on a computer screen? The growth rates for the tumors have been astonishingly consistent for all of us; in another six to eight weeks, what is blooming inside our skulls will come into full flower. We pass our days stepping in and out of the Lochyers' kitchen, studying the thing that took the place of a man's organs, gazing into its strange eyes, wondering if it sees us the way we see it. And lately, we have begun sharing other dreams. Not all of us together, but three and sometimes four at a time, we have stood in various locations throughout our old neighborhood, at the ends of driveways, outside the VFW, on the path to the psychiatric center's grounds, and watched our foreheads part in a rending of flesh and cracking of bone, an eye slicked by liquid as gold as fresh oil staring from each jagged aperture. We have felt ourselves crossing into an old dream no longer a memory, but a stepping-stone to the place we used to live in, the neighborhood where this terminal garden was seeded, long ago in 1979, in lilac season.

For Fiona

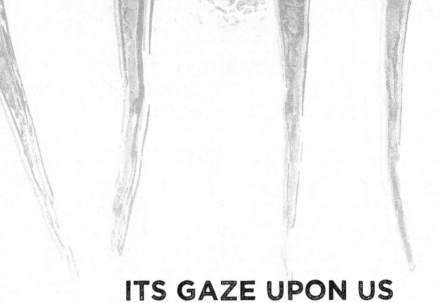

ITS GAZE UPON US

BY LAUREL HIGHTOWER

It was hard for Robin to remember how things were before The Opening. She recalled the event itself, the way every news source in the world capitalized the occurrence, using the same ominous reference. She'd seen it running along the bottom of the screen, below the faces of talking heads having trouble keeping their cool, their eyes hollow, hair out of place, twitching and uneasy the same as the rest of the population.

That scared her more than anything else about the way the world changed. Robin was used to uneasiness, a current of anxiety running beneath her skin, never truly relaxed unless she was at home with Tully, the doors and windows locked against the outside world. Anywhere else and she was a ball of nerves, but she was used to that. Watching the rest of the world slowly descend into her own personal hell turned her insides to ice, her stomach sinking and breath quickening. This was real. Not just real, but very, very bad. It wasn't going to be another swift soundbite that outraged or frightened half the populous, then blew itself out in a day or two of fiery online discourse. Things were changing, and Robin didn't like change even in the best of circumstances. A giant, purple-lidded eye opening in the western sky one summer day was decidedly not the best of circumstances.

There was no sound, no explanation or lead up. Just a change in the light, as though a cloud had passed between the sun and the earth where Robin squatted weeding her garden. The touch of the shadow quickened her heart, made her break out in a sweat. She looked up, shading her eyes with one hand, and for long seconds stared at the ripple of dark clouds that hung, completely static, unmoved by the strong breeze that should have shifted its position. Her heart thudded in her ears and she pushed off the ground, straightening, her gaze never leaving the strange formation. She had a clear view of the sky when the ripple split down the middle, a v-shaped opening stretching it to either side. She wasn't breathing, could feel the burn in her chest but couldn't make her lungs work. Anxiety filled her veins with adrenaline and she watched, motionless, as the split widened to reveal a single, fiery eye staring fiercely from above.

"An eyelid," she mumbled, tearing her gaze from the thing. The purple ripple had been the thing's eyelid, it was the only thing that made sense, and the only thought she could cling to while the rest of her body tried to shut down.

The day stayed cemented in her memory not just because of The Opening, but as the last time things were even close to normal. Robin couldn't recall what normalcy had felt like, just that it had been, and never was again. Tully came home from work early that day, spewing gravel in her truck as she fishtailed up the long drive to their little ranch style home. There was nothing useful on any of the news broadcasts or websites, only a confirmation of what she'd seen. An eye. *The* Eye. When they made the cautious trek to town, to settle into a booth at Rose's and compare notes with their neighbors, it was the same story. Confusion, fear, endless arguing over what it could mean.

Nothing good, Robin knew that, but how she wished she'd been wrong.

The crackling of a walkie talkie pulled Robin from a dead, dreamless sleep. For the first few seconds she wanted to cry, weep at the loss of those precious hours of real, actual rest, deeper than any sleep she could recall in the past two years. When it crackled again, she sat up, heart thumping, her gaze searching the darkness for the pinpoint red glow of the handheld unit, plugged into its charger across the room.

She listened, trying to keep her breath quiet, hoping she'd been mistaken. She couldn't think about what it would mean if someone really was trying to reach her. It couldn't be good—the only good thing in Robin's life had disappeared with the other walkie almost a year ago, and as desperately as she wanted to believe Tully would return someday, her practical mind wouldn't even consider the possibility.

More static, and the low fade of a voice. Robin's heart quickened and she reached for the handgun she kept on her night table. Someone must have found the radio, or taken it from Tully by force. Maybe she'd even given it away, throwing out the last possible tether to her needy, neurotic wife. Robin pinged between dread that Tully was dead, and a gut cramping fear she'd been left behind, abandoned in the end-times.

She pushed out of bed as silently as she could, crept first to the boarded windows that blocked out any trace of light, from the moon or otherwise. The nails were secure in each one, unsurprising since Robin tested them every Tuesday. Next, she checked the two doors, the heavy wooden front door that hadn't been opened in over a year, and the smaller kitchen door she used to come and go. Both were latched and dead-bolted, a heavy metal bar across the base of each, preventing ingress even in the event the locks gave out. She'd installed them after a near miss eight months ago, and each time she looked at them her body reacted, sweat pooling in her palms, her breathing going shallow and erratic, like she could still hear the rhythmic, concussive thuds of something battering the front door over and over. She made a conscious effort to pull her mind away and checked the fireplace, the flue long ago closed, a metal cap on the top of the chimney. All was well, nothing out of place, no dirt or feathers to suggest something managed to find an opening.

Robin returned to the bedroom, to the hissing speaker of the little white radio that was her only connection to the outside world. She sat in the beat-up easy chair where Tully used to drink her coffee every morning, and listened to the static with a hammering heart. If she strained, she could hear low talking fading in and out, but couldn't make out anything being said. The adrenaline slowly leached from her system and her eyes grew heavy—it was amazing, the level of fear a person could grow used to. She fell asleep in Tully's chair, back into the dreamless dark.

"...the hastas are blooming over on the far side of the lake, do you remember planting those? I told you it was ridiculous—thought they were weeds."

A honk of laughter shook the little walkie talkie unit and shot Robin straight up from sleep. She stared with wide, clear eyes at the unit, listening to the *shush* of static that meant Tully's voice hadn't been the tail-end of a dream. The noise-gate was open, which meant someone was on the other end.

The white noise continued, an innocuous fuzz ratcheting her tension with each second, her body so tightly wound it hurt. It was Tully—had to be. No one else laughed like that, and the nature commentary—that was their thing. Robin never liked her wife's explorations, her insistence on walking the outer perimeter of the county. A holdover from when things like land boundaries mattered, but Robin supposed it wasn't any more silly than her continued reliance on the Roman calendar. Everyone had to cling to something to forget The Eye, to quash the deep dread that one day, the gaze would fall upon them, too. So, Tully had talked as she walked, describing everything she saw, what had changed and what hadn't. She always said it was so Robin could find her way if she needed to, if Tully weren't around. In her worst moments, Robin wondered if her lover had been warning her, preparing for her imminent departure.

She pushed away the intrusive thought and kept her attention, every ounce of her hope and will on the radio. Tully's voice had last come from it a year ago now, too long to be anything but dead. She'd been walking the creek on the northern edge of Possum Holler, detailing the squadron of geese she'd found bathing there, then her voice cut off mid-description. There was no cry, no question or indication that Tully saw it coming, whatever it was, but Robin knew danger didn't always look dangerous. A lot of times it looked like neighbors, shop owners you were on a first-name basis with, people you'd known since kindergarten.

Like a lot of small towns, Possum Holler was hard to leave. No matter how many times Robin swore she'd get out of this place, move somewhere bigger, more metropolitan, it never quite happened. It wasn't because the place was some idyllic haven, either. Small town America was romanticized by city dwellers, but towns like hers often meant poverty, limited job prospects, ancient trailers spilling yellow insulation along the sides of narrow, winding roads. Robin didn't know if it was loyalty or inertia that kept people in Possum Holler, but she'd lived long enough to be grateful they'd never moved. So far, The Eye's gaze had passed over them, intent on heavily populated areas. No one knew exactly what happened when The Eye turned toward you, because nothing was ever the same, after.

The radio's static kept going, never once abating, as though someone held the talk button down. Nothing else came from it, and eventually Robin rose stiffly from the chair to take a piss and start her morning routine. Everything took longer today, as she stared obsessively at the walkie talkie, running the sink only in brief spurts so she didn't miss anything.

It was odd that Possum Holler still had running water and electricity. No phones or internet; those had gone down almost immediately, most within the first twenty-four hours of The Opening. They'd stockpiled drinkable water and candles, flashlights and batteries, but other than the occasional heavy storm, they never lost power. Somehow that was more disturbing than being cut off from those modern conveniences. Maybe because a lifetime of post-apocalyptic media led her to expect a return to simpler times; no electricity or water, a camping trip that never ended. It wasn't that she'd be happy if they stopped one day, and she lived in expectation of it happening, holding her breath each time she turned on the faucet. But somehow, the idea of the rest of the world going on as usual out there under the gaze of The Eye was so much more disturbing. She pictured heading into town and seeing all the people she'd known her whole life lined up with vacant expressions, empty smiles, and so many extra eyes... a nightmare version of Main Street.

Robin had no idea who was keeping everything running—she hadn't seen a soul since that time eight months ago when the locks almost gave. She'd wondered, in the first few minutes of the assault, whether she ought to see who it was. Maybe it was a neighbor in need of help, or even Tully, home at long last and too tired or disoriented to remember the right knock sequence. But as that battering went on, Robin knew it was all wrong, and when the thuds became wetter, squelchy and muffled, she huddled in the pantry and covered her ears. Next morning, there were matted bits of hair sticking out from thick gobs of dark blood, interspersed with bone shards and what might be brain matter covering the center panel of the door. She never saw who tried to get in, but she pictured it every day, how it must have looked when an unknown number had swung a human body like a battering ram, head first. She hoped whoever it was had been dead, but she had her doubts. Some folks hadn't waited for The Eye to look their way before losing their marbles.

Robin ignored her usual chore list for the day. It was Friday, which meant gardening in the morning, an outside perimeter check of the house in the afternoon, and blindfold practice in the evening. This last was probably a useless exercise—even if she couldn't see The Eye, she was always aware of it. An uncomfortable itch too far beneath the skin to scratch, an unseen weight on her shoulders, and worst of all, the fluttering. That was what she called it anyway, the feeling like one of those phantom hairs you can't see to push out of your face or pluck off your arm no matter how hard you try. It was constant, tickling at the back of her neck or sometimes her cheek, and she was powerless to stop the accompanying mental image of butterfly kisses. Those sweet, innocuous flutters of a child's lashes against her skin, but on an impossibly large scale. The Eye, that great, pulsating, slit-pupiled orb, close enough to brush her skin. If she let herself think about it, she wasn't too far off from using someone as a human battering ram, herself.

Except she didn't feel any of that today. It was a realization that came gradually, when she absently scratched an itch on her forearm and the feeling went away under the pressure of her nails. She looked down and saw a tiny red bump, a bite from something bloodthirsty but oh so *normal*. Nothing else itched. No weight pressed her shoulders down, and no feathery brushes (*lashes*) threatened her peace. Robin hadn't felt sustained relief like this since before The Opening. The only time the influences of The Eye let up were the brief instances when it closed. Robin thought of it as blinking, the stormy purple ripple of lid closing over the roving fire, offering the shortest of respites before The Eye opened once more, its gaze trained somewhere new. This was much longer—thinking back, she hadn't felt it all day, and that aligned with her deeper sleep of the night before. Even in dreams, The Eye never stopped watching.

The realization didn't make Robin feel better. She wished she could believe it meant something good, that a solution had finally been found by some underground bunker of scientists. She didn't know what science could do about a giant Eye in the sky, but she had to believe someone, somewhere was working on a solution. But Robin had long known hope as her enemy, and tried to banish it. She always ended up disappointed—since The Opening, nothing had ever gotten better, only exponentially worse.

But did the change in how she felt have anything to do with Tully's possible reappearance? Had The Eye perhaps closed long enough for her lover to find her way back home? She hadn't heard anything but static for hours, but she hadn't tried communicating, either. Every time she thought of pressing down that button, of sending her voice into the swirling ether, terror iced her out, froze her hand and her throat. Her little spot of Possum Holler had kept her safe, out of the path of the unknowable changes taking over the rest of the world. She didn't want the attention reaching out could bring.

"You worry too much, Tweety."

Robin jerked, the walkie talkie bouncing from her hand. It landed on its right side, depressing the talk button for less than a second before cutting it off, and she closed her eyes and prayed.

"Was that you, Tweety bird?"

Tully's tone was loving, filled with joy, and Robin could almost believe she really was on her way back. For the first time she thought of how her wife might feel, returning after a year's lonely absence, wondering whether Robin were still alive. For the space of a breath, she let herself hope, even looking around the kitchen, wondering what ingredients she had to make a welcome-home meal. An ache throbbed through her arms and shoulders and her chest hitched at the thought of wrapping Tully close, pressing her face into those riotous curls. Her leg muscles tensed, wanting to be up and doing, running to meet her wife halfway.

She was already out of the chair when she remembered the unit's range. Beyond what was promised on the packaging, they'd tested it themselves, many times. Just under two miles was where the signal failed, their voices fading out softer and softer until they were consumed by static. Like she'd heard last night, low tones pulling her from sleep. It was the sound of someone at the very end point of the radio's range.

Yet that had been hours ago. The digital clocks in the kitchen and next to the television still worked, though Robin could no longer be sure how accurate they were. She'd had to reset them a few times after brief power outages, and each time had to guess. They were out of true, but consistent to each other, and a glance at the glowing blue numerals above the stove told her she'd first heard the radio more than fourteen hours ago. There was no way it would take Tully even a tenth that long to travel the maximum two miles.

Robin stared at the walkie on the floor where it had slid under the kitchen table. The red light winked at her from the shadows, and her heart kicked up a faster rhythm, anxiety washing over her. Something was wrong, with all of this.

"You should see the wildflowers down here! You know that little cleft in the rock, the one that looks like a mustache? It must have got seeded somehow, because it's going nuts. There's those little daisy-looking ones, and the purple ones, and even some of those, what'd you used to call them? Balloon flowers? They must have gotten picked up from your pots."

Robin crossed her arms over her chest and hugged herself tight. She could close her eyes and picture exactly where Tully was, about eight-tenths of a mile to the south of the house. Which based on her last transmission, meant she'd had to have circled around, passed the little clearing where Robin waited.

"I bet you haven't been out here even once, have you?" Tully asked.

Robin realized she couldn't hear any sound of movement from the other end. The noise gate had been open this whole time, the static a constant companion, so if Tully were moving, she'd have heard something. Breathing, the crash of brush or the crunch of last year's fallen leaves. There was nothing, so what was she doing?

"Did you even come look for me?" Tully asked, and Robin winced, her eyes squeezing shut against the stab of guilt.

She had gone to look after Tully stopped responding, but not immediately. It took her over two weeks to work up the nerve to leave the house, and another eight days before she could make it to the stream bed Tully had been describing when her voice cut off. There was nothing to tell her what happened there, whether her wife was alive or dead. Just a peaceful spot dappled by sunlight through the soaring trees overhead.

"It's okay, hon. I get it. It *is* scary out here, until you get used to it. But new things are always scary, aren't they?"

Get used to *what?* Being outside, the current state of the world? Madness?

But Tully didn't sound insane. She didn't even sound annoyed, she just sounded like Tully. Every inflection, the words she used—there was nothing to indicate anything wrong with the voice coming through the radio.

"I wish we'd had more time, Robin. I know you need to warm up to things, process changes before jumping in the deep end. Although I suppose you've had two years by now, so if you're not warmed up you never will be." She gave that honk of laughter again, and Robin's hands shook. More time for what?

"Do you hear them yet?"

Robin frowned, feeling cold. She heard nothing but the hiss of static from the walkie—until she did. A sound that stole her breath, froze her in place. A scraping, followed by low thumps, coming from below. The cellar.

"If you don't, you will soon. Time is very short now, if you want any choice at all in the matter."

Robin kept expecting her lover's tone to change, to grow sly and insidious, reveal that whatever was on the other end of the radio wasn't Tully. But it didn't happen, and she bent to pick up the handheld. She carried it with her to the cellar door and reassured herself it was bolted closed. It didn't have a security bar, though. It wasn't an outside door, and she hadn't thought to add one after the last time.

"It's not your fault, babe. You've done really well, all things considered. Staying inside, taking yourself out of the world, it was never going to be a permanent solution. You know that."

Tears welled in Robin's eyes, a mix of panic and loss tightening her chest. More thumping from the cellar, then the unmistakable sound of a footstep on the bottom stair. Robin whimpered and backed away from the door, patting the handgun in the belt at her side.

She went to the boarded kitchen window, the one with the best view of the treeline where Tully used to emerge after each of her explorations. She hadn't been able to stop herself prying off that lowest board every day to look for her lost love, and always thought it was the weak point, that if something came for her, it would be through that window. Now she laid it carefully on the counter, standing on her tiptoes to peer out.

For the space of a breath, she hoped. The willows that stood at the very edge of the denser growth swayed with movement, and she expected Tully to step out from between them any second. But the movement went on, and no one emerged. Disappointment and fear crashed around her shoulders and Robin held back a sob.

"It's not that easy, I'm afraid," said Tully, her tone full of empathy. "I wish it was. I wish I could do it for you, babe, but it doesn't work like that."

Robin flinched at the sound of heavy steps ascending the cellar stairs. She turned, pressing her back against the sink and holding the radio to her chest.

"It's kind of like tripping. The experience has a lot to do with who guides you through it, right? Only I guess with shrooms you have a choice whether to do it or not, and here… not so much. But believe me, if you come to me, you'll have a much better trip. I can't vouch for what's coming up those stairs."

Robin spun and squinted out the window again, but still there was nothing.

Only… was it darker than it had been a minute ago? She glanced at the clock—early afternoon still. But it was definitely getting darker, the shadows lengthening at the tree line as she watched. She leaned as far to the left as she could, looking in the direction she'd been avoiding for two years now, dreading what she would see.

The Eye. Closer than she remembered ever seeing it, as though it loomed over her very house. The dark purple ripple of lids were only open a crack, but there was no doubt—The Eye *was opening*, and it was looking at her.

"It's almost here, Tweety. Are you ready?"

Tweety. That same use of her pet name tugged at her heart, tried like hell to resurrect hope. But there was no hope—Robin had long known it. All she had left was avoidance, staying out of the gaze as best she could.

"But you can't anymore, babe. Come to me. I can't promise it'll be okay—I wish I could. But it's still the best choice."

Tears spilled down Robin's cheeks, her breath frantic as her gaze moved from the treeline to the cellar door and back again. Something thumped and she screamed, pulling the gun from her belt with one shaking hand, refusing to set the radio down for even a moment.

Closing her eyes, she pushed her thumb against the talk button. "What's it like?" she asked hoarsely. It wasn't what she wanted most to know—*are you okay? Where have you been? Why did you leave?*—but right now it was the only question that mattered.

"That depends," said Tully, and still her tone was soft and warm.

"On what?"

"On how hard you look."

Another thump at the cellar door, and the knob rattled. Robin folded in on herself, bent at the waist, gun and radio both held close to her middle. She edged toward the back door.

"What the fuck does that mean?" she almost screamed. This was when it would happen, when whoever was on the other end of the airwaves would reveal the cheat, ooze horrible things into her ears until she went mad, too.

"Have you ever thought about what The Eye sees?" Tully asked softly.

Tears dripped from Robin's chin, her nose too clogged to breathe through. "What?"

"The Eye. Think of the size of it, how enormous it must be for it to appear so large in our sky. It has to be somewhere out there in the atmosphere, right? And if there's one Eye, chances are there's another. What do you think it's looking at?"

The cellar door shook in its frame against the onslaught of whatever was on the other side and Robin pressed herself against the kitchen door, breathing hard through her tears.

"I don't know, I don't fucking know!"

"Us," Tully said. "It's looking at us, all of us, the whole world all at once. He sees the falling sparrow or some shit, right?" Another honking laugh, but lower, sadder.

Robin pushed the button down again. "You're telling me this thing, this fucking Eye that's caused the end of our world, it's God's eye? That's what you want me to believe?"

"Not God, as you see it, no, but *a* god, maybe. Something big and old and unknowable."

"So the fuck what? How does that help me now?"

"I'm trying to tell you what it's like. When it looks at you… you see what it sees. Do you understand?"

"No!" screamed Robin as another impact cracked the cellar door, a splintering sound she felt in her bones. Her haven was falling apart, almost breached. She couldn't be trapped in here with whatever was coming, so what choice did she have?

"The whole world, all at once. That's what it sees, and that's what fills your mind when the gaze falls on you. You see everything it sees—all the pain, all the hatred and murder and rape and death and desecration—everything across the span of the earth, you see it. Is it any wonder people go mad?"

Robin tucked the handgun under her arm to fumble with the deadbolt, offering an unintelligible prayer through gritted teeth. "Are you mad, Tully?" she asked once she'd gotten it open, poised to flee.

Tully laughed again. "Do I sound mad?"

It was an exchange they'd had too many times to count. Robin, emotionally stunted by her upbringing, unable to read other people for cues, constantly worried she angered and annoyed anyone she came into contact with. Tully, the one person who'd never laughed at her fears or belittled her, assuring her every time. *Do I sound mad?* she'd ask, and Robin would stop to think about it, as she thought about it now.

No, Tully didn't sound mad. She sounded like herself, only the words she said made no sense, but then, nothing had since The Opening. What did Robin know about the world as it was now?

"Why aren't you? If everyone else goes crazy, why not you?"

"It's not everyone else, not by a long shot, but yeah, the odds ain't great. Most people get overwhelmed—it's hit after hit after hit, pain and hate and it kills every ounce of hope you ever carried. But if you can keep looking—if you don't give yourself up to it, there's a way to be okay."

The shadows outside the window grew deeper—something fell from the sky. Soot, maybe? It was too dark to be rain or hail, and whatever it was, it floated like snow. At the same time, something long and black slithered from beneath the cellar door, lashing from side to side, testing. Or maybe tasting, Robin didn't know.

"How?" she howled into the radio, yanking at the door and sobbing when it didn't budge. She remembered the security bar and flung it up and out of her way just as the cellar burst open behind her. She leapt out onto the back porch but stopped at the edge, staring out into a world she no longer understood.

"This is gonna be the hard part, Tweety. You're going to have to hope."

"*What?*" she shrieked for what felt like the millionth time in her life. Everything, always had been a constant confusion for her, even before the world went to hell. She didn't understand what people meant half the time, or why they did what they did, and had relied on Tully to be her interpreter. And right on cue, Tully was here, guiding her through, but still nothing made sense. "How? How the fuck am I supposed to have hope in the face of all this?"

"That's what I meant by looking hard, hon. For every horrible act, every atrocity, every hurt, there are good things that counteract. They're so hard to see, so hidden, and most people shut down before they get there."

The sky darkened to night and Robin shivered in the sudden chill. Wet squelching sounds came from the kitchen behind her and she edged as far as she could without actually leaving her porch.

"We're out of time, babe," said Tully, her voice cutting in and out, static rising. "I wish I could hold your hand, but I have faith in you. Find the hope, and I'll be there on the other side."

The radio fell silent, the red light blinking off, and Robin was alone. She sobbed all the harder, the choice feeling impossible. How could she leave her home, the only place she'd ever felt safe? She didn't *want* to see the rest of the world, the pain that pulsed there everywhere she looked. She'd spent a lifetime hiding from it because to look straight at it was to know despair. Yet she felt The Eye opening, felt its gaze settling upon her, the weight of its knowledge bearing down on her fragile psyche.

Something groaned behind her, a guttural, animal sound, and she felt the heat of carrion breath on her neck. Time was up—she had to go, even if she couldn't control what happened once she did. She searched the treeline one more time, but in the pitch darkness she could see nothing, so she closed her eyes and stepped off the porch.

Lashes, she thought, feeling the feathery brush against every exposed inch of skin. That was what was falling from the sky— lashes. She pushed back the revulsion, lifted her finger parallel to her mouth until she felt one drift down and stick there. It was light, like the softest feather, and it tickled her flesh where it touched. Eyes still closed, she took a deep breath and blew. And for the first time in her life, Robin wished for hope.

SOMETHING FISHY

BY ANDY DAVIDSON

I

I try to tell Mazie about Pastor Roy.

We're in the little cinderblock outbuilding down the hill from the church, where the kitchen is, filling juice cups with alligator blood out of a turkey baster and nibbling Chiclet-sized bread squares. It's Mazie's job, every third Sunday, to prep the Lord's Supper, out here beneath the janky lights and moldy ceiling tiles. It's my first time helping. We suck the blood out of a plastic gallon milk jug from the fridge. Sure, it's weird, but that dead alligator hanging upside down in back of the building with its throat slashed and a bucket underneath it drawing flies is really the last thing on my mind because I've never been alone with a girl, especially like this, in some dim, holy place, and right now, that girl is Mazie Johnson. Who has prickly straw-blonde hair and sad eyes and wears ugly homemade skirts and white socks that bunch around scuffed loafers and she's beautiful. I have loved her since the first time I saw her.

I lay it all out, how Pastor Roy's throat swelled up like a clown balloon stretched over a helium tank during last week's invitation, when we were all supposed to have our eyes shut. The skin below his jaw bulged, a whole forest of veins in there. Me and Mazie was standing at our usual pew down front, as the piano played and everyone in the church swayed gently, waiting on some poor soul under conviction to start crying out in tongues. On the bench behind us we had our programs and our rawhide bracelets given out by one of the church ladies. They had little beads with letters that spelled out "I" and then this heart followed by the word "Dagon." I didn't know what a Dagon was, but I'd only been visiting the Church of the Unending Plain about three weeks, and you could fill a Dixie cup with what I knew about the Bible.

"There's something fishy about him," I tell Mazie.

"You'll understand it," she says, "all by and by." The words come out religious and sad, like she's trying to tune in truth on a sinner's radio. The blood runs over the edge of a little plastic cup into the silver tray, drips out of the baster onto the yellow countertop. Then onto the linoleum.

I go over to the metal sink—it stinks of reptile—and snatch the roll of paper towels from beside the Palmolive. I get down on my hands and knees and wipe up a few red dime spots from the floor. Down here with the dead roaches and spiders and silverfish, it's easy to want to look up at something better, so I do. Mazie's on a stool and I stare at her calves where her skirt has bunched behind her knees. Her muscles are soft. Blue runners of lightning beneath fish belly skin.

Mazie lives with her older brother and crazy mother next door to me and Daddy in the Bottoms, a cul-de-sac of shit-box trailers at the edge of the Ouachita River, where the muddy water sometimes rises and sends us all paddling out of the woods in boats. Most every night, I lie awake thinking about Mazie and fall asleep and dream of sneaking across the gravel lane by moonlight into her open window. Beneath the sill is a piece of plywood set over two sawhorses where her brother, Jimbo, skins squirrels, and in the dream, I climb up there and slip the screen loose and Mazie's hand reaches out and pulls me into her bed, and I shed my underwear onto the carpet like a skin and pretty soon I'm jerked awake by the old hot and sticky pumping into my shorts—

She's at the sink, running water through the baster, rinsing it. It's gushing red.

"Hand me a paper towel, would you, Junior?"

I pass her the roll, and she tears a handful.

"You given any more thought to what we talked about?" she wants to know, shaking water from her fingertips and changing the subject from our mutant pastor.

"What, getting baptized?"

She leans against the sink, nods gravely as she dries her hands.

"I don't like going under water."

I've told her this story. How Daddy took me to the county pool when I was eight and threw me in there with all the kids splashing and screaming and Daddy yelled, "Swim or drown!" Without a doubt, it would have been the second one if that teenage lifeguard hadn't dove in and fished me out. Daddy got banned from the pool after that. Which is kind of funny, since his job as a game warden is to basically ride around in a boat all day on the river, giving tickets to people who fish without a license. I guess he wanted a son who could jump from a boat and rig a trot line like Tom Sawyer, and instead he got a fat kid likes to read *Conan* comics and draw Skeletor while he eats a whole bag of mini Reese's cups. Life isn't fair, I'd like to say to Daddy sometimes. But he already knows that.

Mazie gives me a look of solemn pity, like she knows something I don't, like there's really nothing at all to be afraid of, and if she said that to me right now, I guess I'd believe her. But she doesn't. She just smiles, touches my shoulder. I look at her hand there, her fingernails bitten ragged, and think: *No feeling like this has ever been felt.*

She holds out two silver platters of wafers. I take one in each hand, watch her stack the trays of blood cups then cap the stack with an enamel potlid from beneath the cabinet. She tucks her chin against the lid and holds the stack at the bottom, and I walk behind her out of the kitchen, wafer platters thrust out like the scales of justice. I am her acolyte. Forever.

The screen door slaps behind us as we head up toward the church, which is a squat bunch of concrete blocks on a pile of red dirt next to the river. No windows. Slanted tin roof drifted with pine straw from the trees above. A little rock path down to the river, where they do their baptizing on a sandbar.

They have an artist here, at the Church of the Unending Plain, who paints murals. He did the one in town on the brick wall of the Feed & Seed, over on Peacock Street? A boy in overalls walking behind his daddy as the old man slaps the reins of a mule. The mule's pulling the plow and the boy's head is down and it almost looks like he's crying. It doesn't set right. But most people don't even see it.

To be honest, I don't think much of this person's abilities.

That said, I suppose he's painted his masterpiece here on the white cinderblocks of Mazie's church. Down near where the red mud stains the wall, there's a bunch of weird, naked men that look like creatures from the Black Lagoon. It's like it's all underwater.

You can see what's meant to be the river's surface just above the church door, where there's painted two old boys in a boat fishing, and the one in back near the motor has a knife and his face is all screwed up like he's hearing voices, and maybe what those voices are saying is, "Stab that other fucker right there between his shoulders." Down below, one of the creatures is noodling a big ass catfish, only it's hard to tell if what he's inserted into the catfish's mouth is an arm or something else. The number of fish-men cavorting among the stobs and stumps is twelve, so I figure these are the Twelve Disciples, but I don't really know who the Twelve Disciples are. It's just words I remember from Vacation Bible School at the First Baptist Church when I was small, and Mama was still around and wanted to sleep in four days a week all June. We each got a Bible verse to memorize and got fed Goldfish crackers if we memorized it right. I wasn't good at remembering, so I just snuck a handful of crackers when that teacher's back was turned.

Anyhow.

Inside the church, the congregation is singing, and Mazie and me slip through the double metal doors and into a little vestibule, where we set the Lord's Supper on a folding table. On the other side of a second pair of shut doors, bodies collapse into pews. Pastor Roy's voice starts up a second or two later at a low rumble, and pretty soon he's raining down stones of righteous fury on Our Society Today. As in: Our Society Today is run by Baby Butchers and Queers and Evolutionists, and it all sounds pretty terrible, when you say it like he says it, like we're overdue a good Apocalypse. But then Pastor Roy's voice changes, and his words turn into that gibberish they all spout here at the Church of the Unending Plain—

Ymg' ah mggoka'ai, brothers ng sisters, zhro llll ah bthnknahor!

Painted along the walls of the sanctuary are more fish-men—

and fish-women, too, who are just as anatomically correct as the men—and they all trudge in a long, solemn line through bubbles and mud. Up near the ceiling, monstrous alligators float belly up, boiling clouds of blood from broken snouts and ragged holes. The fish-people slouch on, hunks of alligator meat in their webbed claws, all the way to the front wall of the church, where a huge stone altar is painted. Up on that altar, facing the congregation and kneeling, is a naked girl with a human body and a fish head. Standing at her right side is a little fat white boy with a regular human head. He's naked, too, and has a tiny little pecker. On her left is this stupendous fish-man, head square as Pastor Roy's, and he's got the biggest fish-dick you ever saw. Like, he's really happy to be included, you know? The girl in the middle, she's holding hands with the fat boy and the fish-man, like they're all one happy nuclear family.

The congregation—poor bottom-dwellers, a few rich folks like that paper mill jackoff from town, even the junior football coach from the high school—they're all raising their hands above their heads, like they're stretching their arms out to that girl in the picture, and Pastor Roy he's up there between them and her, unspooling the hurt on the world.

Mazie and me stand on one side of the sanctuary doors, listening, her round face inches from mine, and I can smell the Ivory soap and mildewed fabric creeping out of her like a wild vine—

C' uh'eog l' fhtagn nglui!

Mazie's eyes slip shut and her lips begin to move in what I can only figure is a silent prayer. She presses a nail-bitten hand over her heart and sweat springs out along her hairline and I catch the scent of something sour and funky. Meanwhile, her eyes tick-tick-tick behind her lids and suddenly there's a quaking in my own head as I start to breathe that scent in, and I want to reach out, to touch her, it's like I can't help myself, first the downy fuzz atop the ridge of her ear, then the mole at the base of her jaw. My hand inches toward her—

Soon ng og soon ymg' ephainilgh'ri join ya llll gn'thor's edge!

But she slips away before I can touch her. Through the doors, sliding silently onto the back pew, next to an old lady with drooping knee-high pantyhose, who shuffles over to make room.

I follow.

I'll always follow Mazie.

Three weeks I've been coming here now, just to be near her.

She's like those painted shafts of sunlight that slant like knives through the dark waters of these church walls. She cuts deep.

The preacher preaches on, and Mazie's hand tightens around mine.

II

She knocked on a Saturday, three weeks back. Daddy was off at work, cruising the river for the state, wearing sunglasses and grinning at girls from behind his mustache like he was Ouachita County's own Magnum P.I. Me, I'd eaten a whole bag of Doritos that morning while watching Road Runner cartoons. I opened the door to Mazie in my socked feet. By then, I had moved on to a package of red Twizzlers, which I was holding in one hand. Fingers dusted Nacho orange.

I knew Mazie only in that way you "know" people you live next to, the ones you never speak to, or wave at. She and her brother, Jimbo, and Mrs. Johnson had started renting the trailer next door last fall. Where they came from, we didn't know. Most everyone in those half dozen trailers kept to themselves. Except we all couldn't help knowing a little bit about the Johnsons, because every few days, Mrs. Johnson—who was a large woman, edging toward gigantic—wandered out in her housecoat and left the front door wide open behind her. She'd go off into the trees, waving her arms and talking like a loon. Directly, a Deputy Sheriff would bring her back. Jimbo, he had a job at the plywood plant. On weekends he rode his dirt bike through the woods, and you could hear him all day, whipping around out there in them woods like a nest of hornets rocked loose.

As for Mazie, kids at school talked about her. Kind of like they used to talk about me, I guess. Kids are bastards. Still, I listened to it all. Tried to parse the truth from bullshit. How she never smiled (true). How she never talked to anyone (true). How, in homeroom, Jimmy DeLong saw a cockroach run out of her right loafer one day, when it slipped free of her heel (bullshit).

She wore brown and gray skirts and baggy sweatshirts all that winter and kept right on wearing them into spring. Her clothes swallowed her bird-girl's frame. Her long straw-colored hair was tamed by a tattered pink band and fell in a single golden sheet to her waist. When she sat in a desk, that hair spilled around her like a cape.

Back in March, the school nurse had come seventh period science and we'd put our heads down and held our breaths as her old Black Warrior combed our heads. Rex Swanson called that pencil the "Head Hunter," and he'd sit in the back and make moaning sex noises all through the exam. That day, it was Mazie who had to collect her things, and out she went, head down, pushing up the worn elastic sleeve of her sweatshirt where it slipped from her elbow.

They had to call Mazie's brother to pick her up, and when she came back to school the next day, she had a shorn head, like a spring lamb.

A week or so later, I saw her wandering around by the junior band building at lunch, hair all gone, picking little yellow flowers that grew wild. I sat eating a peanut butter sandwich out of a *Welcome Back, Kotter* lunchbox on the football bleachers. I'd never seen an episode of that show, but Mama had given that box to me, said it was hers when she was a kid. Watching Mazie, I realized we were both trying hard to be invisible, to slip through them spaces where other kids and grownups don't look. For instance, some older kids in letterman jackets sat a stone's throw away from me on the bleachers, and their laughter just whipsawed past me like shrapnel. Not a pair of thick glasses among them, not one wearing secondhand jeans, the thighs worn thin from so much friction. No shoes half a size too small, rummaged at the Salvation Army because their game warden Daddies spent their paychecks on beer and satellite and dirty tapes down at the Crossroads IV convenience store. I ate quietly. All the while watching Mazie out there in the shadow of the building, beyond the fence. Desperate, suddenly, to be seen by her.

At first, I kept the screen door shut between us.

She stood at the bottom of the concrete steps, untangling her fingers from where they were clasped at her waist just long enough to push a phantom lock of chopped hair behind her ear. It had been a little over a month since it was cut, and it had come back in like the fuzz of a baby bird, uneven, untamed. It stirred something in me, that short hair.

She said, "It's Junior, right?"

"Right," I said around a Twizzler.

"Hi, Junior," she said. "I'm Mazie. I live right over there." She pointed.

"I know," I said.

"Well, why don't you come out here where I can see you."

It wasn't a question, the way she said it, so I opened the door and went right down the steps. It had rained the night before and the dirt was wet and my socks soaked it up and it made my feet cold and heavy.

Mazie backed up a few steps, kept her hands twisted together. "You like Twizzlers."

I shrugged.

"Red's the best," she said.

I held out the pack of Twizzlers and bit the one in my mouth off and chewed and said, "I don't like the black ones."

Somewhere, out in the woods, Jimbo's bike was buzzing like a chainsaw.

She pulled a piece of candy from the bag and bit into it and I watched it turn her fingers sticky, and she said, "Junior, I came here to ask you an important question. Do you believe in life after death?"

Stupidly, I nodded. Maybe I was thinking of this movie I'd seen on Cinemax, where Chevy Chase gets killed and comes back as Benji and has to solve his own murder, only from inside the body of a dog.

"Do you believe we each have a purpose in life?"

I hesitated, then shook my head.

"Why not?"

I swallowed. I said, "If you'd asked me what my purpose was a week ago, I'd have said it was to draw. Like cartoons, but—"

"You mean like Walt Disney?"

"Whatever. Only I took this test where you had to draw a turtle and I mailed it off and it came back and they said I couldn't draw a turtle to save my life. They said I should go to trade school and just learn how to weld or something." I was babbling like a damn idiot, I knew it. But she only nodded, gravely, like I'd just told her the ultimate tale of woe and misery. The truth was, they'd said I had potential, but it wasn't like that meant I was Leonardo da

Vinci. I figured anyone had potential as long as they could pay an instructional fee.

"Don't you want to be more than what someone else says you oughta be?" she asked.

I blinked. I had never thought of it that way. I nodded.

"You know The Church of the Unending Plain?"

I said I did not.

"It's upriver a ways, back in the woods. Past that bait store."

"Where they sell comic books," I said, thinking of the banana-flavored Moon Pies I'd get there when me and Daddy went fishing.

"Well, that's my church, and we just started up Revival. And Pastor Roy has asked the youth of the church to each personally invite one young person. You're the person I thought of."

"You thought of me?"

She blushed, cast her eyes down.

"Sure, I'll go," I said.

She stuck her hand out, stiff as a plank, and I shook it. Then she went back across the lane, candy in hand, and that was it.

I went inside and peeled off my socks, threw them in the bathroom hamper, and went to my bedroom and lay on my bed and stared up at the ceiling. "Mazie," I said, softly. "Mazie Johnson. Mazie Johnson."

I said it again and again, quiet like that.

Like it was a prayer I'd only just learned.

III

After the Lord's Supper, the whole congregation shook my hand on the way out the door, telling me how glad they was to see a young man like me taking an active interest in church. I'd helped

Mazie serve, and that impressed people, I guess, me passing the bread plates at one end of a pew while she doled out blood cups at the other. In fact, you might say it turned out to be one of those star-making performances like you hear about in movies. The eighth grade football coach even squeezed my shoulder, told me I was built like a bull, said it was a shame I'd never get the chance to go out for his team next year. Which might have struck me as odd, except I don't get compliments like that very often, and well, I'm not ashamed to admit that it made me proud. I wish Daddy had been there to hear it.

On the walk home through the woods that day, fish-copper taste of alligator blood still on our tongues, me and Mazie don't say much. The river mutters and the wind blows and the trees above us creak. There's something bugging her, whereas I'm in a pretty good mood. In fact, I've just about forgotten about Pastor Roy's weird balloon gullet, or the odd rubbery feel of his skin when he shook my hand, and I'm thinking I might have even been Under Conviction today, so I'm fixing to start whistling like a real pecker head when Mazie tells me she doesn't want to sit down at the front anymore, like we have been, the last few weeks. After today, she says, she thinks she might just prefer the back pew. It's fine by me, I tell her. Then I say something stupid like, "Hey, you can worship God anywhere."

She doesn't talk again. In fact, we get home and she doesn't even say goodbye. Just peels off the lane into her trailer and shuts the door.

I don't see her that whole week. Every day, I go over, I knock. Jimbo slams the door in my face on two separate occasions, and once, Mrs. Johnson asks me if I'm there to cook her some chili or kill the cockroaches. After that, I don't go back.

Come next Sunday, though, like nothing's wrong, she's waiting for me out in the lane, and we set out walking. I tell her I've been thinking about church all week. How much better it made things, just to know you had a spiritual family. Like when Daddy told me I wasn't good for nothing but strapping on a feed bag and eating us out of house and home? I just went into my bedroom and shut my door and thought good thoughts and pitied him for being a poor lost soul. Or how when Rex Swanson caught me walking past his trailer to the mailbox station, I just let him put his big hot hands around my throat and squeeze until he got bored, and you can't even see the marks now. I tell her I figure today might just be the day I join the Church of the Unending Plain. Become a permanent member.

"That's nice," she says, but she won't look me in the eye.

"What's eating you?" I ask.

She looks at me sharp. Like I've shoveled up a nerve.

"Today," Pastor Roy says, voice booming, "I want to talk to you all about the Mire."

He's at the front of the church, standing perfectly still on a low stage built out of plywood and two-by-fours. Square head, hair like a mowed yard. He's clutching a big phone book of a Bible in his hands. Leather bound, the pages are brittle and dry and made of some paper ancient as the Pyramids.

"The Mire!" he cries, and stamps an alligator skin boot. "We walk in it daily, friends. We trudge in it. We slog in it. We've been stranded in it, ain't we? Here in this, this, this, this *putrescence*... for as long as we can remember. Beyond all recall of when or why! Can I get an a-men?"

Mazie and me are in the back pew, like she wants, and the first "a-men" pops from our left, a woman's voice. I spot her right quick where she's nodding her head, frayed hair pulled back in a ponytail.

She's skin and bones beneath a red sleeveless T-shirt. She hugs herself, shivering in the heat.

Pastor Roy's getting revved up now. He's pacing back and forth on his platform like a cat in a cage. His arms start to swing. He slaps that big old book. "Life wrecked us here long ago. Each of us was born out of a diseased womb onto a plain of utter despair. What we have not suffered, we have caused, and what we have not caused, we have surely suffered. Loneliness. Depression. Diabetes. Cancer. Divorce. Hell's own heartaches, each our own."

His voice flies up like a flock of startled birds.

"Would that we had each of us been turned to slime in our mother's bellies than to suffer one more minute of degradation here in this loathsome world!"

"Preach on!" someone cries.

I don't see who it is this time because I'm thinking about Mama and Daddy's last big fight, the one before she left. How I watched it all from the kitchen window, them in the backyard, going at it over something. Their fights always started out over something real—Mama was drunk and burned dinner; Daddy was late and forgot to take his gun off before coming inside—but the worst ones, the reasons just got all twisted up over several hours like kicked bedsheets, until finally it was just name calling and "I hate you!" and "Why don't you take a long dirt nap!" and things like that. This fight, Mama told Daddy she didn't want me. Said she never wanted kids and if she could have afforded it, she'd have gone right up to Little Rock and had Dr. Giggles—that's the name she said, I swear—cut me right out of her.

So now I'm thinking about Pastor Roy's message, and how right it feels. How we're all trapped in some Mire that won't let us be better than we are. Pretty soon, he plonks down the steps and starts working the aisles, touching people on the shoulders, dropping his voice real low and friendly and recounting all their troubles like he's naming all the animals in his garden. He snaps me back when he says, "But I am here today"—and now his voice settles down into a holy, precious tremble, like a warm, idling motor—"to tell you, friends, there is good news. There is good news!"

"Hallelujah," someone says.

"And that good news is this!" He waits until the room is hushed. "That is not dead," Pastor Roy says, "which can eternal lie."

He points behind him, to the picture of the girl, the fat kid, the fish-man.

Beside me, Mazie has begun to tremble.

"Did you hear me? I said that is NOT dead, which can eternal lie. Can I get an a-men?"

"A-fuckin-men!" the eighth grade football coach hollers.

"Oh, I feel the spirit taking me, brothers, sisters! Time's winged chariot draweth near! Lo, the Eternal One is about to wake from a long, dark slumber! And the world will soon know that our Lord and Savior is NOT dead. And the world will soon fear and tremble, and all those sinners out there will find themselves gnashed between the teeth of a great and mighty storm!"

"*Vulgtmah ah!*" someone cries.

"You're right there, Brother Glen," Pastor Roy says. "But none of this can happen, until one more soul comes down to this altar and takes his place among us!"

Now, he's pointing back over his shoulder, specifically at that limp-dicked fat kid with no clothes on, and suddenly it hits me: that boy looks an awful lot like me. I feel a tingling in my stomach. A sudden pain in my head, as this thing, this presence, this *eye*, opens inside me. My heart begins to pound. Sweat prickles all over. Oh yes, I am Under Conviction.

Pastor Roy opens his mouth and lets fly a shotgun blast of mad babble.

"*H' mgah'ehye ahf' gn'th'bthnk ephainourish c' uh'eog dagon nog mgyogor!*"

I clap my hands over my ears, then my mouth.

Imagine two voices, one outside, one inside, the one whispering while the other screams. The one that whispers finally telling me, gentle as can be, what them ugly words mean. And boy, does Pastor Roy keep on trucking. He says it all over and over and over, and I put my head between my knees, trying not to throw up—

Mazie's hand makes circles on my back.

Invitational music floods the church and the congregation stands. Old Miss Doris is at the electric organ, fumbling through four, five verses of "I Surrender All." Only the lyrics are in that ragged language: "*Nilgh'ri l' dagon Y' surrender, nilgh'ri l' h' Y' freely goka.*" My eyes are clinched tight and my head's humming, as if Mazie's brother is looping my skull on his bike like it's the Globe of Death. Mazie whispers my name, a question at the end of it, but I don't have an answer. I press my fist against my temple. That yammer in my head—

If I look up, if I stand, I know I will see Pastor Roy's black eyes locked on mine, and if I meet those eyes, I'm done for. I'll slide out and walk the aisle—

"Stay with me," Mazie says, hand moving from my back to my neck. Into my hair.

I hear his voice, welcoming new members. A man and wife who join by profession of faith. The man's asked Dagon into his heart this very day, he'll be baptized next Sunday night. But these are not the ones, not the final soul, brothers and sisters, no, there is still one more!

I look up at that fat boy and it's too much, like some magnetic pull, I am wanted, I am needed, I am foreordained—

"Don't go," Mazie whispers. Breath hot in my ear.

She grabs a handful of hair and turns my head, kisses me on the mouth.

I feel her tongue, like a nine-volt Eveready to the tip of my own—

The eye inside my head bursts wide open and sees the two of us together on the river in the dark, in my Daddy's bass boat, whispering downstream between the cypress stobs toward the fading daylight. Mazie's up front, working the trolling motor, and I'm standing naked in the middle of the boat, like that painted idiot up on the wall, and she looks at me and I share the secrets of my heart. I tell her about Mama's drinking, the hidden bottles in the cupboards, the ones beneath the trailer in the Igloo cooler. How hard it was, being the fat kid with the drunk Mama who couldn't buy the right size T-shirts out of the Sears catalogue, how she always bought the size she *wanted* me to be, how Daddy's ashamed and says I got tits like a girl and my name oughta be Missy, not Junior, and all the while I'm clutching at my body, trying to hide it from Mazie, but Mazie only gets out of her boat seat and lifts her sweatshirt over her head and she's not wearing a bra and her breasts are small and dark and I can't hide my own titties at the same time as I try to cover up what's happening down below, but my hands refuse to drop down there because my titties, somehow, are so much worse than my twig becoming a branch, so she steps out of her homemade skirt and we're both naked and bare now, together, and there's thunder, hot pink lightning that sears the sky, as the river beneath the boat clouds up gar-black, and she puts her arms around me, and I put my arms around her, fingers light against the mole-peppered skin of her back, and she pulls me against her, nuzzles my neck, and a flash of lightning sears the night, and in that flash I see something change in Mazie's eyes, turn molten, shine, and her hands become rough and scaly against my skin, and her wide mouth cracks open to reveal the wet, sopping gullet of a fish, only it's lined with teeth, about a million teeth, each barbed and sharp as Daddy's fishhooks—

Down front, Pastor Roy smiles and spreads his tree-trunk arms and shouts those awful words again, only this time they're in English: *Let the innocent whose blood would nourish our queen Dagon come down!*

Mazie yanks hard on my wrist, and we're flying out the doors. I can feel the preacher's eyes clawing after me, but we're gone.

We run full out for a while, until I yell slow down, and after that, we walk. Down the narrow carpet of rotten leaves and reaching hardwoods, slicked in brown fungus and mold. All around us the trees are big and gnarled and their rough bark shows high mudlines where the river rises. We don't talk, not at first. My head's killing me. I stay in back of her, my button-up shirt untucked, tail rumpled. Sweat beneath my arms. Face red in the spring heat. After a while, she stops and watches the woods behind us, like something's followed us from the church, is lurking in the shadows of the pin oaks and cypress. We stand there in the gloom.

She says, "I'm sorry, Junior," and her voice trembles. She bites her lip. She sits on a fallen tree and drops her head into her hands. "Oh, I'm sorry. This is all my fault."

"What I saw," I say. Out of breath. Touching a finger to my temple. "In here. What was it?"

"The future," she says. She won't look at me. "Or something like it."

Her white socks have delicate lace collars full of beggar's lice.

I drop at her feet, self-conscious at first. Then I begin to pick the sticky seeds away. I pluck one and it pulls her sock so I can see the skin beneath it, a weird, mottled red and orange. My fingers brush it. It's rough, like snakeskin. It's not a rash. "Mazie?" I ask, looking up.

She stares at me, like I'm the dumbest thing in all creation, which I guess maybe I am. Her eyes change. Her pupils get big, get black. She looks *through* me. Beyond me. Beyond this place, this life. This world. She gets to her feet and lifts the hem of her sweatshirt over her belly, draws it up high, just beneath her small breasts, and holds it there with her chin.

I rock back on the pine straw, staring at the sheen of scales across her stomach. Each the size of a saucer. Sunset reds, fiery orange.

"It's happening quick now. Pastor Roy says it'll be over by next Sunday—"

"How?" I croak. But I'm already thinking of that painting—not the girl, not the fat kid, but the fish-man, black doll's eyes wide with some unknowable feeling, some terrible satisfaction. That huge fish-dick like a Louisville Slugger. It's too awful to imagine—

She takes my hand and places it against her belly. Over her scales.

"They're cold," I say. I jerk away.

"I wanted this, Junior. I came to this church and they loved me, *he* loved me, and it's like this, this was always here, waiting for me. Like it was all…"

"…meant to be," I finish.

"Don't you feel that way?"

"I feel like I was tricked."

She yanks her sweatshirt down. "I didn't trick you. I invited you. And you came." She starts off, toward the trailers.

"So, what happens?" I call after her. "You eat me or something, after you turn into a fish, and I'm just supposed to be okay with that?"

"You should be so lucky!" she spits.

"Hey, you aren't special!" I cry after her. "You're just a stupid girl who got duped into making a stupid choice for some dirty old fish-dicked man! And maybe just killed the world while you were at it!"

She whirls. Stabs a finger at me. "What did the world ever do for you, Junior Grubb?"

I stare at her, fuming, working hard to come up with an answer to her question, but it hits me, all at once, how right she really is. Sure, it feels wrong, just to say it, that you'd rather the world go ahead and get the hell on with ending, but whatever Pastor Roy had done to Mazie, whatever sack-of-shit thing he'd done, I can't really disagree with his police work when it comes to one simple truth: it sucks here, this plain of utter despair. It's sucked for a long time, actually.

Mazie sees it on my face, and I think, ever so briefly, about running away from her. Getting as far from here and her church as I can. But where would I go? There'd be no Mazie there, wherever that is. I pound the ground, pulp the leaves, and once the pounding starts, it doesn't really stop—until she's there, bending low beside me, taking my hand, touching my hair, whispering soft words. She tells me she's sorry. I tell her the same. And after a while, I get up, wipe my face, and hand in hand, we walk back to the Bottoms, like two doomed kids in some hopeless after-school special.

IV

The week passes. I try not to eat so much chocolate, have a carrot or two. Do some push-ups. To taste my best, is how my thinking goes. I don't see Mazie, but it's not because we're either of us still upset with the other. It's more an unspoken agreement, like how a bride and groom can't see each other before the wedding? Mazie doesn't go to school, but I do and when the bus drops me off each afternoon, I go over and sit on the squirrel station beneath her window, and she sits in the shadows in there behind a half-drawn shade and tells me all the places she's got parts growing. How it's always something new, like a plant grows when you're not looking. She says she can walk around the house with her webbed hands and feet making balloon noises and Mrs. Johnson, she's so far gone she doesn't even notice. "Does it hurt?" I ask. "Not really," she says, but I can tell it's not entirely the truth. She says the hours are gloomy and long when I'm not there, because all she has time to do is think. Mostly about her brother, who is her one regret. She hasn't said boo to Jimbo this week. He's working graveyards at the mill. He's not a bad person, she says. He always did right by her. It's tearing her up, I can tell, the idea that his destruction might be among the first she wreaks, simply because he sleeps in the bedroom next to hers.

"Maybe he'll make it," I say. "Some folks have got to."

"Says who?" Mazie says.

"Movies," I say. Thinking about this one where robots take over the world and there's a few raggedy survivors who band together and invent time travel. "Who knows. Maybe one day someone'll even defeat you. Like create some cyborg to fight fish-monsters and all the other weird shit you're about to unleash."

"You're funny, Junior," she says.

Her voice has this kind of warble to it, like she's underwater.

"Maybe it'll be Jimbo," I say, and that's the end of that conversation.

Saturday rolls around and over breakfast, I ask Daddy if he wants to go fishing. He doesn't say much at first, standing at the sink and rinsing out his bowl of Cap'N Crunch. "Really fish?" he finally says. "Or me fish and you just sit there and read funny books?"

Really fish, I tell him, so we go.

We're on the river in his bass boat and he's brought a six pack, is kicked back in the front swivel seat, rod hanging over the edge, and I get out a cane pole and bait it with a worm. I loop the worm three times over the hook, like he showed me, and try not to blanch at the yellow goo that squirts out. I catch a bream and Daddy whistles at the size, even though it's not that big. When it comes time to take it off the line, I don't pass it to him, like usual—I've always been afraid of getting finned—but instead I run my hand down the slick back, flatten out the fins, work the hook free with the other hand, and toss it into the live well, where it thrashes and splashes, and I wonder what it will feel like when Mazie puts her teeth into me.

It was a good day.

Late that night, I tried, one last time, to talk to her. To tell her all the stuff I hadn't said yet. Because who knew what would happen, come tomorrow. I stood outside her window and called to her, but that heavy shade was drawn down. I went to the back steps and peered through a pair of sliding glass doors and there, sprawled in a reclining rocker in her housecoat, was Mrs. Johnson. She saw me staring in and her eyes were wide and scared and her hands gripped the chair's arm rests like she was an astronaut bound in place by unimaginable forces. I waved and went away, feeling bad I had startled her.

Later, I wondered if it had even been me who scared her.

Sunday, after services. Pastor Roy's shovel hand cups my head. The brown river water is warm like a bath and laps at my knees. I look up at the congregation of leering faces all along the riverbank and there are some who wear glasses and the sun flashes in their lenses and makes their eyes dead, and their smiles are terrible and toothy and the water makes a little trickling sound and downriver at the public ramp someone's motorboat just won't start. Pastor Roy talks a while about how I am the last convert the Church of the Unending Plain will ever know, how tonight, when my blood is shed and the great storm breaks and the eternal vortex opens it'll be the end of all suffering and Dagon will emerge in new form to claim his Queen and lots of other crap I don't hear because I'm thinking mostly about how I'm fixing to go under water, and I'm thinking about that day at the county pool and how Daddy told me a few days later he was sorry for what he did. At last, Pastor Roy shuts up and that big hand slips down to my right shoulder, the other under my left arm, and suddenly I am beneath the water and it is dark and a million dry throats are crying out for a single drop of water to touch to their tongues, only their tongues have been ripped from their mouths, and then I'm staggering up onto the sandbar, soaked through and dripping, and I glance one last time at those horrid faces, their hands brought together in applause for the last soul they will ever win, and nowhere among them do I see Mazie, and I'm grateful for that, that it's not going to happen right away, because I'm not quite ready yet, to meet her in her new form. I have one last thing to do. But just the thought of her face, her spirit, her white lace collared ankle socks, resolves me yet again: this is the way.

There's something I haven't told you.

Something I did before leaving home for church that morning.

I went into my Daddy's bedroom where he was sawing logs after frying up last night's fish and getting stone drunk on a case of Budweiser in celebration of finally having the son he'd always wanted. He'd marveled, I reckon, at how I helped him clean and gut those fish. How I used a knife and not a spoon to scrape the scales, then thumbed that knife through four or five fish heads until they crunched. It felt good, knowing I had at least made him happy, given him something to remember me by. For all the brief time he had left.

I still didn't have a clear picture of how it was all going to go.

But there was one thing I was going to hang my hat on happening.

I went to Daddy's dresser and unsnapped his gun holster where it lay among his belt and badge and slipped out his Glock and popped the clip to be sure it was loaded—of course, it was—and then I took it out of there and tucked it snugly into my backpack, beneath my post-baptism towel.

What I'm planning to do, you'll want to think it's for Mazie. And if you do, you go right ahead and think it. I can't stop you.

Really, it's just for me.

A lady in jeans and an airbrushed T-shirt that says "Yes, Dagon Loves Me" leads me back to Pastor Roy's office. I drip a wet trail down the narrow, cinderblock hall. She opens a door and hands me my backpack, tells me I can change out of my wet things in here, then leaves me alone. I stand for a second, staring around. Pattering river water on the preacher's cheap-ass carpet. High up, there's an AC unit, but it's switched off and the room is like a hotbox in the spring humidity. The preacher's desk is big and metal and the homemade shelves behind it are lined with books on marriage counseling, plus a few weird things I'm betting you just don't find in most preachers' libraries. Mounted over the shelves is a marble-eyed catfish the size of a small dog, thick with cobwebs.

I set my backpack on the lime green couch opposite the desk and it hits me, suddenly, that it was right here, on this couch, where it happened. Above the couch there's a picture, a painting on canvas by the same artist who did the murals, and it's got the same yellow-haired woman from the altar, only in this one she's less exalted, more defiled, because that big fish-man from the sanctuary, the one with the Louisville Slugger? Well, let's just say he's stepping up to bat, and the woman, she's thrown back against a cypress stump and her eyes are scrunched and her mouth is open in what looks like the loudest scream you ever heard, and there's water running down that monster's thick, beefy thighs and a big fin that runs all down his whip-scarred back.

Maybe it was like that. Maybe it wasn't.

I'd like to think she came to it on her own terms, that it wasn't about meanness.

Either way, it doesn't change what I'm about to do.

Footsteps outside the door. Voices.

I remember the wet jeans I'm wearing. The T-shirt clinging to me, showing off what Daddy might call my "Missy bags." I peel the jeans, kick them aside. I've got my shirt over my head when I hear the office door start to open. I clutch the shirt close to cover my tits, then drop it down to hide my Hanes underwear, which I realize have been made whisper-thin by their soaking. Back to my chest. I can't decide.

The door opens.

"Junior," Pastor Roy grins.

He stands dripping wet in his long white robe, eyes crawling me. Then he shuts the door and digs around in his own duffle bag, which is in the leather swivel chair behind his desk. "Best change, son, before you catch cold."

He begins to strip his clothes.

Like Mrs. Johnson in her recliner, I'm frozen.

Beneath his robe Pastor Roy wears a plain T-shirt and gym shorts. He shucks these and suddenly he's naked, and his bulk seems to fill up the entire corner of the room where he's toweling off his legs, his chest, his head. His dick swings there like a club, though it's hardly the size of a baseball bat. He sees me staring and goes still. Lets the towel drop into his chair. He runs a hand through his wet hair and says, "You ever whistle in the dark?"

When I shake my head, he grins.

"You know what that means, whistling in the dark?"

Another shake of the head.

He reaches for a dry T-shirt in his bag. "Our little Mazie," he says, pulling the shirt on over his head. "Boy, she can tell you what it means. Well, she *could*, if she could still talk—"

That's when he sees what I'm holding in my hand.

He hesitates, a flicker of something, it's not fear. Recognition, maybe.

I thumb off the safety.

"You ever see that famous picture, Junior, of them sheep?"

Overhead, the lights hum and flicker in their fixture, and the room is suddenly too bright, too real.

"A thousand sheep, lying dead in a field. Somewhere in Montana. Killed by lightning. Some mineral in the ground, conducts electricity.

Sent it through 'em, fried ever last one. Bzzt! I think about that sometimes, when I'm up there. Preparing the way. All those bodies warming benches. Imagine how that feels, to hear a great clap of thunder when you're speaking the dark god's truth."

Outside, like he's called it down himself, the sky cracks open.

"There are sheep," he says, and the words sound funny, like his throat's welling up with water. "And there's the lightning. I am not the lightning. I never was. Which do you think you are, Junior?"

Pastor Roy rears up on the balls of his feet and arches his back and spasms. Something wet spills like lamp oil from his mouth. He staggers against the corner of his desk, then reaches up to the top of his head with one wide hand, digs his long fingers into his scalp, and rakes it. Flesh tears, as the thing inside him steps out onto the carpet, and Pastor Roy's skin sloughs onto the desk in a heap, and what I'm looking at now is a scaled, pale-slick demon, and his neck is wide and bulging and joins his shoulders in one solid fleshy mass and his wide-set eyes are black pin points, his lips fat and rubbery. Long black whiskers uncurl wetly from his chin, and his fingers open into webs and end in sharp claws. His feet are wide, splayed fins. His big fish-pecker jumps and stands out straight and arrow-shaped and sharp, and that gets me, more than anything, makes me stare slack-jawed with horror, dimly aware that the Pastor-Roy-fish is still speaking, out of that wet, black throat that drips. "Our Mazie, she *is* the lightning, and that is why He chose her *l' h' ah uh'eog!*"

I understand every word of it.

...To be his queen.

And suddenly I feel it, the utter emptiness of it. The loss of Mazie to another.

To the thunder.

The gun bucks in my hands and the Pastor-Roy-fish flops

backward onto his desk, a crater where his bulging throat once was. There's not much blood, just the reek of fish and that wild, river smell that breaks from the Ouachita after a hot summer rain. He lifts his giant head toward me and speaks, one last time, the words broken in his ruined throat.

"Go," he says. "Be hers."

Lightning, thunder, as Pastor Roy passes a final sigh of air and water.

I look down at the gun in my hands.

I forget dry clothes, my backpack.

Wearing only my underwear, I toss the gun and run.

V

The wind kicks up an eddy of leaves and dirt as I duck and weave through the woods. Twigs and roots jab my feet. Branches rake my chest, drawing thin runners of blood. Briars snag my shins and thighs. The trees overhead sough and bend and thunder splits the sky and the day darkens to midnight. By the time I make it the mile or so back to the cul-de-sac of the Bottoms, I'm bleeding all over and my throat and sinuses are raw. I hock a lump of spit and step out into the gravel lane.

The wind has knocked down the transformer that powers the half dozen trailers. Wires buck and spark in the road like pissed off snakes. All windows are dark. No one's in sight. A loose door somewhere bangs in the wind. I make my way around the edge of the woods to miss the downed wires. Mazie's brother's dirt bike is on its side, sputtering gray exhaust. Had Jimbo come home early, tried to get one last ride in, before the storm? Or had he fled, when he saw her?

The sliding glass doors at the back of the trailer are wide open. Fanned in blood.

Poor Mrs. Johnson slumps wide-eyed in her chair, guts spilling out of her housecoat.

In a heap near the pine-paneled living room wall, Jimbo's a broken, twisted mess. There's a broomstick on the floor beside him, like it was the only thing he could grab before she got him.

I stand there in the dark living room, shivering. The air burns with the metal scent of blood, beneath it mold and a thousand cigarettes. I listen for any signs of life. At first, all I can hear are fat, heavy drops of rain plunking on the metal roof. Seconds later, the skies open a vein and the roar is so loud I almost don't hear the crash of glass from the back bedroom of the trailer.

"Mazie?"

Slowly, I feel my way along the hall in the dark and nudge open a room I have dreamed of entering, a room I never believed I would actually see.

A flash of lightning.

Mussed bedcovers. Empty bed.

A pile of something on the floor that might have been clothes, tangled up in skin.

A draft of cool wind.

Broken shards of window glass, wet with blood and rain.

I ease out onto the plywood squirrel station, which immediately collapses under me and sends me sprawling in the mud, which goes squelching into my underwear. I follow her tracks—wide, webbed—where they lead off past my own trailer, into the trees, down one of Jimbo's dirt bike trails, all the way to the river's edge, where they disappear, the bank already falling away in the downpour, the water out there rising.

"Mazie!" I scream. Afraid she's left me. Afraid she's gone.

Afraid there's nothing special at all anymore, about the way this ends.

Lightning flashes, and I see a shape, humped and big-headed and strange, knee-deep in a whorl of river water.

She turns. Her eyes flash like headlights in a graveyard.

I remember, suddenly, that first night of Revival. Twilight, after the service. Pastor Roy on the church steps, gripping hands and slapping backs. His hand on her shoulder, a little longer than it should have been, touching the back of her neck. He kisses the top of her head. People stream out, drift away. We set off into the woods. Kick over crawdad mounds and swat at spring's first lightning bugs. At some point, we break into a field beside the river, and she picks dandelion blooms the sinking sun has set ablaze like the tops of a tiny, fragile city in the grass. Her breath sends the blossoms sailing. The wind gathers them up and throws them higher, up toward the blue sky, the invisible stars beyond, some high and lofty place I will never be. "Thanks for going to church with me," she tells me, that day.

Another flash of lightning and she's gone.

I drop to my knees. Begin to sob out her name.

But then she's there, crawling over the lip of the embankment—no, not crawling, just coming, moving on all fours in a way that's perfectly natural, given her new shape, and now her face is inches from mine and we're both there in the mud, naked and pitiful, glorious and new. Her eyes are wide and round and golden. Her lips small. In place of her nose, a red snout flecked with orange, like a sunset, and when she turns her head I can see the long-scaled shape of her, the green dorsal fin that begins at the top of her head and runs the length of her. Gills flutter along her neck, and I reach out, helpless not to, and touch her. Smooth back the fin. No fear of the spines. She can never hurt me. Never. Her eyes close, and she makes a sound, kind of like a trilling, before she settles down onto her knees, and together we sit in the mud and hold hands and touch heads like two children in a fairy tale.

There's a sound, out there in the river, a rushing, sucking, whirling sound. Probably Pastor Roy's eternal vortex, the Eternal One, making his entrance. Biggest fish-dick of them all. That's okay, I tell myself. I'm here. With her. She glances over her shoulder—what used to be her shoulder—as the sound out there gets louder. The river spinning itself up, a gate opening, I guess, like in that movie, the one where the duck has to fight a bunch of interdimensional lobster monsters that come to Earth in a tunnel of cosmic dust. Daddy and I watched that movie. He said the duck looked fake. I thought it was okay.

I kiss Mazie's lips.

She blinks a big, fish-eye blink.

I tilt back my throat and shut my eyes against the rain, squeezing her webbed hands tight.

Her mouth opens wide, revealing what I'm sure is a long, deep tunnel of teeth.

Down in there, somewhere, is the world I've dreamed of knowing.

THE GIFT OF TONGUES

BY AO-HUI LIN

"**A**in't nothing to be afraid of." Miss Annie's voice is coaxing, even as the hand wrapped around Myra's upper arm tightens into a band of steel, dragging her towards the crib next to Pastor Paul's desk.

Myra peers into the crib, hesitant, as if the mere sight of the baby will strike her forever blind. The baby, Agnes, stares at them, her eyes darting from Myra to Miss Annie and back. Myra cannot escape the notion that she is being judged and, as Agnes breaks eye contact, found wanting. Agnes sighs as if disappointed.

"See, she likes you!" encourages Miss Annie. "Pick her up!"

Myra notices that Miss Annie makes no attempt to pick up the baby herself. Indeed, Miss Annie has stepped behind Myra to apply light pressure to Myra's back, pushing her forward over the infant. Myra, only fourteen but with a decade of experience caring for her siblings, reaches into the crib and with a practiced move, bringing the swaddled babe up to her shoulder, Agnes's head cradled against her neck.

"What's up, pretty baby?" Myra coos in a sing-song voice. Agnes reaches out a chubby fist to tug on a lock of Myra's hair and puts it in her mouth.

Miss Annie beams and pats Myra on the shoulder. "I knew she'd take to you like a duck to water. From now on, you come every day and take care of little Agnes, and I will give you twenty dollars each and every time," Myra knows this is too much to pay a girl to watch a baby, but she doesn't know if the wage is an act of charity, the church helping out its newest orphan, or if it is an enticement to stay after so many other caregivers have run away, making the sign of the cross and warding against the evil eye.

She has little time to think about it. In the space of a heartbeat, Miss Annie has ushered her to the door and out to the parking lot in back, snagging a canvas knapsack from a table along the way. "You have everything you'll need in there," she says as she hooks the bag onto Myra's free wrist. "Pastor Paul needs to concentrate on his sermon for tomorrow, so don't bring the baby back until after sundown," she warns right before she closes the door with a *thunk*, not quite on Myra's face, but close.

Staring at the closed door, it takes Myra a few seconds to gather her wits. Then she shrugs the knapsack over her shoulder, adjusts her hold on Agnes, and sets off toward home.

"Well, pretty baby, I guess it's just you and me."

When Myra steps through her door into the gloom of the front hall, the babble she's been directing at Agnes gets louder and faster. Myra's still not used to the eerie silence that has replaced the constant din of six people living in a tiny four-room house, and she's grateful for an excuse to make some noise.

Agnes, for her part, is completely mute. Not a gurgle, a whimper or a laugh escapes her lips. But Myra knows Agnes can talk. She's heard it. The whole town has heard it, as have plenty of folks from other towns what come to listen to Agnes during Sunday services. Agnes is the reason the Deer Lick Pentecostal Church of God can pay Myra $20 a day to take care of her. Myra takes Agnes straight to the kitchen, to the highchair her brother Jakey used to sit in. It's a little too big for Agnes, who's about the size of a one-year-old, though she can sit up fine when she wants to. Jakey was almost two and a half last time he sat in that chair, not more'n a month ago. Myra straps Agnes in before rummaging through the knapsack. She pulls out a couple of jars of baby food. Carrots and some nasty green pea thing. She wrinkles her nose and sticks out her tongue.

"Blech. Agnes, you don't want this, do you?" she asks. Agnes blinks owl-eyes at her but says nothing. Myra goes to a kitchen cabinet and brings out a dusty box of graham crackers. She looks inside, pleased to find an unopened sleeve. She pulls it out and rips it open, breaking the cracker sheets along the perforations and placing the rectangles on the tray in front of Agnes.

"These were Jakey's favorite", says Myra, her voice catching on her brother's name before she forces out a more cheerful note. "He liked to dip them in milk. I don't have any milk but..." She's foraging through the bag, and comes up with a baby bottle. She tips the contents into a glass and makes another face at the chalky grayish liquid. "Oh well, it's the best I can do." She takes one of the graham cracker squares and dunks it into the formula before handing it to Agnes.

Agnes takes it delicately between thumb and forefinger and nibbles on it. "Good?" asks Myra, and she's not sure if Agnes gives a little nod, or if it's gas.

Myra pulls up a chair. Now that she has someone to talk to, she can't seem to stop, even if it's someone who never answers back, or maybe because of it. While Agnes eats her snack, Myra finds herself talking about baby Jakey, and her sister Sarah.

"We used to call her Sarah, full of Grace, on account of because she ate Momma's pet chicken named Grace...anyway, Daddy accidentally ran over it with his truck and we had to cook it. And Hester, who was second oldest and riding shotgun that day everyone went to the store. Except Myra 'cause she was mad at all of them for..."

"Huh," she says, "I don't even remember why I was so mad."

She doesn't talk about Momma and Daddy because that hurts too much.

By the time she's got it all talked out of her, Agnes has finished the crackers and the formula and the carrots and the nasty pea mush, had a fresh diaper change, and taken a tour of all four rooms of the house. And now she is snuggled in Myra's embrace. The baby's stone expression never changes, but her eyes seem to note every detail, and Myra likes to think that Agnes has absorbed every word she's heard.

She delivers Agnes back to the church well after sundown, and returns home, hoarse, tired, and twenty dollars richer. She takes her pillow and her blanket and curls up in the hammock her daddy had hung in the backyard, unable to sleep inside where her ghosts still talked to her at night.

The next morning, she goes to church, same as every Sunday. The church is packed to bursting, the young and healthy mostly relegated to standing in the back or alongside the outer edges of the pews, the sitting spaces reserved for the old and infirm. Pushed against the wall near the pulpit is Baby Agnes's crib. A few people on the benches crane their necks to catch a glimpse of Agnes, while the old church ladies glare at the gawkers before they blush and turn their eyes to their feet, instead.

Pastor Paul's sermon is full of fire and brimstone, and on each thunderous repetition of "Hell", one or two parishioners jump out of their seats and collapse into the aisle, convulsing, screaming "Jesus!" and "Oh, Lawd!" Pastor Paul, the sweat plastering wisps of hair to his face, pounds on the pulpit, making the Bible jump and jitter. People weep, holding their arms out, palms open, fingers outstretched, as if they can pluck God's blessings from the air. Choruses of "Amen!" and "Hallelujah" shake the wooden rafters of the old church roof. Myra sits still, not joining in, praying that she will one day feel God speak from within her, but for now, hearing nothing except an empty deadness.

Pastor Paul comes to a final, shouted "Amen!", which is answered by the crowd, and then for a second everyone is quiet. And in that moment of silence, Baby Agnes's voice booms out, deeper than any baby's voice should be.

It has a curious cadence, each syllable inflected as if it is meant to be a standalone sentence. Agnes has pulled herself to standing using the slats of the crib, and from her open mouth pours a litany of sounds, rising and falling, the glossolalia transfixing the audience. Old women fall to their knees, crying. Young men lay on the floor, shaking. Miss Annie, sitting in the front pew, turns to look at Myra, gives her a small nod and a meaningful look at the crib.

Miss Annie has explained that this is part of her duties, as if Myra hasn't seen the ritual for all the years of her life. Myra stands and moves to the crib, picks up Agnes, who clenches her little baby fists and waves them around as she screams the incomprehensible words. A spectator might be tempted to laugh; Agnes has all the appearance of a tiny toddler raging at the loss of an ice cream cone. Myra carries the angry baby into the crowd, where the parishioners reach out to touch her dress with trembling hands. The two of them shuffle closer to those seated in the pews; Agnes strikes out with her tiny hands, balled into fists, knocking people across the face, in the eyes, snatching at hair and clothes with a strength shocking for one so little. An old man receives a blow across the face, knocking off his glasses, and he gasps, tottering to his feet and tossing his cane away. A young child is boxed on the ears and starts to scream, his mother crying as the child reacts to the commotion as if hearing it for the first time.

In the space of three minutes, there is no more, Agnes falls silent, her hands relax, and she leans into Myra as if too tired to stay awake. The parishioners plead for her to wake up, to continue the words of God, to heal just one more person, but Myra whisks her away to the pastor's office. Behind her, she hears the deacons moving among the flock and the rustle of cash money and the clink of coins into the collection plates.

After a while, Miss Annie and Pastor Paul join her in the office. Miss Annie sits at a desk and rings up the Sunday's take, an amount that sounds impossibly huge to Myra's ears. Pastor Paul pats Agnes on the head, who ignores him, and chucks Myra under the chin. "You did well, Myra. Best haul we've had in a while. You have a way with that child."

Miss Annie sighs. "It's good, but not like the old days. I remember when Agnes first came, and we realized she had the gift of tongues and the healing touch. People would line up for miles come Sunday."

Pastor Paul taps his hands down in a "now, now" motion. "Annie," he intoned, "Give thanks in all circumstances, for this is the will of God. Besides, you know the social services people would be all over us if we were attracting such attention. Who ever heard of a ten-year old infant?" Paul peered from under his bushy brows at Agnes, still snoozing in Myra's arms. "It sure is a mystery."

"God works in mysterious ways, Pastor." agreed Miss Annie. "Shame about that state lady, but we was lucky, too, that they never sent anyone else after she…" her voice trails off as Pastor Paul gives her a warning look and murmurs, "Little pitchers…"

Myra says nothing, even though everyone in town knows the story of how Agnes was left abandoned in the poor box, and how the church took her in, but she ain't grown a speck in the ten years she's been the draw at Sunday services. And how early on the lady from state social services came to look at the baby and said it was a case of "failure to thrive" and she was gonna take Agnes away to get proper medical care. And how her car got hit by a hog truck and no one else ever came asking questions, not about Agnes and not about Myra neither. Most of the people from outta town think it's a different baby, year after year. But in Deer Lick, they all know she's the same Baby Agnes what got left nearly ten years ago.

Miss Annie gives a little shudder, like a cat is walking over her grave, and tells Myra to take Agnes out and don't bring her back until suppertime. Myra does as she's told, and when she and the baby are out of the church, away from listening ears, Myra whispers into Agnes's ear, "Don't you worry none. I'm gonna stay and take care of you. I won't go away like the others." In that moment, she isn't sure if she's only talking about all those other caretakers who'd left Agnes, one by one, unsettled by their perpetually infant charge.

Agnes presses her lips to Myra's ear and whispers back. Myra is so startled she nearly drops the baby right there in the street. Agnes's hands tighten around Myra's neck when she feels the sudden shift in Myra's hold, and the whispering stops. Myra rushes back to her house, locking the door behind her, and settling the baby in the high chair in the kitchen.

"Agnes, what did you say? Were you talking?" Myra is no longer sure exactly what she heard. As far as she knows, Agnes has never spoken a word outside of church services. "Please, say something again!"

Agnes looks around, reaches an open hand toward a cabinet, opens and closes her fingers. Myra looks frantically around before understanding. "Graham crackers? Would you like a graham cracker?" She scrambles to get the box down, spilling crumbs on the floor in her haste. She gives a few Agnes, who consumes them with single minded intensity. Then the baby, crumbs still clinging to the corners of her mouth, begins to bellow that rolling, lilting refrain from earlier.

Myra falls to her knees in front of the baby and runs her hands down Agnes's arms. "Agnes, is God speaking through you?" Agnes pauses for a moment, black eyes bright like a bird, as if to say yes, then continues with her chanting. Unlike at the church, this goes on for much longer than a few minutes. Myra listens intently. She's heard Agnes speak in tongues for nearly her entire life, and it still makes no sense to her, but she knows instinctively that this is the voice of God.

"God, I don't know if you can understand me. I don't speak the same tongues as Agnes. But if you can, please tell my Momma and my Daddy and Jakey and Sarah and Hester that I love them?"

Agnes pauses again. And when she speaks, the voice is softer, soothing, even though the sounds still make no sense. Myra waits for another pause, participating in the rhythm of a conversation she doesn't understand. When she gets a chance, she adds, "Please tell them I'm sorry I got mad that day." Agnes reaches out to touch Myra's cheek. "Tell them I wish I'd been with them no matter what."

As Myra cries ugly, gut-wrenching sobs, Agnes continues to babble. Eventually, Myra takes Agnes out of the chair and they lie on the rug in the living room and fall asleep, Myra wrapped around Agnes.

Miss Annie is relieved when Myra offers to take Agnes home for the week. It's the week before the 10-year celebration of Agnes's arrival, and Annie and the Pastor have so much to do in preparation. "You're a good girl, Myra," she says, while handing Myra a small wad of twenties. "Make sure you get Agnes whatever she needs, you know, formula and diapers and what-like. We've got a pretty new dress for her for Sunday, and you can take some extra clothes out of the poor box for her." She eyes Myra and adds, "Take something for yourself, too."

Myra doesn't mind her shabby clothes, and she doesn't want something from the poor box. Momma taught her how to do the laundry and mend, and she can do better than the cast-offs that people give to the church. She takes Agnes home and they explore the boxes under Momma's and Daddy's bed. There are little dresses handed down from her to Hester to Sarah, and Myra gets out the sewing machine and fixes them to fit Baby Agnes. She thinks about making a dress for herself, too, for Agnes's big celebration, but there's nothing to start with except one of Momma's dresses, and Myra isn't ready for that.

She still can't sleep in the house, but it turns out that Agnes likes sleeping in the hammock with her. The two of them lie together and stare up at the stars, talking at each other without comprehension. Agnes's words sound happy to Myra, even excited, and Myra finds herself telling Agnes stories from when she was littler. Myra even tells Agnes about the first time she remembers being in church and hearing Agnes speak the word of God.

All night long, every night, Agnes whispers in Myra's ear, and Myra's dreams turn the sounds into words she can understand.

She imagines that Agnes is saying, "I will save you" over and over again, and she knows it is God, letting her know that he forgives her for wishing that she had died with the rest of her family on that trip to the store.

She sleeps so well, better than she has in a month that, come Sunday morning, she doesn't wake up until the sun is beating down on the two of them as they sway back and forth in the midmorning breeze. She bolts upright, nearly tipping both of them from the hammock, and then rushes to get them both washed and dressed. She is breathless when she arrives at church, having run all the way with the baby in her arms.

Miss Annie raises a hand and slaps Myra across the face. "Girl, you nearly gave me a heart attack. Where have you been? And what is Agnes wearing?" She snatches Agnes out of Myra's arms, while Myra stands there, a hand to her cheek. Without waiting for an answer, Miss Annie strips the dress Myra altered off of Agnes, leaving red marks on the baby's arms in her roughness. Agnes doesn't cry. She never cries. But her eyes are black pebbles in her face, as hard and dark as onyx. Annie wrestles Agnes into a new dress, a thing made of scratchy lace and polyester, with yellow flowers and bunnies. She ties a baby bonnet on Agnes's head, and it looks ridiculous; a yellow duck bonnet shadowing Agnes's habitual sour baby expression. It occurs to Myra that she hasn't seen that expression for nearly a week, but here it is again.

Out of patience, Miss Annie takes one last look at Myra and sighs. "I wish you'd picked up something pretty for today. Well, no time for it now. Go on. Get out there." Myra leaves to take her place in the pews while Miss Annie puts the final touch on Agnes, a pair of baby booties tied with pink ribbons.

Pastor Paul's sermon lacks the usual nods to damnation and evil. Instead, he trots out homily after homily about gratitude and unexpected gifts from God and, though Myra doesn't quite understand the connection, not hiding lights under a bushel. He ends with a prayer thanking God for delivering Baby Agnes upon Deer Lick, and produces a tiny cupcake with a single candle in it from behind the pulpit.

Everyone looks expectantly at Agnes, but she is completely silent. After a long, awkward pause, Pastor Paul laughs and beckons to Myra. She comes up to the pulpit and he gives her the cupcake, telling her under his breath to take Agnes away. She takes the cupcake and picks up Agnes, while he says something in a loud voice about Agnes deserving a day of rest, and he hopes everyone else is ready for a party.

Myra decides to take Agnes out the front door of the church, rather than back through the Pastor's office, so that Agnes can see the sun and enjoy her cupcake under the trees in the churchyard. The congregation parts to let her through, but they stay behind, anticipating the promised celebration and the food that's been set up on the table against the back.

As they step out into the light, Agnes turns her face up and opens her mouth, and that deep, unchildlike bellow emanates from her again, louder than Myra has ever heard it. It nearly deafens her, and she's about to put Agnes away from her to save her ears, when a shadow blots out the sun. Wind gusts across the churchyard, the trees shiver, and a boom overhead has Myra ducking for cover, holding on to Agnes with a grip like a vise.

Above them hovers something giant and pulsating, a creature or a machine or a demon – to Myra, it could be any of those things. Screeching noises emanate from it, like metal grinding against metal, or the screams of a thousand tortured souls. She feels a *whomp*, a burst of pressure so strong that it erases all sound, and then the church is torn apart, disintegrating as if in the path of a tornado, although the cyclone is contained within the perimeter of the church's walls.

Giant fleshy appendages emerge from the monster, thick and glistening like tongues, tasting the air above the churchyard. Almost everyone had been inside the church, and there are no remains, building or otherwise, visible. Those who had been milling about outside begin to run away, but the tongues snap out, licking the people up and tossing them into the vortex of wind that swallowed the church.

One of the tongues flick toward Myra and Agnes. Myra's eyes are closed, her mouth moving in prayer over and over again.

Agnes is speaking as well, in her God-touched language, and Myra knows that this word of God will be the last thing that she hears. She shields Agnes with her body and braces herself to be reunited with her family again.

Myra feels cold slime pressed against her neck, her back, and she screams in terror. Agnes screams… in triumph. And as they are carried upward, captured and enfolded, Agnes whispers her secret language into Myra's ear, and this time, she understands.

It's not God who will save her, but Agnes.

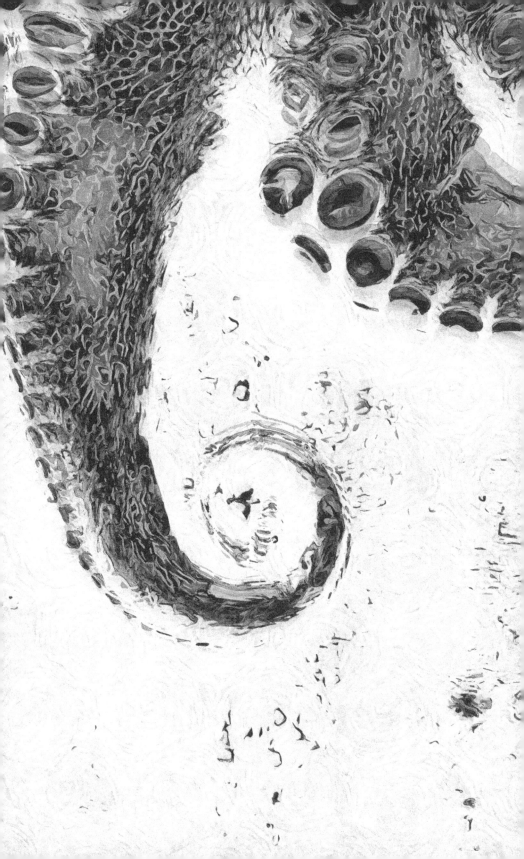

HOMEOWNER'S ASSOCIATION OF UNFATHOMABLE HORRORS BEYOND THE STARS

BY JAY WILBURN

Rachel Rathburn experienced the sense of dread settling upon her spirit as soon as she entered Scully, Alabama. The town lay closer to some major cities than others, but not truly within a reasonable distance to anything. At the final gas station, the ground was dry, making the grass wiry and crisp under her sandals. Seeds bit underneath her soles and irritated between her toes. Pollen assailed her nose and dried out every dark passage from her sinuses down throughout her body. Trailers spotted the forsaken land with men waiting for factories to reopen and women picking up odd work to close the distance between budgets and bills for their families.

Back in the cab of the truck again, Rachel's father drove the U-Haul through the gates of their walled community situated between squalor and vacant lots. As a small plane buzzed an approach to an unseen landing strip behind the back wall of their subdivision, Rachel wondered if the wall was high enough to keep out a determined redneck who might decide he wished to scale the fine brick to see how the one-percenters lived. She also thought she should have spent more time studying rather than drinking to avoid moving home at the moment her family relocated to Alabama.

She cut her eyes at her brother to her left and her mother in front of her. Rachel thought if word got out her father was here to close down more factories and sell off the pieces one truck and plane load at a time, she would be even less likely than usual to make friends.

They pulled into one of the driveways with a rumble that jostled everything packed into the back. Rachel leaned up far enough to see over the seat and her mother's shoulder. The cloth upholstery was hard and smelled of absorbed sweat and grease.

Sod clung to packed clay in unnaturally green squares. Mulch so brown and crisp that it appeared to be dyed with blood lined the curves of beds along the walk with perfect precision and organic geometry. Saplings stood erect aided by support twine in the midst of the slaughter colored beds.

Her father had purchased a pink house in the midst of lime green, baby-powder blue, and shades of white that defied description. Every neighborhood seemed to have one tacky, pink house and the Rathburns had moved into this one.

Men in jeans cinched too tightly under their paunches set aside fast food cups and bags along the edge of the garage before they stepped out into the unforgiving sun and humidity. The Rathburns climbed out of the U-Haul and the heat in the air punched Rachel in the face. She circled around the edge of the drive, keeping her mother, brother, and father between her and the men.

They were an unusual breed of humanoid. Shoulders slumped in a way that hollowed their chests within their dirty tank tops and humped their backs. Their eyes took on a wrinkled squint that would not suit them for any work other than their current condition in Alabama. It would be impossible to transmute them into suits and northeastern law firms. No amount of soap or schooling would disguise them as anything other than what they were. Open mouths showed misaligned teeth and gave the sound of wet, phlegm clogged breathing. There was no other word for these dirty, dusty creatures than that of redneck.

Their eyes drifted as if it hurt to focus upon people or concentrate on any one idea for long. Paint-spotted boots scuffed along the driveway and then the creatures peeled open the accordion door on the back of the truck.

Rachel's brother wandered into the house without looking up from his phone. She could not fight the impression that the place had consumed him and he had wandered into its jaws willingly.

A plane took off behind the neighborhood with a claw-like scream against the sky. As the private jet lifted away from the scorched earth of Alabama, Rachel dearly wished to be in one of those seats sipping whatever they had on ice.

The workers tromped about the truck and hauled off oaken antiques clutched between their digits while balanced upon the tilted wheels of dollies. One creature with a sunken chin and a prominent Adam's apple stepped by carrying a box marked: Rachel's delicates. His fingers disappeared into the darkness of the slots on both sides, hiding what he might be feeling. She swallowed as she watched and made note to be certain that box was still taped and all the contents intact once it was left inside. What she would do if she found it tampered, she was not sure.

"Come inside," said her mom.

Rachel blinked. The sun left her dizzy and seeing purple and green spots wherever she tried to focus her vision. Her mother called it glistening, but Rachel felt downright greasy between her clothes and her skin. She had not tanned while away at school, so she had no base in place to protect herself from Alabama sunburns. She might quickly become leathery and shriveled like these creatures her father had hired.

She turned for the shadows provided by the empty garage, but the line of movers stepped back out from the cavern darkness into the light again. Rachel moved aside to give their passage a wide berth. They lumbered forward with heads down, forming ridges with the protrusion of their spines from within freckled and scaly skin.

Rachel swallowed and looked away. She spotted the outline of her father within the garage, fiddling with hooks upon a pegboard. She had not seen him personally use a tool since she was a child, so she was not sure what he intended to hang upon the wall there.

The buzz of the next plane took on a lowering tone which told her the craft was small and descending upon them. She knew the sun would impact her eyes again, but she could not resist the urge to look anyway. Small and silvery, the craft reflected more sunlight into her face for her troubles. She imagined the plane serving some drug cartel, looking to feed the despair and desires of the unemployed dregs of Scully. Some of them probably worked distribution and sales for the illegal drug trade now that men like her father had closed the factories. She thought most of their drugs were of the variety cooked in sheds and closed garages and probably not imported.

Scrapes and shuffles closed behind her, so Rachel sidestepped into the rough squares of sod to avoid physical contact with the creatures that labored for her father. Two hauled the kitchen table and a third carried a box of plates with his dirty fingers in the slots on both sides once more. She would not be able to picture anything else other than these beings touching the table and plates as she ate her breakfast in the mornings.

"Why did we have to ride in a U-Haul, if you were hiring movers anyway?"

Her father cut his eyes from the work at the peg board. "I do not trust them to drive with our things."

But to touch them, she thought.

As the noise of the cargo plane died behind the wall, more light and motion drew her attention to the street. These creatures dazzled where the movers disgusted. Their skin was as porcelain and in the sun they appeared to lose their edges. They were almost impossible to view directly or comprehend. They seemed to be somewhat feminine and wearing pantsuits. The new, glowing procession mounted the driveway carrying casserole dishes.

Rachel's mother stepped out of the house fanning herself as she glistened heavily. "Hello. Welcome."

The leader of this line of high creatures said, "Welcome to you and your family, Mrs. Rathburn."

"I use a hyphenated name for business purposes," Rachel's mother said. "I sell candles and facial creams."

The women exchanged looks over their casserole lids. "Not from your home, we hope, dear. That is most definitely against the bylaws."

The smile wavered on her mother's lips. "No, not really. It is all on-line."

The women turned upon one another in a tight circle. They muttered among themselves all at once either in a language that Rachel's ears and mind could not process or in a tone that did not carry over the air so thinned by the oppressive heat. They turned out once more. "We will have to check with the HOA board to see if such a thing is allowed."

"Using the Internet in our own home?" Her mother forced a chuckle. "Surely."

The women's frowns seemed to dull the blinding glow of their pure skin.

"We shall see."

"Very well." Rachel's mother extended her hands accepting one casserole after another in a precarious balance one upon another on both hands and the forearms.

The women exchanged another look. "Your fence is over the property line. It will need to be removed."

They turned away and filed off the driveway without awaiting a response. A plane roared upward and through purple spots, Rachel longed to be upon it.

Her mother glared at Rachel's father and he turned away before she could say anything. "Gentlemen, would you mind terribly taking a break from the move to see to our boundary violation? I will compensate you handsomely, I promise you."

The creatures exchanged looks and one of them translated. "He will pay us to tear down the fence."

They slouched toward the fence and began their destruction. The white plastic rocked back and forth under their assault with the look of flimsy weakness, but the hold of something much more stubborn. The sections and supports split into sharp tears that threatened to eviscerate flesh, but the fence collapsed piece by piece as the obedient creatures pressed their attack on the barrier.

A plane hummed in and Rachel tracked it through a floating green spot. Some doctor was probably accumulating his flying hours on his small plane on his day off, she decided.

A man cleared his throat and Rachel spun about to see a white polo shirt, khaki shorts, and skin tanned beyond bronze to orange marching toward her. She glanced back long enough to see that her mother had retreated inside to deal with the onslaught of casseroles. The house had consumed once more. The man seemed deliberately muscled to leave an impression in his shorts and a polo.

Her father exited the garage and extended his hand. As he bowed his head to the blaze of light from above, it gave him a submissive stance that Rachel was not certain her father meant to portray. The new fellow locked hands with Rachel's father and turned his hand about a quarter inch over the top of Mr. Rathburn's hand. Their hands remained clasped and her father squinted as he glanced from the handshake to the neighbor.

"Your air conditioners are a problem."

Her father contorted his hand to slither in free of the grasp. "How so?"

"The units stick out from the sides. That's not allowed. It'll have to be resolved or you'll get a letter."

Rachel turned to see the window units protruding as metallic warts from the living room and the kitchen on the side. They gave a rattle and hum she had not noticed before. The drone of the machinery and the gurgle of chemicals drawing energy from the very air itself blended with the airfield noise of approaches and departures.

People weren't meant to fly, she thought. The words traveled through her mind like temporary fog and she could not explain what spawned them. On its heels, she thought, *People write letters because there is no threat of swordplay any longer.*

"We don't have central air," Mr. Rathburn said. "They were installed before we moved in. They were there when we bought the house."

The man shrugged. "The guy before you was quite a monster. We had to place a lean on his property because he would not remove them. It was very ugly and the house was taken out from under him. Nasty business. My wife is on the board and she's drafting up a letter now. I just came to give you a chance to deal with it before it came to all that."

"It's a hundred degrees out."

The fellow wiped his forehead and nodded. "I know. Relentless, isn't it. She told me to ask you to wash the casserole dish before you return it, please."

"Of course. Tell her we said thank you … and it was delicious, of course."

Welcomed with the poison of life, thought Rachel.

"Very kind of you." The husband of the board member turned to leave with his hands in his pockets, pulling the shorts tight over the curve of his cheeks. "Welcome to the neighborhood."

Her father stepped out into the grass of the side yard. With one hand over his eyes, he waved above his head with the other. Distorted shadows danced across the sod squares around his feet.

One of the creatures mauling the fence met Mr. Rathburn's eyes and wandered forward at his beckoning. "Sir?"

"I need the window units taken out. Can you assist me with that?"

The angular being cut his eyes back at the house, making Rachel think that some magic hung over the air conditioners wherein they could only be seen when one specifically looked for them and decided to see them. "A hammer can break most anything that duct tape can fix. Can we salvage the copper?"

"If you'll accept that as partial payment. Sure."

The creature wandered behind the garage and Rachel heard the hammers begin to steal the cold air from inside. She thought she should probably get out of the sun, but it would soon be as hot inside as out, so what was the point really?

She heard the metal door of the mailbox scream open and closed. Rachel turned and saw a young, porcelain-skinned girl in a flowered sundress. She might have been a few years younger than Rachel herself. Rachel raised her hand to wave, but the girl turned and shuffled away diagonally through the street.

Rachel stared at the mailbox a moment before she crossed the driveway toward the street. With the air conditioners silent, she heard the roar of engines between hammer blows. Two aircraft crossed in the air – one coming, one going.

In the mailbox, she found an unsealed envelope. RATHBURN blocked in black penned characters across the front. She thumbed open the flap and slipped out the folded page. It was typed and mentioned both the fence and the unsightly units. She assumed that meant the air conditioners, but the vague wording left a lot open to interpretation. The final paragraph addressed the house itself. Pink was not an approved color and aluminum not an approved material. It all had to come down.

She walked up the drive and her father stepped out to meet her. She handed over the letter without trying to explain. She watched his expression shift darker as he processed all the information. He did not look up from the page before walking around the side of the house.

Rachel watched three more planes rise into the air. They were all leaving.

Who doesn't have central air, she thought in the absent manner in which her thoughts seemed to be forming and passing. The heat was doing a number on her ability to form complete sentences.

The house screamed and she took a step away. The sun-wrinkled creatures that had touched her things and hammered apart the fence and air units for her father, now used pry bars and sledge hammers on the structure itself. She watched without comprehension as the siding peeled away from the insulation in drastic curls. Tentacles of pink siding with primer grey underneath reached above the roof and twisted around at her like mindless claws. More pink from the exposed bags of insulation spilled out puffy and sharp. She knew if she touched the threads of fiberglass, she would be cut thousands of times and itch without end.

Green and purple spots overtook her vision and prevented her from focusing on the unreal destruction. She could not wrap her mind around this being her home. She could not move her feet to go inside the stuffy belly of the pink clawed beast, but she did not desire to remain in the Scully, Alabama sun to bake alive.

She could not form sentences in her thoughts any longer even in the misty, disconnected way she had done before. All the edges blurred out of her vision and the house became shapes and colors that defied description. Her madness was surely heat exhaustion and a trick of the light, but it was madness just the same. She did not remember having a brother.

The engine noise changed tone, but she could not lift her eyes to look this time. She could not form a judgement of whether the craft approached or escaped. Rachel could not form a coherent wish to be upon the craft and out of the driveway any longer. She stood facing the house without really seeing it.

Soon she only saw the spots and Rachel whispered, "Stars? Not meant to voyage far ..."

When she fell and struck her head on the concrete, she did not feel it. One of the movers set aside his tools and lifted her in his hairy, sweaty arms. Like her delicates and the family's kitchen table before her, he carried her inside to become part of the home. She remained lost in a sea of blackness within her mind, ignorant that she was moving at all.

EVERYTHING AFTER WE KISSED

BY LUCY A. SNYDER

The water's moving fast, it's so cold, *I can't swim I can't swim oh God —*

Stop.

Don't breathe.

Hold on.

Time slows down. I am caught between heartbeats, hanging in the moonlit turquoise dimness. Above and below, dark abysses wait, comforting as cold wombs.

Do you remember that day when we were five? When we were alone in the Sunday school room? I think one of the big girls was supposed to watch us, but there was a boy who wanted to talk to her out in the hot South Carolina parking lot. So, she left us alone in the dim coolness of the repurposed double-wide trailer playing with my collection of mermaid dolls, and I thought you were pretty and I guess you thought I was pretty and then we were kissing like I'd seen people do on the TV at the laundromat. But maybe you were kissing me like you'd seen your ma kiss your pa because your folks were pretty strict and you never got to watch TV, not even when your ma had to do the wash.

I wish I remembered more about the kiss. About what it was like to touch you that first time. I know that it happened, because of what happened after. But trying to remember the kiss itself, it's like minnows slipping through my fingers in dark water.

The thing I don't want to remember is the thing I remember in high definition: your uncle Lonnie roaring down on us like a curse from God. Shouting about perversion and damnation. The hiss of his belt whipping through the loops of his Wranglers, and then all that hard leather lashing down on my back and my legs. Cutting my flesh. Yours, too. The thing I remember clearer than my own pain is you screaming, begging him to stop.

We were fucking *five*. It sounds crazy to tell people what happened. To tell people that a guy who claimed to uphold the Holy Word would do that to a couple of little girls over a kiss. But the scars on our legs and backs don't lie. We were both in bandages for *weeks* because of it. And nobody said boo about what he did, not even after the minister told my parents it would be best if they found another church to attend, since I was the "corrupting influence".

My older brothers and sisters blamed me for ruining the friendships they'd forged at church, and forever after I was the outsider in the family. It didn't help that our mother had a talent for playing all us kids off on each other; her quiver was full, and she had to keep us arrows sharp and ready to draw blood. Before the kiss, I was the baby of the family, the golden child. Afterward, I was either invisible in our crowd of eight or I became the scapegoat when things went wrong. My father always seemed to be working, or sleeping… I can't say he was ever really present in my life. He didn't make anything worse, but he never made it better, either.

You and I never saw each other again in that little town. Nobody protected us. Not our bodies, not our minds, and certainly not our souls.

Our kiss is why I never learned to swim. I was still in bandages when the aquatics programs opened up at the YMCA in the spring. That summer, when I might have had a shot at learning to swim at day camp, my parents instead sent me to a place where I had to sit and pray and listen to what would happen to an impure woman in Hell. The shame they put in me was glowing plutonium that settled in my bones. After that, I was afraid to show my body in a swimsuit lest it make me impure, or cause impure thoughts in a man who happened to see me. I stayed inside and read my Bible, because that seemed safest. To exist, but not really live, in the hopes that I would be rewarded by Jesus after I was dead.

I did every goddamned thing they told me to do, and it was never enough.

I spent the whole rest of my childhood believing that I was broken, born with a deep spiritual sickness — even though God doesn't make mistakes! — my soul malformed and doomed to hell. Believing that my only hope was to cast my true self aside and hide my secret heart forever while I praised Jesus as loud as I could. I prayed for Christ to make me whole and pure and turn me into the kind of woman a good man would want for a helpmeet.

And then, when I was 18 and getting ready to go off to Bob Jones University, the youth pastor Brandon called me into his office.

He started rambling on about how he was called to witness for the Lord, and part of me had started to tune him out when suddenly he was on top of me on the couch, whispering, *Oh, you're just so pretty, I can't help myself* and even though I hadn't said a word he clamped his hand over my mouth and pushed me down into the musty brown couch cushions. I didn't know what the hell was happening and I just froze up. Once my recoiling mind had registered that this seeming impossible, terrible thing was reality, he had mostly cut off my breathing with his meaty, sweaty hand and I was afraid that if I tried to fight back, he'd strangle me for real.

The physical pain was awful. But the betrayal was the worst. There he was, the ministry's golden boy, chosen above all others to lead the rest of us on the path of righteousness. And on a whim he'd taken from me the only thing I'd been told gave me any value in the world whatsoever. Just because it made him feel powerful to defile me in a way he was sure I'd never reveal. I could see it in his face as he hurt me.

Afterward, he wouldn't look me in the eye. He told me to stop crying, clean myself up and leave. I just asked him *Why?* over and over. He pretended like I wasn't saying anything. He only just told me to leave, and so I did.

But the dam holding back 13 years of rage was starting to crack.

Two long days later, my body shivering like I had the flu, acid rising in my throat, I went to the minister and reported the assault. I tearfully poured my heart out to that man. What did I expect? That he'd defend me as a good shepherd defends his sheep? That he'd unleash on my behalf the kind of Biblical justice he'd been preaching at us for years? Or that he'd merely extend a shred of sympathy?

But I received my second betrayal instead. He started lecturing me about the sin *I'd* committed by leading on a fine young man who'd been called to God. *My sin.* My sin of sitting there, hands folded in my lap, politely listening to a pompadoured bumpkin bloviate on and on about his personal relationship with Jesus and his oh-so-holy mission before he decided to push me down and violate me.

My sin, apparently, was just the simple act of existing in a woman's body.

I had given all I had to give and still this man expected me to erase myself entirely? The dam inside me was breaking fully open, the concrete cracking side to side like an open, toothless mouth screaming into the dark voids between the stars.

And then the minister was telling me that I had to be *careful*, that I had to be *quiet* and not say anything to anyone else about this, or people would get the *wrong idea* about me.

"You made a mistake, but nobody needs to know that you're not a virgin," he told me. "I don't want to ruin your future. I'm just going to pretend we didn't have this conversation."

At that point, I didn't give Shit One about my future or anyone else's.

"But what about Brandon?" I asked, my voice flat. "I know I'm not special. So, he's probably done this before." The truth of it struck me as I said the words out loud. He'd hurt me so *casually*. It wasn't his first time. "He's raped girls before. What are you going to do about that?"

The minister started spluttering a bunch of *how dare you* and *he's a fine boy* and *he would never* and I just stood up, grabbed my purse and walked away.

I kept walking down the highway until I got to the Flying J truck stop, bought a Coke, and sat at a booth silently weeping and staring out the window at the clear blue skies, wishing I could disappear up into them. I wasn't sad so much as I wanted to drown the minister and Brandon and everyone who turned a blind eye to their cruelty in the deepest, darkest trench of the ocean. That included my folks, because I figured that if I told them what happened, they'd side with the minister and declare me used goods, too. If they hadn't come to my defense when Lonnie beat me, they wouldn't do it now.

I'd been there for about an hour, assuming I'd become invisible, when a black-haired lady trucker wearing a Dixie Chicks tee shirt, snakeskin boots and skinny black jeans came up to my table and gently asked, "Are you okay, honey?"

I shook my head *No* and started crying harder. She slid into the booth across from me and introduced herself — her name was Annie Fernandez, and she'd been driving a rig for six years right out of high school. She was born in Argentina and moved to Fort Worth with her parents when she was just a year old. Soon, I was telling her everything I'd told the minister. And more. She didn't try to shush me, even though the cashiers and cooks milling around behind the food counter were sneaking glances our way and whispering to each other.

"It's awful what they did to you," she said when I finished. "Do you want me to take you home?"

"No." I furiously rubbed the tears out of my eyes. "I want to get out of here and never come back. I'm 18 and I don't have to be here anymore."

I thought about what it would be like going off to Bob Jones, and it just made me sick all over again. The place would be crawling with guys like Brandon — why wouldn't it be? It was perfect for them. There would be plenty of old men like the minister to protect them. Church and all the purity and piety attached to it was just a rigged game that men got to play against women, I realized, shocked to my very core at that cold truth. My parents and the preachers had all raised me to see the world in black and white, and in that moment at the truck stop booth, Christianity suddenly seemed the blackest of the black. How much of what I had been taught was nothing but a lie to make me be an obedient sheep for their wolves? I felt as though I was completely unmoored, drowning, but instead of being afraid or despairing I was nothing but angry. Angry at Lonnie and Brandon and the minister, angry at my parents… and angry at myself for not seeing any of it sooner.

I swore — and I'd never allowed myself to swear out loud before, and the transgression made me feel strangely elated — and slammed my fist against the Formica table.

Annie gently put her hand over my quivering fist. Her nails were painted turquoise to match the polished stone in her sterling silver belt buckle.

"You don't have to go home if you don't want to." Her voice was gentle and her brown eyes were glistening with sympathetic tears. "My mom and I got caught up in a cult when I was thirteen, but we got out… and I know what bad religion can do to your head. You can ride with me a while if you like. See the rest of the country. Get your sea legs under you."

And so that's how I ended up traveling around the country with Annie in her big rig for the next five years.

The first thing she did after I got in her semi was to drive to the nearest pharmacy to get me a morning-after pill, which she said should still work even though it had been a few days. It made me feel dizzy and a little nauseated, but I didn't throw it up. Two weeks later, she took me to a free women's clinic in Detroit and explained the situation so I wouldn't have to tear my soul open describing it to strangers. All I had to do was nod while she advocated for me. We sat there in the crowded waiting room for an hour, and I used the time to write a letter to my parents on some motel stationery that Annie had, telling them what Brandon had done, and what I thought of the church, and telling them I never planned to come back home and that they shouldn't worry about me. I didn't mention Annie for fear that they might make trouble for her.

She held my hand while the lady doctor took my blood, swabbed my cervix, and poked and prodded at my healing flesh. Thankfully, I didn't need an abortion. But Brandon, that Christian paragon of self-control and purity, had left gonorrhea brewing inside me. So, I got a shot of ceftriaxone and a bottle of doxycycline for the road.

Annie, knowing what I'd been through, was endlessly patient with me. I learned that she was a trucker because she loved being on the open road. Her mother's people were Romani who lived all over Scotland and Spain before they settled in Argentina, so she figured traveling was in her blood. She taught me how to drive her rig before she ever so much as laid a hand on my knee. The first time we kissed, we were pulled off to the side of the road amongst a seemingly endless sea of whispering corn in Nebraska.

And when we kissed, I thought of you. Tried to grab onto those dim memories and pull them to the surface. I couldn't, of course, and so the kisses I shared with Annie got all mixed up in what little I could recollect of you.

When we were parked above a cliff off the moody Oregon coast, she took me up the ladder to the futon in the cramped sleeping compartment over the cab, and my heart was beating so fast I worried I might faint. As a teen, I had dared not think of sex — certainly not with another girl. And I didn't care to think much about doing it with a boy. In my parents' world, sex was something a woman only did after marriage. It seemed like something you endured to keep your husband happy and for the sake of making babies for God. I'd never pictured it as something enjoyable, something I could ever let myself want... but I wanted sex with Annie very, very badly. The idea of it terrified me, but every molecule in my body was keening for her.

And more than that, I wanted to do it as my own personal "fuck you" to Brandon and Lonnie and everyone else. I desperately wanted to purge the poison they'd put in me.

Annie had already made it clear to me that what Brandon had done to me didn't count as losing my virginity in her book, because sex was something that two people chose to do together.

"Think if he'd stabbed you with a dirty knife," she said. "That's not sex. Him stabbing you with his infected dick doesn't make it any sexier. It was assault."

I didn't believe her when she said that, but I didn't contradict her, either. And deep down, I didn't believe that having sex with her would be anything other than scratching an itch. My hormones were just going crazy and it was something I needed to get out of my system.

But making love with her was... miraculous. I don't use that word lightly. It wasn't just that it felt completely *right* in a way that nothing had before. The feel of her body pressed against mine, her soft breasts moving against mine... it was as if I had been made for this. She taught me all the parts of myself that I had been told were dirty and ugly and never to be touched or named. And they were beautiful, because she was beautiful, and she made me feel beautiful.

I had never come before except maybe in my sleep. In my dreams. Annie had barely put her hands on my vulva when I felt like I'd been hit by lightning, my entire body twitching and every neuron in my brain exploding with pleasure. I gasped and started crying and she held me tightly in her arms.

"Sh, sh, it's okay, I got you." She gently rocked me in the hug and planted a light kiss on my sweating neck.

I tried to form a reply but could only emit a moan.

"Some women are one-and-done," she whispered. A touch mischievously. "But I think most of us can take another spin. Sometimes way more than just another. Think you're up to finding out?"

I managed a nod.

Smiling and looking tremendously pleased with herself, Annie went to work on me again. And I discovered that I had a practically endless capacity for orgasms. She set me on wave after wave after wave. I lost count, and nearly lost consciousness.

Somewhere around twenty or thirty, I had a vision. You and I were sitting knees-to-knees on the thin carpet of the doublewide's Sunday school room, just like we had the day we kissed. The room was dim, filled with chilly mist. My eyes wouldn't focus on your face.

"Look," you said, pointing to the corner of the room.

I followed your point. The walls were silently falling away, and instead of a bright hot South Carolina summer, the world beyond the trailer was a dark, moonless ocean. The stars burned unnaturally bright in the black velvet of the sky, reflecting off the ripples and bubbles of something surfacing from the depths a few yards away.

"The Deep Mother," you announced.

A woman with skin the color of a shark rose from the stilled ocean. She was tall, beautiful, terrible, with red-flaring gill slits on her neck. Below her waist where legs should have been were eight thick octopus arms studded with pale suckers. I wanted to run away, but there was nowhere to go.

"You have always been mine." Her lips moved, but I'm not sure she actually made a sound. "No false gods or prophets can take my place."

Suddenly the distance between us disappeared. Her damp, muscular arms slithered over me, cold and thrilling. The Deep Mother took me down into the dark sea with her, and as the water closed over my head, I tried to scream but could not.

I never slept well again after that dream. My insomnia made me feel detached and slow, and I started to have brief periods where I blacked out and lost time. I didn't tell Annie about the blackouts because I didn't have insurance. If she knew, she'd take me to a doctor, and I knew she didn't have the money. I felt okay, otherwise; I reasoned that if I had a brain tumor or something, I would get headaches, and I didn't.

She started worrying about my reflexes after a bad near miss with a tiny red sports car outside Oklahoma City. I had my commercial driving learner's permit by then, and she was officially my teacher. She made me a passenger for those next few weeks. I don't know if my mental state made a difference in what happened next, but it probably did.

We were back in Texas, traveling south down Highway 90 when we spotted a roadside farmer's market set up in the parking lot of a shuttered K Mart. It was a clear, mild fall day and we had the windows down a bit; right after we saw the market, the scents of steaming tamales and frying churros wafted into the cab.

"That smells really good." Annie craned her neck at the market. "What do you think?"

"I haven't had a decent tamale in forever," I replied. "We have time to take a lunch break, right?"

"An hour. No more." Her tone was stern, but a smile played at the corners of her mouth.

She pulled off the road and parked in the rear of the lot. We visited the tamale vendor, but her batch was still cooking, so we poked around the flea market stalls and generally spent a very pleasant half-hour… until we heard shouts of "La migra!"

Black-uniformed ICE officers swarmed into the market like a dirty flash flood into a desert gulch. People scattered, tried to run. Cops shouted and drew weapons on kids, old men and middle-aged ladies.

A little girl of maybe eight or nine dashed past us, and an ICE agent in mirrored shades that made him look like a bug grabbed her by the neck and lifted her clear off the pavement.

Before I'd even had time to process what I was witnessing, Annie ran forward, hollering, "She's just a little girl, you prick!" And when she grabbed at his arm, he barked for backup, and suddenly three guys had dogpiled her.

I tried to help her. I yelled something stupid like, "Stop, she's a citizen," but a cop grabbed me, too, locking my arm behind me and forcing me to my knees on the hot blacktop. They hauled Annie away to one of their square black vans while I screamed helplessly after her.

The cop torqueing my elbow let me up after another roughly pulled my wallet out of the front pocket of my jeans and checked my ID. But by the time they told me I was free to go, the others had taken Annie away along with many of the people from the market.

I illegally drove our load to its destination in Brownsville. Spent the next three days in that stinking armpit of a border town calling various agencies to try to find out what ICE had done with Annie.

But because I wasn't a blood relative, or her legal wife, nobody would tell me much of anything. I swallowed my distaste and tried to pretend to be her sister, but that fell apart as soon as they started asking ID questions. All I could do was hope that someday she'd call my cell.

I didn't know what to do with myself. I couldn't sleep. Life without Annie… it was inconceivable to me. There were a few thousand dollars in the account we shared. Enough to move someplace new, or to deal with a small medical emergency. I could take my CDL test and become a solo driver… but did I really want that? What *did* I want, besides Annie?

That third day in Brownsville, I was so anxious and restless I decided to go through the rig to clean and organize all our stuff. We'd kind of let things go for a few weeks. I had to get way under the seats to retrieve lost drink bottles and granola wrappers…

…and that's when I found a small mahogany jewelry box inscribed with the words "Mare Matrem." Sea mother? I felt a chill.

That chill deepened when I opened the box and found a silver medallion the size of a quarter. It rested cold and heavy in my hand. On one side was an etched address: 42 North Main, Playa Baja, California. The other side was a bas relief image of a pretty mermaid sitting on a cliff under a full moon. But in place of a fishy tail, she had octopus arms for legs. Just like in that weird dream.

My skin was crawling at the memory of my nightmare, but I was also halfway turned on. I decided to take a walk to a nearby McDonald's to try to clear my head with some coffee. While I was there, I connected to the free WiFi and looked up Playa Baja. It was a small beach town just south of the Santa Lucia Mountains. Some professional surfer I'd never heard of was famously from there. Searching the address on the back of the medallion took me to a website for The Velvet Curtain, the local theatre, which hosted live plays, concerts and movies. It seemed the town mostly survived on money from tourists heading to and from wine country. The pictures all made it look very pretty: the conifer trees a glossy green against perfect blue skies, the beach a clean stretch of creamy white beside the cerulean ocean.

As I sat sipping sour coffee in that dingy plastic booth and browsed those idyllic photos, I grew fixated on the idea of visiting Playa Baja. Texas felt like a suffocating tarpit; I wanted to be away from it. Annie's routes had only rarely taken us out to Cali. We'd never been to that part of the state. If I took a short visit, maybe I would learn something about Annie's past while I was there? I reasoned that I could leave the rig in storage in Brownsville. And pay her back when I saw her again.

The Greyhound route passed by The Velvet Curtain on the way into town. The marquee advertised a midnight showing of a movie called *Cthylla*. I'd never heard of it before; I guessed it had to have some kind of special cult following.

The bus dropped me bleary and disoriented just a few blocks from the theatre. I'd slept maybe two hours the entire trip, and my deprivation gave everything an unreal air. The town looked so pretty compared to all the dingy flyspecks we'd stopped at along the way that I had the unshakeable feeling I'd walked onto some elaborate Hollywood set.

A block away was a five-room bed-and-breakfast called Pillow & Toast: a pink Craftsman-style house with a broad front porch. Yelp and Google both said it was the cheapest, cleanest place to stay. The owner was a pretty blonde woman in her 40s named Jody. She wore designer clothes, so I guessed the B&B business was good. She had a stack of flyers for The Velvet Curtain beside the register. After I pre-paid my room in cash, I pulled the heavy little medallion out of my pocket. It still seemed cold despite how hot I'd gotten on the bus.

I set it mermaid-side up on the check-in counter. The moment the metal touched the polished wood, I started to feel dizzy. "Have you seen one of these before?"

Her perfectly-waxed eyebrows rose ever so slightly. "I have. Where did you find it?"

An intense wave of vertigo washed over me. I gripped the edge of the counter to steady myself. "My… my girlfriend Annie had it."

Jody fixed me in an unreadable gaze. "Annie Fernandez?"

"Yeah." More vertigo, and my vision doubled. "Did you know her?"

"Of course. I knew all the girls who went to the midnight shows."

It worried me that suddenly Jody seemed to have eight dark, shiny eyes.

"What… what is it?" I asked.

"It's a lifetime pass to see *Cthylla*. Did you come here to go in Annie's place?"

The walls of the inn fell away like cheap cardboard backdrops as the counter collapsed beneath me. Darkness poured in. I dropped like a silver ingot into swirling black saltwater.

I came to inside the theatre; after a brief moment of disorientation, I realized I recognized it from online photos. I was sitting in a crowded row on a stained red velvet seat as the light from the huge screen bled down on us all. I looked around; the seats were filled entirely with young women in bathing suits and bathrobes or beach wraps to ward off the air-conditioned chill.

At that moment, I realized that I, too, was wearing a red bathrobe and bathing suit that I didn't remember owning and didn't remember putting on and *oh god what had happened to me while I was blacked out...*

The girl sitting to my right distracted me from my panic by grabbing my hand. She had curly auburn hair and a dusting of freckles under her bright blue eyes. I knew nothing about her but I decided she was adorable. "This is so exciting! Is this your first time?"

"I — I guess?" I patted my robe with my free hand, trying to ground myself in physical sensations, and discovered that my cell phone was in my left pocket and nearly fully charged. That made me feel a little better. Whoever brought me here would have taken my phone away if they were up to no good, wouldn't they?

"The Deep Mother rises!" a woman intoned in stereo from the screen.

That snapped my full attention to the movie. A group of red-robed women stood on a dark jetty as ocean waves crashed around them. Beyond them, the octopod sea goddess from my dream rose tall and majestic from the restless water.

My head swam, and I thought I was about to black out again, but I didn't.

"This is my favorite part!" the auburn girl squealed.

The lead woman, who carried herself like a priestess, dropped her scarlet robe and stood there completely naked, holding her arms out to the tentacled goddess.

"Cthylla," chanted the women in the film.

"Cthylla," echoed the women in the theatre.

The camera zoomed in on the priestess' lovely, proud face. She closed her eyes. "Oh, Deep Mother, take me."

"Oh, Deep Mother, take me," breathed the audience.

The glistening goddess embraced the naked priestess, and her moist purple tentacles slithered up her bare legs to her ass and her breasts and —

— the girl holding my hand pulled me to her and started kissing me and part of me wanted to fight her off but another part of me was completely into kissing this pretty stranger while the priestess moaned and writhed in ecstasy above us and —

— I felt myself fall backwards, down, down into dark water.

I came awake standing on the beach. The moon shone bright and full, so I could see for what seemed like miles in that cold light. There were maybe fifty young women standing there in their robes and bathing suits… and at the front of the line, I saw a woman my age whose tanned legs were crisscrossed in white scars. White scars from a brutal beating with a belt she suffered when she was very young.

I felt like I'd been hit by lightning. I *knew* it was you with every fiber of my being! How had I found you at last, after all those long years, 1800 miles away from our home town?

The Goddess brought us together, a voice in my head said. *This is fate.*

Someone announced something — the blood rushing in my ears made it impossible to make out the words — but you dropped your robe and shimmied out of your swimsuit and started walking down to the waves crashing on the sand. All the other young women followed your lead.

I took off my robe… and my phone started playing the Dixie Chicks' "You Were Mine" in the pocket. Annie's ringtone. A tiny voice told me I needed to stop and answer it, but you were wading into the water and I wasn't going to lose you again.

I dropped the robe, kicked off my flip-flops and ran toward you, hoping I could catch up to you before you got in too deep, because I was acutely aware I couldn't swim. But as terrified as I was of drowning, my anxiety at the thought of you disappearing forever was even worse. I had so much to ask you. So much to tell you. I couldn't surrender this chance to talk to you no matter what.

I'd only ever waded in streams or stuck to the shallow end of hotel pools. I had vaguely imagined that the sea would be like a swimming pool, just big and salty. I was wrong. This water was *powerful*, and so cold it seemed electric in its force and shock. And it wasn't just the power of sheer size that I felt. Perhaps what I felt came from ancient instinct, the red sea in my own veins faltering in the vastness of its prehistoric birthplace.

I splashed on in despite my fear… and the undertow yanked my legs right out from beneath me. It pulled me down to the sandy bottom, shell fragments cutting my back and my legs, as it dragged me into deeper water. I kicked and flailed, trying to get some kind of purchase, trying to figure out how to swim, but all I could do was sink.

Exhausted, lungs burning, I stopped fighting. The strong moon far above lit the water around me in a dark turquoise, and I suddenly had the feeling I'd been trapped inside a jewel. And I thought, *Well, at least I will die in a pretty place.*

Something large and dark loomed close, and I felt the brush of suckered cephalopod arms curling against my legs. I thought I heard a woman singing some weird melody, and the sound sent a thrill through my whole body. But then I remembered that people hallucinate when their brains run out of oxygen.

This is it, I thought. *This is the end.*

But the thing I couldn't quite see circled me three times, then jetted down to the murky deep.

And then I saw a naked woman swimming toward me, graceful as a mermaid, her scarred legs powerful and sure.

And you swam right up to me, your face inches from mine, and when I looked into your eyes it confirmed to me that you were who I thought you were. You remembered me, just as I remembered you.

You kissed me, and I kissed you back, your chilly tongue exploring my warm mouth. You breathed the ocean's dark blood into me... and suddenly, I could take a breath. The cold felt like comfort. These depths felt like home.

You helped me tear off my constricting swimsuit as our bodies changed: webbing, fins, gills, scales. It hurt more than anything I'd ever been through... but it was glorious.

And when it was over, I gazed into your bulbous, lidless, huge-pupiled golden eyes and thought you were the most gorgeous thing I had ever seen.

I took your cold paw in mine and we swam into the welcoming darkness.

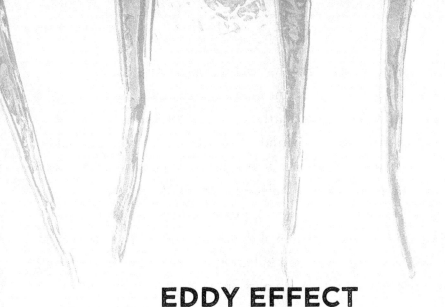

EDDY EFFECT

BY REBECCA J. ALLRED

Olivia slides into a corner booth, ignoring the "Please Wait to be Seated" sign, and flips her coffee mug right-side-up, bringing it down just loud enough to rouse the woman dozing behind the cash register. Aside from the occasional gust of wind and resulting chime of bells, the diner is almost silent. She and the waitress are alone.

No surprise there. The surprising bit is that Gemini Falls boasts a 24-hour diner at all, but Olivia is glad for it.

A lunch counter separates the waitress from the rest of the room. A dozen booths line the periphery. Those designed to accommodate larger groups straddle three corners, but her booth, the one farthest from the door, is the smallest of the lot: a cozy nook built for two.

The waitress shuffles around the counter and crosses the room. Little crackles of light, just barely visible, spark round her feet as she walks. She's wearing oval glasses with dandelion-yellow frames and a uniform the color of pre-chewed bubblegum. Her thin, blue-violet hair is done up in a beehive, and her lipstick matches exactly the vermillion embroidery above her left breast.

Olivia considers asking the waitress to join her for a cup of coffee. Instead, she moves her purse into her lap, comforted by the weight of the gun inside, and scoots farther into the corner.

She is in the midst of a kind of protracted, accidental suicide. Against her better judgment, Olivia got involved with a ruthlessly ambitious stage director and helped him track down and secure an original printing of an old French play that turned out to be more than just an obscure, career-making text. The thing that resided inside its cursed pages had first killed the director (killed, or worse), and then promptly set its mad sights on her.

Until now, she hasn't dared stop for longer or more often than was absolutely necessary. Olivia hadn't planned on stopping in Gemini Falls at all, but while the rest of the town seemed deserted, all buttoned up with the lights turned down, the cafe glowed with gentle intensity. A luminous oasis amidst a desert of night, offering succor and respite. Olivia is ashamed to admit it. It doesn't make much sense given her predicament, but the reason she stopped here boils down to the fact that someone left the light on.

"Might I interest you in the daily special? Perhaps a slice of pie?"

The waitress is older than Olivia guessed, and she speaks with all the enthusiasm one might expect from a woman whose golden years are measured in graveyard shifts at an all-night diner. She stares at Olivia, eyes betraying a weariness reserved for the terminally captive—familiar in a way that makes Olivia's head spin.

She's holding a pot of coffee and a small blue plate bearing a piece of pie.

"Just the coffee, thanks."

The waitress nods, fills Olivia's cup, and sets the pie down across from her before shuffling back to the stool behind the register, kicking up more ethereal sparks as she goes.

Inside Olivia's head, a carousel spins out of control, dizziness threatening to collapse into wholesale vertigo. She grips the edge of the table with one hand and sips at her coffee. It's hot and bitter. Grounding. She sips again, and again, deliberately experiencing each unpleasant drop. At last, the carousel inside her head comes to a rest, and she's able to reach for cream and sugar. Relieved, she adds generous amounts of both.

Cream sinks beneath the coffee's surface, receding as if in retreat before rising again in a burst of milky tendrils. Insentient, still they writhe in protest, oblivious to the inevitability of their own dissolution. Olivia traces a multitude of paths cut by the lactescent spirals, and with a few passes of her spoon, sends them all spinning into extinction.

Finding the sweetened coffee acceptable, Olivia notices the pie, bright red cherries bulging from between layers of flakey, golden crust, so plentiful they spill out onto the blue plate beneath. She decides she would like a piece after all. Olivia repositions the pastry and scoops one of the cherries into her mouth.

The door swings inward, admitting a wind born of darkest night. The bells above the entryway tremble. The lights flicker and dim. Darkness seeps into the cafe, overtaking it, as if whatever is attempting to enter radiates an inverse light.

He's found her.

Olivia tries to rise. Fails. Her legs have forgotten how to stand.

Olivia slides into a corner booth, ignoring the "Please Wait to be Seated" sign, flips her coffee mug right-side-up, and waves impatiently at the old woman nodding behind the cash register. It's impossible to stay in one place for longer than absolutely necessary. She's running, yes, but it's more than that. She's losing faith in her ability to judge time and space. Lately, they only line up when she's on the move, taking every opportunity to coalesce and intermingle whenever the need to eat, sleep, or refuel the car arises.

From her tiny booth, farthest from the entrance, she can see everything. The door. The bells. The lunch counter between the register and the rest of the room. She notes the position of every table and booth. Every inch of cracked and faded tangerine upholstery. Every fiber of the pea-green shag. Every detail is a riff on the familiar, because every link in this endless chain of gas stations, rest stops, and roadside cafes so closely resembles the last they might as well be the same.

Roused by Olivia's aggressive, one-armed flail, the waitress shuffles around the counter and crosses the room. A trail of minute sparks follows in her wake.

She is even older than Olivia had guessed. Much older. Her mouth, painted to match the vermillion script embroidered above her left breast, is ringed by creases arranged in concentric circles. Her recessed eyes are visible thanks only to the magnification lent by a pair of oval glasses with dandelion-yellow frames. Above them, a tower of blue-violet hair further accentuates the waitress's already considerable height. The ill-fitting uniform she wears might once have been pink, but it too has been chewed up by the years and is now the shade of stale bubblegum.

For a moment, Olivia considers inviting the waitress to share a cup of coffee. Instead, she scoots farther into the corner and shifts her purse onto her lap, taking a small comfort from the weight of the gun stowed within.

She hadn't planned to stop in Gemini Falls. Would have

passed through without so much as slowing, but for the darkness. Impenetrable as liquid spite, it drowned her headlights, forcing her to navigate the streets at an excruciating crawl. Amidst the blackout, she couldn't help but spy the cafe; it glowed irresistibly, a solitary point of beauty in an otherwise endless sea of night.

"Are you interested in the daily special? Or maybe another slice of pie?"

In one hand, the waitress holds a pot of coffee, in the other, a small blue plate of cherry pie. She awaits Olivia's answer with an air of indifference. Her eyes exude an apathy born of tedium and stagnation.

Nauseated by an uneasy sense of recognition, Olivia frowns. Shakes her head.

"Just the coffee. Thanks."

The waitress fills Olivia's cup, deposits the pie in front of her, and retreats in a flurry of electric crackles.

Olivia sips the coffee. It is too hot. Too bitter. Her stomach clenches. She grabs the cream and sugar and dumps a generous amount of each into her cup. A bouquet of tortured appendages blooms in thick, milky plumes, an imitation of the noxious waves twisting her midsection into a fist. She refuses to obey the uncanny urge to allow herself to vomit and stirs the swirling mimicry out of existence.

The sweetened coffee settles her stomach almost immediately, and Olivia decides the pie might be a good idea, too. Cherries, fat to the point of bursting, glisten between sheets of sticky crust. A few, livid as bruises, lie beside the main slice in a puddle of congealing juice. She sweeps a straggler into her mouth, and events twist back on themselves, infinite variants of this same moment spiraling out and away into a vast, unfathomable void.

Olivia looks to the door with expectant dread. In a few seconds, it will burst open, and bells, jostled on wind like the stale breath of a corpse, will sing an agonized hymn. Constellations of black stars will saturate the room with terrible, unsane splendor.

He's coming.

The door flies inward, admitting a gust of wind, somber as a funeral procession. Bells hung from the entryway chatter nervously. The lights flicker and die. Darkness squeezes all remaining light to a single fixed point.

Olivia tries to cry out. Fails. Her throat has forgotten how to scream.

Olivia tiptoes behind the counter, lifts a pot of coffee from one of the warmers, and slides into a corner booth, ignoring the "Please Wait to be Seated" sign. She doesn't wish to disturb the tall, ancient woman dozing behind the register any more than she wishes to be disturbed. Olivia inspects the waitress with a growing sense of unease. She of the dandelion-yellow glasses and blue-violet beehive. Her uniform, drab except for a vermilion slash above the left breast, hangs from her frame as if she's begun to shrivel inside her own skin. Olivia shies from a pang of familiarity and pours herself a cup of coffee.

Gemini Falls is the last place she imagined stopping, but given what's chasing her, it felt like bad luck to pass by the only wellspring of light in an otherwise endless night.

In that endless night, the cafe windows are transformed into a bank of slick, black mirrors. Countless iterations of Olivia reflect back and back and back. She wishes she could whisper through them to an earlier version of herself. Warn her when to look away.

Olivia opens her mouth, as if to confess this vital knowledge, but she feels the waitress's sudden appearance beside her. Confirmation comes in the form of a dozen more reflections. The hairs on Olivia's arms rise as *deja vu* surges through her like an electric current. She scoots farther into the corner, repositioning her purse onto her lap, but the weight of the weapon inside brings no comfort.

"Here's your pie."

The waitress slides the small blue plate across the table. Moldering cherries bulge from between strips of crust as thin and pale as damp tissue paper. Bloated and bruised, the skins of several burst, oozing juice like clotting blood.

Olivia lifts the cup to her lips, a premonitory compulsion bordering on lunacy, and pauses to recollect the coffee's bitterness before it has the opportunity to blanket her tongue. She looks to the door in dread anticipation. Reaches blindly for the cream and sugar and succeeds in dumping a generous amount of each into her cup and onto the table. In a few seconds, the door will swing open. There will be wind and bells and darkness.

The carousel inside her mind is spinning nonstop, and her intestines knot like razor wire. She grips the table with one trembling hand and again, dutifully, raises the cup to her lips. She swallows every sweetened drop. The coffee restores some of Olivia's balance, and the pain in her guts lessens, but she doesn't touch the pie or any of the poisoned berries around it.

Olivia turns to the waitress. To warn her of what's coming. Urge her to flee the King's terrible procession before it is too late.

The waitress looks through Olivia and beyond, a legion of possibilities transpiring and echoing simultaneously in her hollow, depthless eyes. Olivia, so preoccupied with what's been chasing her, finally sees the Something Worse that's been waiting for her all along.

The waitress glows from within, becoming ever more radiant as countless electric discharges coalesce around her into a crackling halo of static bioluminescence. Her ancient piscine eyes gleam, shot through with spider-thin vessels gorged with ichor that corkscrew and pulse like threadworms. Strands of blue-violet hair stand out from her head like a fan, drifting in a self-generated electric current. She is an ageless predator, borne silently through myriad centuries. Always alone. Always hungry. Always in pursuit of chance encounters in the infinite dark.

The door flies open, and a choir of bells wails in delirious terror. Wind like a death rattle extinguishing the lights, ensconcing the cafe in a film of near-absolute darkness. Only a single focus of brilliance remains.

There is no King here.

She reaches into her purse, withdraws the gun, and presses the muzzle to her temple, but before Olivia can pull the trigger, a coldness blooms in her stomach. A bitter toxin paralyzes her muscles. Her emotions. Her mind.

The waitress leans down, vermillion lips parting to reveal a throat studded with wriggling phosphorescent protrusions that fade into a deep, lightless chasm.

Olivia's hand twitches, one final act of insentient protest. A light, brighter than any she's ever dreamed, swells toward her like an angel's song, enveloping her in an ear-shattering promise of deliverance. Then it collapses, receding into a single pinpoint of light. It abandons her to the darkness.

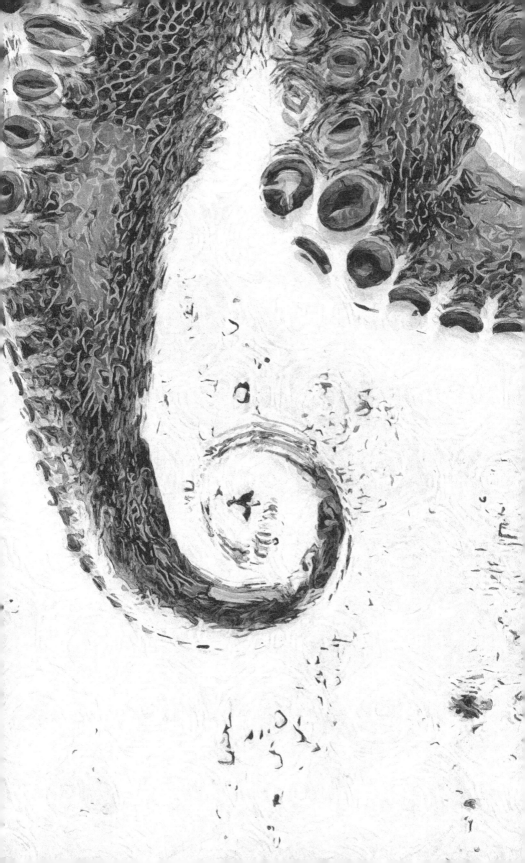

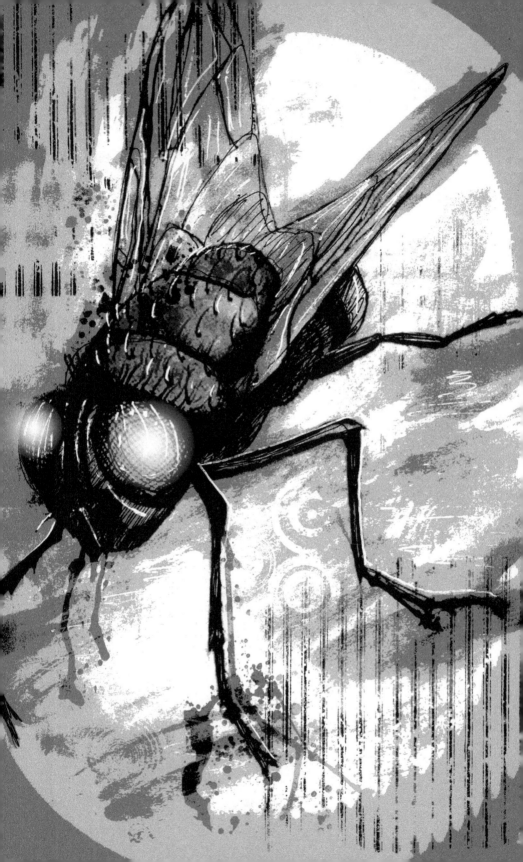

SONG OF THE BLACK FLIES

BY S.A. COSBY

Cici parked the car but she didn't immediately cut off the engine. If she did, the Bluetooth would disengage and she wouldn't hear the end of her favorite song by her grandmother and she thought that would be damn near sacrilegious since they were about to walk into her grandmother's former restaurant.

Cici drummed her fingers on the steering wheel as her grandmother's voice rose and carried the note she had been holding to the stratosphere while her great-uncle Swamp Rat Williams bent and stretched the chords on his steel body guitar until his sister found a place for that note to land.

"Ain't nothing but darkness waiting for me in your arms." Cici sung along with her grandmother as the song ended.

"She really had an amazing voice." Wayne said.

"Yeah, she had like a five-octave voice. Like Mariah." Cici said.

"I know I've asked you this before but it had to be weird for you and your mom when she went missing," he said.

Cici shrugged.

"I was a baby. I don't even remember. I've only seen her in pictures and on a few YouTube videos. It was really hard on my mom and my uncle," Cici said. In her mind she could see her mother crying at the kitchen table every March 22nd. The day her grandmother disappeared.

The story, as was told to Cici by her uncle Josh, was that on the night of March 22nd 1983 Jessie Mae Jackson locked up the Blue Note restaurant she'd opened when she'd retired from the road and had walked to her car around back of the building. Somehow, between locking that door and walking around the corner she'd disappeared. Her cook, Clem Washington, had been standing on the steps of restaurant's porch smoking a cigarette and waiting for his wife to pick him up. He'd told the police he'd seen Jessie Mae walk around the corner. When his wife came by ten minutes later, they'd driven around the corner and seen Jessie Mae's Cadillac Seville still sitting under the sodium arc light fastened to the roof of the building that housed her business.

Jessie Mae was nowhere in sight.

Clem had been the police's first suspect in the disappearance, but Donald Frame, the pharmacist who ran the drug store across the street (the only drug store in Maryville County) was able to back up Clem's claim that he'd been on the steps from the time Jessie Mae had walked around the corner till his wife showed up. Donald was locking his own door and had waved to Clem. Clem had returned the wave and the two men had held a short-shouted conversation until Louise Washington came to get her man.

"Well, I think she'd be proud you were re-opening The Blue Note. "Wayne said. He leaned over and gave Cici a kiss on the cheek.

"Let's go check out our future." Wayne said.

They got out the car and walked up the steps to the front door. Jessie Mae had purchased the former Sinclair General store in 1979 and turned it into the Blue Note. Cici's mom told her people from all across Virginia would come down to the little town on the shores of the Chesapeake to get her down-home soul food. Jessie Mae would get some of her running partners from her days on the road to come and play a gig from time to time. The Blue Note was open to anyone, but the black citizens of the Maryville embraced their native daughter and her new business with open arms.

"Friday and Saturday nights that place would jump. You could feel the building shake from people dancing and laughing," her mother used to tell her.

"People was in there smiling from ear to ear. Damn that Confederate Statue near the courthouse and damn old mean-ass Sheriff Hawes. The Blue Note was a place where you could just... be," her mother had said.

Cici thought if she had anything to say about it, The Blue Note would be that kind of place again.

She unlocked the door and entered the building.

The day she'd gotten passed over yet again for a promotion at McTaggart, Lehman and Trask was the day Wayne had suggested she follow her dreams.

"You've always talked about buying your grandma's place and opening it up again. We've got a nice nest egg saved up. And you're fucking miserable at that place. Let's do it. You'll be a former attorney and I'll be a former software designer and we'll reinvent ourselves as restaurateurs" Wayne had said.

She'd taken a day to think it over but when she got to work the next day and Martin Trask had mistaken her for a receptionist she'd gone to her desk and called Wayne.

"Cash in our savings. We're doing it."

They walked through the dining area holding hands. The decorators had created an art-deco neo-soul dining experience for their hopefully numerous customers. Pictures of Robert Johnson and Son House were placed side by side with posters of the Eiffel Tower and a globe from the 1932 World's Fair. Plush red leather booths lined the walls and deep brown oak tables sat in mute rows in the middle of the floor. In the back, near the entrance to the kitchen, was a small stage bracketed by lush red velour curtains.

"It looks…" Cici trailed off.

"It looks amazing," Wayne said.

"Yeah. Yeah, it does." Cici said.

An hour later some of the staff had arrived. An hour after that the delivery trucks started rolling in with alcohol, cuts of beef and lamb, chicken, and fresh seafood. Cici slid through the kitchen overseeing the preparations of her mother and grandmother's recipes with her heart fluttering in her chest like a butterfly.

This was it. They were really doing it. No turning back now.

Wayne was out front talking to the band they'd lined up for their grand opening. They'd come a day early to check things out and get a feel for the acoustics. Cici went to the office at the very back of the restaurant near the rear exit. When she'd done a title search on the building, she was shocked to find it hadn't been sold to anyone else after all this time. Her mother had quietly paid the taxes on the property for 38 years but had never visited the building since her own mother had vanished.

Cici sat behind her and Wayne's desk and put her hands to her face. Tears like drops of melted glass rolled down her cheeks.

"For you grandma. It's all for you," she whispered.

They were locking up for the night when the old man stepped out of the shadows. His dark brown face was lined with wrinkles that folded in on themselves like a puzzle box. He wore a long-sleeve blue flannel shirt and weathered blue jeans. His hair was cut into a short gray afro that matched his patchwork beard.

Cici thought if it wasn't for the flies, he'd be totally unremarkable.

Large black flies buzzed around him like a living cloud. They crawled over his faces and alighted on his lips like eagles coming home to their nests. They flew in and out of his hair like planes taking off and landing at an airport. Cici could hear the violent buzzing of their wings as the man stood before them with his narrow hands hanging at his sides.

"Can… we help you?" Wayne asked. He stepped in front of Cici. She looked over his shoulder and watched as the man slowly shook his head from side to side.

"You look just like her," the old man croaked.

"I'm sorry? What can we do for you?" Wayne asked.

The old man closed his eyes then opened them again. The irises were muddy as the bottom of a pothole.

"Jessie Mae. You look just like her. Same eyes, same smile," the old man said.

"Hey, man, I don't know what you want but we getting ready to leave." Wayne said.

"You knew my grandmother?" Cici asked.

"I used to work here," the man said.

"You're Clem, aren't you?" Cici said.

"Yeah. I'm Clem," he said.

"You were here the night…" Cici let the statement hang in the air like a piece of rotten fruit on a dying branch.

"Look, you shouldn't do this." Clem said.

"Do what, man?" Wayne asked.

Clem waved his hand at The Blue Note.

"This. Re-open. Some places are just bad. They got a shadow over them that don't never let the light in. Blue Note was like that long before Jessie Mae went missing. When they said it was gonna be opening again, I decided to come down here, see if that shadow had gone. But it's here. Touching everything," Clem said. He was breathing hard and Cici saw with some measure of disgust that the flies were being drawn into his mouth.

"Look, man, you need to move on down the road," Wayne said.

"Jessie Mae thought she could cheat him. But they always come for what they owed. "Clem said. He took a step back, then turned and walked down the sidewalk until he was enveloped by the advancing night.

"Well, that was enough weirdness for a week. Let's get home," Wayne said.

"I wish he would have told me more about my grandma." Cici said. Wayne put his arm around her shoulders.

"Baby, he needs to be dipped in creosote to get rid of those flies. He probably moldy as hell. You don't need to catch MRSA or something from him," Wayne said. He started for the car.

Cici lingered on the steps, her gaze following the path Clem had taken into the dark.

The opening night was amazing.

They were packed from the moment they opened the doors. Cici found herself running back and forth from the kitchen to the dining room to the office to help with orders, get cash for the register and help seat guest. Things were going better than she could have ever dreamed.

The band had played two sets when she heard the lead singer say her name.

"I want to thank the owner of this wonderful establishment for having us here tonight. Ms. Cici Miller!" He said it with a flourish.

Cici paused long enough to wave to the crowd.

"Now, a little birdie told me that Ms. Cici can do a little something with a song or two. You think we can get her to come up and join us for a number?" the lead singer asked. The crowd erupted in applause.

"Go on. You know you want to," Wayne said, appearing at her side.

"Did you tell them I could sing?" Cici asked.

"I might have made a comment or two," Wayne said with a wink.

Cici climbed onto the stage.

"Do you know 'Tall Dark Handsome Man' by Jessie Mae Jackson and the Tupelo Playboys?" Cici asked.

"Say less. We got you," the lead singer said.

The guitarist launched into a sticking, molasses-thick slice of Delta blues. The drummer and the bassist caught the beat and wrestled it to the ground.

"I'll back up the chorus," the lead singer said when he handed her the mic.

Cici nodded and smiled.

She launched into the first line of the song.

"I see a tall dark handsome man coming to make me a woman," Cici sang into the mic.

Cici closed her eyes and dragged the line to its limit, hitting the high note on the end of "woman".

When she opened her eyes, she felt her stomach drop.

The crowd was hypnotized.

That wasn't a euphemism. Every single person in the building was frozen in place. Their eyes had glazed over like wet diamonds, their mouths agape locked between a grin and a grimace. Cici turned to her right. Wayne was frozen in the middle of taking a step. The band was locked in place, their instruments in stasis.

"They are but flies drawn to the ruin of your essence."

She heard the voice in her mind like an echo that reverberated through her soul. Cici dropped the mic and ran off-stage. She stopped in front of Wayne and tried to shake him.

"Wayne, did you hear that? What was that? What?" Cici asked.

Suddenly the whole building seemed to… ripple. It was as if she was underwater and she saw the world around her undulate like a pond after a stone has been tossed into it.

Sound filled her ears once more. Laughter and the clinking of glasses and the playing of the band. The lead singer picked up the mic.

"I… um… sorry, folks. We must have had some technical difficulties with that last song. Let's see if we can get some of you out of your seats," e said.

He didn't mention Cici.

"Babe, you okay? You look like you seen a ghost." Wayne said.

"I… didn't you see me on the stage? Didn't you see everybody just stop moving? Like they were… I don't know, stuck in time or something," Cici said.

Wayne frowned.

"Cici, what are you talking about? Come on, let's go in the back and take a break," Wayne said.

"I don't need a break. I need you to tell me you saw what I saw," Cici said.

"Babe, I don't what you're talking about."

Cici took her hand off his broad shoulders.

"I... I... maybe I need a drink," she said.

The band played on.

L ater, as they were an hour from closing, Cici begin to convince herself that she had imagined that moment on the stage. The voice, the way time seemed to stop, all of it was just a dissociative interlude caused by the stress of the grand opening.

She opened the door to the basement with this thought on her mind. They needed another bottle of chardonnay for the nine-top table. Cici gripped the brass door knob and gave it a slight turn.

The door burst open, knocking her to the floor.

An enormous cloud of black flies poured forth from the basement. It filled the kitchen, then forced its way out into the dining area. Cici tried to get to her feet but the flies covered her face like a death mask. She tried to feel her way around the kitchen until she grabbed something hot and burned her hand. When she cried out, flies flew into her mouth. She coughed and tried to spit them out as she crawled across the kitchen floor.

She tried to remember where the door was by memory but the buzzing of the flies, their wings moving in time like a million small violins playing a song of desiccation, resounded inside her skull.

She could hear people screaming. She could hear the sounds of panicked footfalls as the crowd made a break for it. She could hear the breaking of her heart and the shattering of her dreams.

Wayne swept up the last pile of flies. He had filled two 39-gallon black trash bags with dead flies. The health inspector had shut them down until they could figure out what the hell had happened.

Cici came into the dining area dragging her own black bag.

"This is the last of them," Wayne said.

"Yeah."

She pulled off her gloves and her N95 face mask.

"300,000 dollars Wayne. We put 300,000 dollars into this place," Cici said.

Wayne didn't respond, not at first.

"Babe, we are gonna be okay."

"How? Who is gonna come back and eat in a restaurant that shits flies all over the place? Huh? We're ruined," Cici said.

"We're not ruined. We just have to figure out how all those flies got in here. Once we have an explanation for the health inspector we can work on re-opening."

"For what? Maybe Clem was right," Cici said.

"You know, I've been thinking. Maybe we talk to him. He damn sure didn't want you to open this place. And he was here walking around covered in flies like Pig-Pen. Maybe he pumped them in here somehow. Used a ShopVac to blow them in through a vent or something," Wayne said.

"Why would he do that, Wayne?" Cici said.

"I don't know. But I'd sure like to ask him about it," Wayne said.

Cici thought about what Wayne was saying. Clem had been the only person who was opposed to them re-opening the Blue Note.

"He can't be hard to find. There's only 8,000 people in this town. I'll ask around,"Cici said.

"I already did. He lives over on Town Bridge Road."

Clem's house was a ramshackle trailer with six cinderblocks for a front step and a dying rose bush that served as the extent of his landscaping. Wayne parked the car and started to open his door.

"Let me go talk to him by myself. I don't want to scare him if he didn't have anything to do with it," Cici said.

"And what if he did have something to do with it?" Wayne said.

"In that case, I'll come back out and get you." Cici said, then turned and approached the trailer.

She knocked on the door with three hard raps. Clem opened the door and stepped down onto the cinder blocks.

There were black flies crawling over his face and in his hair.

"I heard," he said softly.

"You didn't have anything to do with it?"

Clem smiled. Flies were stuck to his teeth.

"No ma'am. *He* did it. Just like he made your grandma disappear. Jessie Mae thought she could cheat him. But she was wrong."

"Who are you talking about?" Cici asked.

Clem sat down on his steps.

"You ever heard the story about Robert Johnson? How he supposed to have gone down to the crossroads and sold his soul to the Devil?"

"Yeah, what that got to do with my restaurant being taken over by flies?"

"There are things we call the Devil 'cause to call them by their real name would make your brains run out your ears. To call them by their real name would make your tongue boil in your mouth," Clem said.

Cici took a step back.

"What do you mean?"

"Old things. Older than the Bible. Older than the motherland. Jessie Mae knew their names. Learned from her mama. Taught it to your mama. Thought 'cause she knew their names, she could control them. She promised them things and they... *He* gave her things in exchange for that promise," Clem said.

"Are you talking about voodoo? My mom said my grandma fooled around with that stuff," Cici said.

Clem looked up at her.

"It wasn't voodoo. There ain't no name for it. I used to be with her band back in the day before I was a cook. Played standup bass. She took us into the woods once. Made a circle in the dirt. Took a baby calf out with us. Made us... do things with the blood of that calf. With its body. I didn't see *Him*. I closed my eyes but I heard him. His voice was like the beat of thousand wings," Clem said.

"What are you talking about? I don't know what any of this hoodoo shit has to do with my restaurant. My life is in that building and you talking in riddles,"Cici said.

"It's not hoodoo! It ain't the Devil and it ain't witchcraft neither. It's worse. It's something from way back before the sun was a flame and you done came here and woke it up!" Clem shouted.

Cici took another step back but Clem jumped up with a speed that he shouldn't have been capable of and grabbed her by her arms.

"Jessie Mae promised him the blood of a baby. A baby from her own line! And then she tried to back out! And then he came for her. Crawled up out that basement and took her back with him and if you don't leave, he gonna take you too! Take you to a place where the stars are black and the sky white and the way the corners ain't never right and ain't nothing but death there. And all you ever here is the beat of all them fucking wings!" Clem screamed.

Cici was crying, and then Wayne was there pushing Clem to the ground.

"Get your hands off her, man!" Wayne shouted.

Clem lay on the ground clutching at his throat. A sound that was half a groan, half a gurgle came from his chest. Cici watched as his eyes rolled back in his head. His mouth hung open like a broken drawer.

"Wayne, call 911!"

Wayne took his phone from his pocket. As he pushed the "9" button Clem moaned and sat up still grabbing at his throat.

A fly, the size of a raven, pushed its way out of his mouth.

It's wings, translucent like two sheets of tracing paper, caught the sunlight. It glistened, wet with spit and blood. It flapped its wings once, then twice, then flew straight up into the air.

Cici screamed. So did Wayne. They were both still screaming when he dragged her back to the car and tore off down the road.

Both of them took a Xanax when they got back to the house they were renting on the outskirts of the county. Wayne had tried a few half-hearted attempts at trying to convince her and himself that they hadn't seen a fly the size of a bird crawl out of Clem's mouth but as the Xanax kicked in, he went into the bedroom and stretched across the bed. Cici joined and soon they were both asleep.

When she opened her eyes again the room was dark. The sun had set and she could hear the call of whippoorwills outside their bedroom window. Cici got up and went into the kitchen to get herself a glass of water.

There was enough ambient light from the screen on their smart refrigerator that she didn't feel the need to turn on the light. She got a glass out of the dishwasher and filled it with water.

"Promises are made. Promises are kept."

The voice filled her mind. It stretched her brain to bursting. She dropped the glass. She didn't hear the shards dance against the tile. She didn't see the water itself run across the floor to pool at her feet.

She couldn't speak.

She couldn't move.

Standing before her was a being.

That was the only way her mind could articulate what she saw.

Gray skin like an elephant. A form that was vaguely human but grossly out of proportion. Hands that ended in talons black with blood and sticky ichor. A member that fell to its knees but ended with what appeared to be the beak of a giant squid. But it was the thing's head that made her nose bleed. Made her eyes water. Made bile bubble up from her belly and pour out of her mouth like a polluted waterfall.

The head was that of a giant fly. Huge insectile eyes glowed with a green eldritch flame like St. Elmo's fire. A mouth like a horizontal bear trap opened and closed in slow motion.

"Promises made of blood," Cici whispered finally.

Nearly nine months later they were preparing for their latest sold-out night. The health department had miraculously returned their business license without pushing for an explanation about the infestation. People returned to the Blue Note like nothing had happened. Wayne noticed no one spoke of the incident. They were all too busy congratulating them.

"Is it a boy or girl?" one of their customers had asked the other night.

"A girl. We are gonna name her Jessie Mae." Cici had said. Wayne hadn't agreed to the name but once Cici said it, well, it sounded like music to his ears.

He hadn't noticed the fly that had crawled out of her mouth.

PRAYERS LIKE GENTLY FIRED RAIN

BY JOHN F.D. TAFF

O utside the windows, the fires burn, in the city, the country. Maybe sometime soon, the entire world.

I pray for that, with each shot I take.

Here, though, inside, it is cold, growing colder.

The place is a shambles. Lunch boxes with their Marvel superheroes and Disney princesses, half-eaten food. Books are scattered everywhere. Smiling animals and colorful playgrounds and children skipping rope. Their little pages, their curled covers darkened, leeching the liquid they landed in.

I must have dozed off for a while, my head resting on my knees, connected to my cheek by a thin stringer of drool. I part it, wipe my chin and cheek.

A distant patter has awakened me, growing closer, ever closer.

It is coming.

He is coming.

Finally. Everything I ever prayed for.

I said my prayer, my first *real* prayer, the first one that meant anything, when I shot my sister at the age of eight.

I won't say accidentally.

We lived in Oneida then, and it wasn't a good time to live anywhere in Smalltown, U.S.A. Oneida was a husk, sucked dry by the loss of the mill that went overseas, the auto parts manufacturer that went overseas. Leaving the town like a jilted lover. All to make more money.

Oneida wasn't big, and the loss of those two pillars set the town teetering at first, then in about two years, careening into a pit too deep to recover from. The loss of all those jobs, all that steady income, meant some people, the smarter ones, left. Others, too stupid or too poor to be able to move, plopped right into poverty. They'd never really been too far from it anyway.

My parents were both too poor and too stupid to move from a place that was so obviously, even to my young eyes, dying.

It was as if God himself had left Oneida, packing his bags and decamping for somewhere things were happening, to China or Canada or Mexico or wherever all that commerce, all that money, all that *life* had gone.

We were left with the abandoned mills and plants, the shuttered stores on Main Street, the dilapidated houses, abandoned by smarter parents, the closed schools, the boarded-up churches with their orphaned gods.

My parents were like the town itself, never the most stable. I remembered, even when they were working full-time, food being scarce, the refrigerator empty, the cupboards bare. Plenty of mayonnaise sandwiches, and not even the name-brand stuff, some bargain-bin, off-brand white glop smeared thickly between two pieces of soft, airy, off-brand bread. And Kool-Aid, pitchers of the stuff, gallons, most of the time without the amount of sugar called for in the instructions, just enough to take its bitter, acrid edge off.

My parents spent their money on drugs, mostly alcohol, weed, and later meth. Our house didn't smell like the houses of my friends, with their air sprays and potpourri. Our house smelled funky with a kind of acetone edge, like a skunk had wandered into the chemical factory.

They were not godly people, my parents. After they lost their jobs, their drug use *increased* rather than decreased. Food, never in abundance, pretty much disappeared. Neighbors reported me and my sister wandering the streets on a number of occasions, asking for food.

That led to us being whisked away from them by Child Services, plunked down with Mr. and Mrs. Durrance, our foster family. Our *new* family.

Suddenly, my parents were gone, but food was on the table. *Food.* So much of it, and all the time, nearly whenever we wanted. Now, the sandwiches had meat in them, and the Kool-Aid was full sugar. It seemed everything was full of sugar.

We were blessed.

My parents died shortly thereafter. My mom of an overdose, and my dad of a drug deal gone bad.

As I said, not godly people.

Mr. Durrance, "dad" as he urged us to call him, was a true believer. He had a shrine to our God in his den, a wall of guns the likes of which I'd never seen before.

Dad liked to pray a lot, at the nice, white church they led us to on

Sundays, sure, but more so at the local shooting range on the grittier side of this gritty town. He brought me there often, to shoot little .22 pistols at first, but later larger guns, then rifles. He's the one who opened my eyes to God, the one who first told me *Every bullet is a prayer. Every prayer is a bullet straight to God's heart.*

Dad liked two other things.

One was alcohol, mostly beer. Having been raised by addicts, I knew drug use. While my parents had been completely out in the open with all the drugs they took, Mr. Durrance was secretive. He might have a discrete two or three beers in public, but the majority of his drinking was done in the privacy of his den, late at night, alone with that second thing.

My sister.

While he was bundling me off to target practice and hockey games, he was also spending time with her, when the house was dark and everyone else was asleep.

We were two years into our new family before I noticed anything. *Two entire years*, can you believe that?

She came to me, her big brother, a few times early in the morning, well before we were allowed to get up and watch cartoons on the big television in the family room, eating bowls of whatever sugary cereal "mom" had picked up at the grocery store.

"It makes my stomach hurt," she'd said both times she'd awakened me.

"Of course it does," I'd told her. "Makes my tummy hurt, too. It's all that sugar. But at least we *have* stuff to eat, and we're not hungry like before."

I thought she was bothered by all the junk they let us eat. Still can't believe I said that, knowing what I do now. She had to have heard it as *what he's doing to you is buying us all this.*

She was only ten years old at the time. How could she have heard it as anything else?

I finally understood the evening she woke me up with blood on the hem of her Little Mermaid nightgown.

In an unpleasant flash, I realized it wasn't about sugar at all, at least not *that* kind, and I was angry and scared for both of us, as if her words lit a fire with us at its center.

I'm embarrassed to say I immediately thought if dad was able to do this to her, what else might a few midnight beers loosen him up for?

I cleaned her up as best a thirteen-year-old could, tucked her into bed in her room, which now felt like a soiled animal cage. I kissed her cheek and told her it was alright. It would be alright.

Straight from there, I went to my father's den to ask God for help.

I opened the gun cabinet, which he always left unlocked, removed the shotgun, ridiculously oversized for me. Methodically, I loaded the shells, racked one as he'd shown me.

I left the temple, gun leaning over my shoulder like a Revolutionary War patriot marching off to war, brave and forthright. I crept down the hallway, my bare feet on the blue, sculpted shag, the low drone of the furnace working to keep the cold November air at bay.

Didn't think much, didn't consider what I was doing, what it might mean.

What my prayer might cost.

God seldom shares the cost.

So inwardly focused, I didn't hear the soft swoosh of her door opening, her own bare little feet on the same carpet.

"Cooper?" she whispered.

I spun, caught off guard, and my prayer boomed out in the narrow hallway.

It kicked us apart, like the opposing poles of two magnets. I hit the wall outside our new parents' bedroom, slid to the carpet with my ears ringing and my shoulder sore where the shotgun's butt had kicked.

She landed *everywhere*.

I could see two bare legs, the hem of the new nightgown I'd put her in, completely soaked in blood.

After that, it was all people screaming and sirens and lights flashing. Police and doctors and polite, severe men in suits.

In the end, they blamed it on us, not just me, but her, too. Playing with weapons unsupervised. Mom and dad went along with it all. They wrung their hands appropriately, made all the right prostrations. But they were only too happy to blame us, the fosters.

They gave my dad a slap on the wrist for not locking up his guns, removed me from the home, much to my mom's dismay.

Lots of weeping and wailing, but I clearly remember my dad's eyes as the cops escorted me out of the home.

He knew my prayer had been meant for *him*.

Before the clouds gathered and the fires ignited, I moved through a world I barely understood. Not because I was stupid. I got the world. I just think the world didn't get me much.

I didn't get *me* much.

After thinking about it for years, though, I knew one thing.

The prayer I'd boomed out in that hallway long ago?

That prayer hadn't been meant for *him*.

It had been for *her*.

My next family left me pretty much to myself. Weren't mean or abusive or anything, just didn't give a shit. Oh, they were nice enough, sure, and I was happy to have been taken in.

They knew about me, what I'd done, but their lips were as sealed as my court documents. Besides, they had two other kids they were sucking in government checks for, and I caused no immediate problems. Easy to forget about me.

For a year or so, it was all barbecues and swimming in the public pool during summer and cookies baking and holiday lights in winter. Until, that is, I realized what I missed wasn't the sugary treats, my *real* parents, or even my little sister.

No, what I missed was *praying*. These new-new parents weren't godly people either, not a gun to be found anywhere. So, there was a hole in my life where that used to be, and I sorely needed to fill it. I needed to hold a gun in my hand again.

I needed to pray.

How does an almost fifteen-year-old get a gun? Well, God bless the U.S.A. Aren't we lucky to live in a country that believes in God, prayer, and guns?

One bright Saturday afternoon, I ate an early breakfast of Pop Tarts and orange juice, politely asked my parents if I could borrow the family bike for a ride that afternoon.

They readily agreed, and my mom even pressed a few dollars into my hand to buy lunch while I was out, despite the dirty look the old man flashed at the exchange.

What they didn't know was I'd been stealing from them here and there for almost a year by then. Never enough to notice, and they certainly never had. Because of that, I'd put together quite a bankroll.

I booked to the town's Civic Center, just off the main drag near the roundabout with the Sherman tank and the memorial to the dead soldiers of World War Two—what the new old man called "the last great patriotic war"—at its center.

The parking lot was filled to capacity, and several cops were directing traffic in and out. Gun shows always drew a crowd, and since our little town was the county seat, this show drew people from all over our county, even two or three more rural counties.

The officer flicked his hand in annoyance, directing me to the bike rack. He paid about as much attention to me as my new family.

Good. I was counting on that.

I locked the bike as the old man had shown me, pushed my way into the lobby on a sea of people. It was close inside, hot and stuffy. It smelled of metal and hay and kettle corn, sweat and something even deeper I couldn't place, baser.

The main room was chaos, rows of tables with men and women selling stuff. Mostly guns, of course, pistols as well as long guns, but other stuff, too. Ammo, paper targets, clay pigeons, body armor, sights, custom grips, cases, locks, vaults, cleaning supplies, displays.

Interspersed here and there were tables of nearly all the local churches in town—well, at least the *white* Christian ones—handing out pamphlets and ginning up the crowd to gain new members. Some of the tracts were pressed into my hands by sweaty, beefy, red-faced men who flecked spittle when they spoke. The pamphlets railed against most everything—women's rights, abortions, rock music, Hollywood, the "effeminization" of men. The evangelical pamphlets also issued veiled warnings about Jews and black people.

I was fifteen, I wasn't stupid.

None of that even remotely interested me. I stuffed them all in the trash. They weren't *my* churches, weren't *my* God.

There was an atmosphere to it all, something I'd never experienced. I felt like a pilgrim in the Holy Land. All of this stuff, these wonderful devices to talk with God. I was overwhelmed, like Saul struck by lightning on the way to Damascus.

No one paid any attention to me as I walked the aisles. I mean, it wasn't like I was the only kid there or even the youngest. No one batted an eye as I fingered this gun or that, most not under glass or behind a counter, but right there, right out in the open. Free to examine closely, to touch, to caress like a medieval relic.

I came across a gleaming, well-oiled silver nickel pistol that fit inside my teenage grip as if it were made for it. A .22 caliber, five-shot, semi-automatic Smith & Wesson 61-2, known as a "Pocket Escort." What a wholesome, totally innocuous name, as if it were a friend or a pleasant companion who could also kill people if necessary. But I wasn't interested in it as a *defense*. No. It had a white plastic grip that somehow spoke to me of God and holy places.

That's what I *wanted*. What I *needed*.

I already heard its voice in my head, speaking the prayers I hoped to utter through it. The rhythm of its stuttering pops, the echo of its report like a choir in the nave of some great cathedral.

I told the obese man in suspenders and a suspiciously stained T-shirt I wanted this gun. How much? Just sixty-five bucks. I had enough to buy two, but thought it best not to be greedy. He'd even kick in a case, a few boxes of ammo, and a second magazine.

"How old are you, son?"

I wasn't anyone's son, and that angered me.

"Eighteen," I lied.

He scowled, battling ethics and law against his desire for my money.

"Tell you what, whyn't you bring your pa over here, get him

to sign these papers, and you can have yourself this little pistol?" Bargaining. I liked that.

"He's awful busy," I said, deepening my voice just the slightest. "I'm afraid he'll say no, and I'll lose out on that gun. Why don't I take the papers to him, have him sign them, bring 'em back?"

His scowl deepened, but he was hooked. "You even got the money, son?"

I fished into my pocket, pulled out my wad of mostly ones and fives, but enough to convince him. He pushed the papers over to me.

"You get those papers back before I change m'mind, hear me?"

"Yes, sir," I said. I snatched them, disappeared into the crowd. I took mom's lunch money and bought myself a hot dog, a bag of chips, and a large Mountain Dew at the concession stand. I ate slowly. I had to make it seem as if I actually had to hunt down an imaginary father, convince him to sign a paper letting me get a handgun. But I was anxious to complete the transaction, get out of there.

When I'd thrown the trash away, I used the table of the local Methodist church to sign the papers with my best approximation of an adult signature. I used my real dad's name and our old address.

I dashed back to the table, and the fat man was already waiting. He took the papers, scanned them, pursed his lips. While he did this, I produced the money again, began conspicuously counting it out.

In the end, he slid the gun, already in its vinyl pouch, into a plain plastic bag with two boxes of ammo and a small plastic sleeve holding the other magazine. The duplicate paperwork also went in, but I didn't care about that.

He handed the bag to me, along with a receipt for the money I'd finally passed to him.

"You don't go shooting no one's eyes out with that, you here? Don't want no angry moms coming for me."

"No, sir," I promised solemnly. "Only for what it's made for."

This seemed to flummox him, and I thought it best to get out of there before he called for the gun back and just kept my money. Adults were like that.

Swimming against the tide of people coming into the Civic Center, I finally gained my bike. I unlocked it, then used the chain to lash the plastic bag to the back of its banana seat.

I flew off, away from the congested parking lot, away from the gesticulating cop, down Main Street. Never in my life had I felt so excited, so happy, so absolutely fulfilled.

Soon, I would talk to God again.

I pedaled fiercely toward a wooded area to the north of town, out where the houses and buildings gave way to flat, thousand-acre farms stretching to the horizon. When I reached the woods, I got off the bike and walked it in, so eager to tear the bag open and let the gun speak.

I held out until I was deep in the forest, the dappled sun through the canopy of trees, the blissful buzz of insects, the chirping of birds, a distant train whistle. This cathedral was what my new instrument was meant for.

Unable to hold out any longer, I unlocked the bike chain, pulled the plastic bag free, let the bike clatter to the dirt. I discarded the plastic bag, sent it fluttering between the trees like a ghost, a soul fleeing the scene.

The zipper rasp sounded loud, and I let the case fall to the ground near where I'd set the two boxes of ammo. The empty magazine clicked out into my palm, and I tore open the ammo, loaded it carefully, my hands shaking.

Five rounds, and the magazine clacked into place, such a satisfying sound. I thumbed the safety on the left side off, licked my lips in anticipation. Assumed the stance my previous father had taught me, breathed as he had taught me, even and calm...

...and prayed.

When I really did turn eighteen, I was unceremoniously booted from my parents' home. No tears, no hugs, just get out. You can take your clothes, but pretty much nothing else.

I *did* take the one thing they never knew about.

I already had a steady job pushing a broom at a plant that painted car parts. That job was overnight, so as not to interfere with my school. Hah, right. It paid okay, but I got myself a second, day job to help with finding a place to live.

Within a year or two, I was settled. Had a one-bedroom apartment right on Main Street, over the empty space once housing the town's only department store. I was close to both jobs, close to everything really, and I settled in nicely.

I never once looked back, never once missed any of my families. What had they ever done for me anyway?

Nothing. So, they meant nothing to me.

Actually, I never saw them again, not once, any of them. Strange for such a small town as this.

Anyway, I lived, you know. With some of the money rolling in, I bought more guns. A long gun or two, several pistols bigger than my trusty little S&W Escort. Finally, an AR-15. Over the years, probably four or five more AR-15s.

Jobs changed. Finally got myself a place of my own, a mobile home out on a piece of property right at the edge of town, on a slight rise above the flood plain near the river. Bank had foreclosed on it, and I got it fairly cheap. Previous owners had trashed it a bit on their way out. Eviction does that to some. But I was able to clean it out, fix it up.

Had two bedrooms now.

One for me.

One I made into a temple for my God.

I kept to myself mostly.

I prayed a lot.

Things around me changed over the years, though. The country changed. People changed. Things slid so much I didn't recognize Oneida anymore, much less the country.

No matter how much I prayed. And I prayed furiously, but it didn't work. Somehow my prayers fell on deaf ears.

Television helped. I watched old movies and shows from the Fifties, before things began their downward spiral. Mostly black and white, but who cares? Good stuff. Wholesome stuff.

And the news. I found that news channel, the one real knowledgeable about what was going on and what it would lead to. Damn, if they weren't reading my thoughts. They had their fingers on everything, all of it, all bad, all stuff I knew would bring us down.

All the stuff I'd prayed for but had not yet been answered.

The other thing that helped, at first, was the internet. There, I was able to dig in, lose myself, meet people who thought like me, saw what was going on around all of us. People whose love of guns was a way of life, just like with me.

I fell into it like a cool lake on a hot summer day. People who had my same interests, my same concerns, hated the same, loved the same. It was a joy, and I fell in *hard*. Stayed up late into the night cruising the boards. When the boards died out, there were the social media sites, and I burned through them when they still allowed people like me to have beliefs like mine.

One by one, though, they kicked us out, and we dispersed a little, like the surface of that same pond someone throws a rock into. We came back together just as quickly, on more hidden sites, private groups. The Dark Web. We found ourselves there in these places, and that, too, was a joy for a while.

Deplorables, she called us. Yeah, we were that and more, and we wore it like a badge of honor. As great as all that was—and it was great, every minute of it, because I felt like I had found a home, a great web supporting me in ways my family, real or otherwise, never had—something bothered me. It became apparent right from the start, a niggling little thing like a spot on a mirror that remains even after you've Windexed it.

No matter how much like me everyone on my television and computer were, they *weren't*. Not really. At least not in the way that should have mattered most.

They enjoyed guns. Saw the problems I saw. Had the concerns I had. Hated the people I hated. Prayed to God for the answers.

It wasn't my God they prayed to, though, and this bothered me. I was able to tamp it down at first, but the spot grew, larger and larger until it blocked the mirror completely.

I had to acknowledge their love was the same, but they weren't willing to pray, I mean really *pray* on it. They weren't willing to do something about it, to save the world from all the evils pulling it down.

To save it from itself.

I had to. I had to pray my own prayers. Right the wrongs. Set this country back on the right course.

Watching television one night, I saw the answer.

Ever see one of those commercials where you're asked to support a child in another shithole country for just $1.39 a day?

It was the kids. Always had been.

They were in trouble, and I had to save them.

Just like my little sister, so long ago.

I'd prayed she'd be saved, and she *was*.

Who was praying for those children now? And I don't mean those dirty, shoeless kids in their backwater countries. I mean good, solid American kids, with their baseball cards and Hello Kitty backpacks and missing teeth.

Who was praying for *them*, praying to protect *them*, to save *them* from their country, corkscrewing its death spiral into Hell?

No one.

Certainly not most of the idiots in this country. Not my gun family.

Not even me.

I knew that had to change.

I knew what I needed to do.

There was an elementary school just off Route 3, only a mile or so from my house.

I knew it well, James Madison Elementary School. It was my school, off and on again, when I was a kid. Only one in town. Grades K through six, then James Monroe Junior High, and John Adams High School. All good, solid American names, none of this woke nonsense.

No need to case the joint. I knew the layout of Madison Elementary, knew it well. The u-shaped building with the courtyard at back between the two arms. Kindergarten through grade three on one side, grades four through six on the other. A cafeteria and auditorium dead center.

I also knew there were no "school resource officers" or whatever nonsense words they were using for police in the school. The town couldn't afford them. There weren't enough police to spread that thin in this community.

Good, because I knew there would be problems with me praying in a school. Such is the godless nation we've become.

There wasn't no planning or anything that went into it. I picked out my instruments carefully, loaded plenty of ammunition into a school backpack I'd picked up from the Wal-Mart over in Bonne Terre, a much larger town a few miles away.

When the morning came, I dressed carefully in my best clothes, phoned work (got a recording) to let them know I'd be missing my shift. Apologizing for the inconvenience. They were still finding it hard to staff all shifts because of the pandemic hoax, and me not coming in for… well, *forever*, would cause them problems.

I watched TV until about eleven a.m., then climbed into the car, put the backpack carefully into the passenger seat, drove the short distance to school. I knew the first lunch shift started at eleven-thirty, and I wanted to be sure to get there when there was the maximum number of kids to save.

As I drove, I thought of myself as a child, bouncing along on the green vinyl seats of our bus, no one sitting next to me, feeling alone, isolated. I shrugged that off. Not a memory I care to ponder over.

I parked in the visitor parking lot, just outside the main doors. I took a deep breath as I looked into the windows opening on the cafeteria, already abuzz with kids.

The signs plastered to the front glass doors said visitors must sign in at the main desk. I wouldn't be doing that, and they had no way of knowing since the school was laid out in such a way you could enter the cafeteria without anyone in the office knowing you were there.

The other was a simple graphic of a gun inside a circle with a slash over it.

No school prayers.

Sure. Right.

I hefted the pack on my shoulder, opened the door.

I went in, found no one about in the hallway. They were either in class or attending to the kids in the cafeteria.

Two entrances to that room. The first was near the main doors, and I went inside, bent immediately to set the floor locks in these doors. When I arose, I paused, took it all in.

Place memory took over.

The raucous sound of kids' voices echoing in the cinderblock room, laughing, shouting, being shushed by the cafeteria monitors. The smells of school food—pizza and chicken fingers and cheap government hamburgers, the weird tang of carton milk—whatever they used to clean the tables, the floors.

A woman approached as I made my way over to the second set of doors, bent to lock those as well.

"Excuse me," she said. "Have you checked in at the office?"

I stood, slid the small pistol, my original Escort, from its shoulder holster as I did.

"I'll pray for you, too," I said as I pulled the trigger. Its flat retort cracked in the hollow space, and the woman clutched her chest in confusion, then disbelief. She crumpled to the vinyl floor, and the cafeteria fell silent.

I unshouldered the first of my two AR-15s, checked it, flicked the safety off.

Screams first.

Then the prayers.

They moved away from me in a mass, like aquarium fish from a tapping finger, piled up at the set of doors I'd locked first. No one thought to or knew how to unlock them.

I approached, praying all the while, praying fiercely.

Praying for their safety, this country.

Praying to make it *all* better.

When I saw their faces, I thought of their cartoon lunch boxes scattered across the communal tables, the characters on their sneakers, the art hung all along the school walls, signed with crooked, scrawling names like Tim and Althea and Kimmie.

It nearly stopped me, but I also thought of the poverty outside, the lawlessness, the lies and stealing, all the great people doing bad things. A people in decline. Godless. I thought how these kids would not have to face this any longer. I had prayed for them, released them.

I prayed through several clip changes, then moved to the kitchen to pray for anyone still there. There was no one. The cafeteria workers had fled through the delivery door. Not one had stayed for the children. Typical. I locked that door, my feet slipping on some thick goo from a pan one of the fleeing cafeteria ladies had dropped. I saw my tracks through the glop, bright red impressions of the soles of my feet.

Back in the main cafeteria, I reloaded, heard pounding at the second set of locked doors, strident voices demanding to be let in. I fired a few times through the door, and the pounding stopped.

Bodies littered the floor, slumped over tables, piled against the far doors like driftwood left by receding waters. I prayed for a few of them, still crying out, moving slowly.

When my prayers were done, I went through the cafeteria line, made myself a tray of hamburgers and chicken nuggets, a few cartons of low-fat chocolate milk.

Ate and waited.

Waited for my God.

After my meal, I sat behind barricaded doors, looked out occasionally at the sea of people, the carnival swirl of police cars and ambulances, the bright lights of television vans, the *swoosh-swoosh-swoosh* of helicopters overhead.

My God was not among them.

What hadn't I done? Why had he abandoned me?

Is it just the way gods are? Their god abandoned Jesus on the cross, so I guess I shouldn't be too surprised.

I blew off the negotiator who offered to talk via megaphone. What was there to talk about? My prayers were made. There was nothing more *man* could do.

Eventually, I found myself pushed into the far corner of the room, away from the bodies and the blood. I cradled my Escort, full magazine in place, snugly against my chest.

Knew if my God didn't show here soon, those outside would.

Sometime after midnight, I awoke, confused to find myself still in the cafeteria, in the dark. I smell food that's gone off, the bitter odor of a coffee pot that's brewed to burning, the cloying, metallic edge of drying blood.

I'm roused by a thud reverberating up from the floorboards.

Another.

Another.

A slow series of tremendous shocks, getting closer.

Footfalls.

I rise, go to the windows now, eager to see where everyone is. I mean, God has never been dependable, but police and media? They'd *never* just up and leave.

They are gone.

And I know. I know the something stomping down the dark, tree-lined street is the answer to every prayer I've ever fired off.

More than that.

My God, the only thing that's ever loved me, the only thing I've ever cried out to.

Worshipped.

I can smell it as it approaches, all gun oil and cordite and that metallic slick of blood. As it nears, I see it outlined against the melon-colored streetlights, the fires and destruction it has left in its wake. Its bulk amazing, towering, blotting out the stars in the sky.

It is roughly human-shaped, legs thicker than tree trunks. Its limbs, its broad torso gleam like a god risen from the waters, its skin flecked but plainly metallic. As it stomped closer, I saw it was made of bullets of all calibers, hundreds of thousands of them, millions. Bound together with oozing scabs, vaguely red in the firelight, shifting like fish scale or chain mail.

As I scan up, I see its monstrous face, its eyes huge and larval, practically dripping fire. Or is it hot, hot, blood? I'm not sure. Mouth filled with teeth, shells of the largest caliber I've ever seen, easily as tall as a man. It gnashes those around what I see are body parts, severed arms and legs, gnawed torsos, crushed heads, dripping gore down its metallic chin, to bead on its metallic chest.

It stomps its way to the school's front circle, reaches down and tears off the roof of the cafeteria with one massive hand. Girders snap, concrete crumbles, and debris patters the floors.

With the cafeteria exposed, God reaches in and scoops up several bodies from the pile beached against the doors, lifts them...

...oh.

...lifts them to its mouth, shoves them in, mashes the children's broken and bleeding bodies between the bullets of its teeth, grinds them into a paste of blood and bone and brain, swallows them down.

Again and again, it reaches in, grabs more bodies, chews and swallows until there are none left. Its head twists, and I close my eyes, sure I am next. I will be its body and blood, to be taken in.

But no.

It fixes me with those roiling eyes.

"Pray," it booms with a screech of metal on metal. "Pray to me."

I open my eyes, understand. Slowly, I reach for the AR-15 I hadn't yet used. Fully loaded and ready to go. I retrieve my backpack, still with plenty of ammunition.

Kneel before my God.

It says nothing more, so as I rise, I climb through the rubble near it, make my way out of the cafeteria. All too aware of those giant grasping hands, those grinding teeth.

Without looking back, I set off into town, toward the fires on the horizon.

I am a patriot, a soldier, a saint.

I know. I believe. I *pray*.

We build our own gods with the ammunition of our beliefs.

And those who remain, if any, cry *Hallelujah*!

Hallelujah.

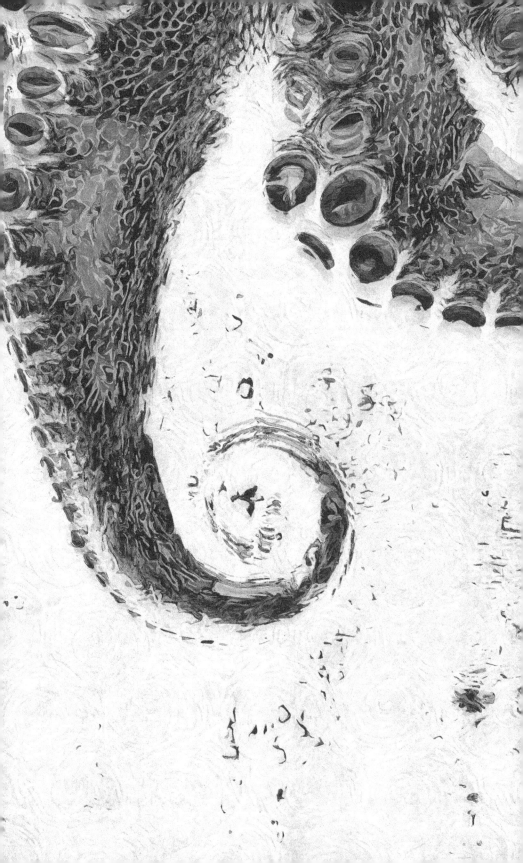

AND SO IT GOES, THE END THAT COMETH SWEETLY

BY MAXWELL I. GOLD

very so often,
I miss the feeling of being alive.

The touch of someone's finger across my cheek, the blade
that strikes the hair on an ancient head, dull perfumes and empty
cabinets with knick-knacks collecting the stale suggestions of
what-if and maybe-so. So it goes beneath a bunker of stars,
I cowered under blankets of withered dreams, the famous last
words of a dead man.

I miss them.
I miss the lights.

The stars, even the dreadfulness which cavorts amongst the
quiet thoughts and candor of friends, I can't help but miss those

awkward stares. The banal wonderment in the eyes of enemies
which crackles like the last bitter embers of a candle.

I miss it,
>   but damn the lights.

So it goes, as the blood turns brown,
>   and the flesh dries up there's nothing I wouldn't give to watch
>   the sands turn to glass under the long, dim shores of tomorrow
>   where nothing matters save for the decayed bones of old gods.

I cursed them.

Even the cosmic flash-death which boils atom and age beneath
its rancid blasphemies was a sweetness compared to the curses,
the flesh-tubes, and bodies that comprised of me.

>   Yet, I miss it.
>   And curse it to the end, that cometh sweetly for us all.

ABOUT THE AUTHORS

REBECCA J. ALLRED is the author of numerous short stories including *Behind the Veil of Pretty Pink Lies*; *When Dark-Eyed Ophelia Sings*; *Mother's Mouth, Full of Dirt*; and *The Last Plague Doctor*. Her novella, *And In Her Smile, The World* (with Gordon B. White) was nominated for a 2022 Bram Stoker Award®. Website: www.diagnosisdiabolique.com

LAIRD BARRON spent his early years in Alaska. He is the author of several books, including *The Beautiful Thing That Awaits Us All; Swift to Chase;* and *The Wind Began to Howl.* His work has also appeared in many magazines and anthologies. Barron currently resides in the Rondout Valley writing stories about the evil that men do.

ROB E. BOLEY likes to make blank pages darker. He lives with his wife and his daughter in Dayton, Ohio. By day, he manages and analyzes big data. Yet each morning before sunrise, he rises to strike terror into the hearts of the unfortunate characters dwelling in his novels, stories, and poems. His fiction has been seen lurking in places such as

Dark Matter Magazine, Pseudopod, Clackamas Literary Review, and Diabolical Plots. His poetry has been known to prowl in publications such as Eye to the Telescope, California Quarterly, Horror Writers' Association Poetry Showcase, and Undead: A Poetry Anthology of Ghosts and Ghouls. He co-founded Howling Unicorn Press with his wife, author Megan Hart, to conjure tales that thrill, chill, and fulfill. You can learn more about this weird figure of the dark by visiting his website at www.robboley.com.

RAMSEY CAMPBELL was born in Liverpool in 1946 and now lives in Wallasey. The *Oxford Companion to English Literature* describes him as "Britain's most respected living horror writer", and the *Washington Post* sums up his work as "one of the monumental accomplishments of modern popular fiction". He has received the Grand Master Award of the World Horror Convention, the Lifetime Achievement Award of the Horror Writers Association, the Living Legend Award of the International Horror Guild and the World Fantasy Lifetime Achievement Award. In 2015 he was made an Honorary Fellow of Liverpool John Moores University for outstanding services to literature. PS Publishing have brought out two volumes of *Phantasmagorical Stories*, a sixty-year retrospective of his short fiction, and a companion collection, *The Village Killings and Other Novellas*, while their Electric Dreamhouse imprint has his collected film reviews, *Ramsey's Rambles*, and his study of the Three Stooges, *Six Stooges and Counting*. Their latest collection of his tales is *Fearful Implications*. His latest novel is *The Lonely Lands* from Flame Tree Press, who have also recently published his Brichester Mythos trilogy. His other novels from Flame Tree include *Fellstones*, *Somebody's Voice*, *The Wise Friend* and *Thirteen Days by Sunset Beach*.

CLAY MCLEOD CHAPMAN writes books, comic books, children's books, and for film/TV. You can find him at www.claymcleodchapman.com. S.A. COSBY is an Anthony Award-winning writer from Southeastern Virginia. He is the author of *All the Sinners Bleed*, the New York Times bestseller *Razorblade Tears* and *Blacktop Wasteland*, which won the Los Angeles Times Book Prize, was a New York Times Notable Book, and was named a best book of the year by NPR, The Guardian, and Library Journal, among others. When not writing, he is an avid hiker and chess player.

ANDY DAVIDSON is the author of *The Hollow Kind, The Boatman's Daughter,* and the Bram Stoker Award®-nominated *In the Valley of the Sun.* His stories have appeared in numerous anthologies, most recently in the Shirley Jackson Award-winning *The Hideous Book of Hidden Horrors,* as well as the Stoker-nominated *Human Monsters* and *The Year's Best Horror,* edited by Ellen Datlow. He lives in Georgia where he wrangles cats with his wife, Crystal.

KRISTI DEMEESTER is the author of *Such a Pretty Smile, Beneath,* and the short fiction collection *Everything That's Underneath.* Her short stories have appeared in *Black Static, The Dark,* among others, and she's had stories included in several volumes of Ellen Datlow's *The Best Horror of the Year, Year's Best Weird Fiction,* and Stephen Jones' *Best New Horror.* She is at work on her next novel. Find her online at www. kristidemeester.com.

MAXWELL I. GOLD is a Jewish American multiple award nominated author who writes prose poetry and short stories in cosmic horror and weird fiction with over half a decade of writing experience. Five-time Rhysling Award nominee, and two-time Pushcart Award nominee, find him at www.thewellsoftheweird.com or on social media by his handle at @cybergodwrites.

LAUREL HIGHTOWER is a Bram Stoker Award®-nominated author from Lexington, KY. Her books include *Whispers in the Dark, Crossroads, Below,* and *Every Woman Knows This.* Her novel *Silent Key* is forthcoming from FlameTree Press. She has more than a dozen short story credits to her name, including publications through Burial Day Press, Cemetery Gates, Dark Hart Books, and Brian Keene's Patreon. She has also co-edited three anthologies: *We Are Wolves, The Dead Inside,* and *Shattered & Splintered.* She's a bourbon girl with an affinity for rescue animals and a tendency to hand out unsolicited advice on being kind to yourself.

PEDRO INIGUEZ is a horror and science-fiction writer from Los Angeles, California. He is a Rhysling Award finalist and has also been nominated for the Pushcart Prize and Best of the Net Award for his speculative poetry. His work has appeared in Nightmare Magazine, Never Wake: An Anthology of Dream Horror, Shortwave Magazine, Worlds of Possibility, Tiny Nightmares, Star*Line, Space and Time Magazine, Speculative Fiction for Dreamers, Savage Realms Monthly, and Infinite Constellations, among others. He can be found online at www.pedroiniguezauthor.com

JOHN LANGAN is the author of two novels and five collections of stories. For his work, he has received the Bram Stoker and This Is Horror awards. He is one of the founders of the Shirley Jackson awards, for which he serves on the Board of Advisors. He lives in New York's Mid-Hudson valley with his wife, younger son, and towering ziggurats of books.

ERIC LAROCCA *(he/they)* is the Bram Stoker Award®-nominated and Splatterpunk Award-winning author of the viral sensation, *Things Have Gotten Worse Since We Last Spoke*. A lover of luxury fashion and an admirer of European musical theatre, Eric can often be found roaming the streets of his home city, Boston, MA, for inspiration. For more information, please visit ericlarocca.com.

AO-HUI LIN enjoys finding terror in the day-to-day of domestic life, particularly in motherhood, which is why she doesn't want her children reading her fiction. The truth was frightening enough. Her work has appeared in various venues, including Drabblecast, Defenestration, Everyday Fiction, Jersey Devil Press, and the anthology Daughters of Icarus. When she's not at her day job, writing AI software to take over the world, she can be found haunting the coffee shops of Chicago, Illinois or online at https://aohuilin.blogspot.com

T.T. MADDEN *(they/them)* is a genderfluid, mixed race writer of horror, sci-fi, and fantasy. They've been writing scary stories ever since, as a toddler, they tried to climb their mother's bookshelf to get to her copies of Stephen King. They have published dozens of short stories, most recently in Pyre Magazine, Grim & Gilded Magazine, and anthologies by Bag of Bones Press. Their genderbending mech/kaiju novella, The Cosmic Color, is being published in 2024 by Neon Hemlock. They can be found on most social media as @ttmaddenwrites.

LUCY A. SNYDER is the Shirley Jackson Award-nominated and five-time Bram Stoker Award-winning author of 16 books and 120 published short stories. Her most recent novels are *Sister, Maiden, Monster* and the forthcoming *The Star-Stained Soul*, both from Tor Nightfire. She also wrote the novels *Spellbent, Shotgun Sorceress*, and *Switchblade Goddess*, and the collections *Halloween Season, Garden of Eldritch Delights, While the Black Stars Burn, Soft Apocalypses, Orchid Carousals,* and *Installing Linux on a Dead Badger*. Her writing has appeared in *Asimov's Science Fiction, Apex Magazine, Nightmare Magazine, Pseudopod, Strange Horizons,* and *Best Horror of the Year*. She lives near Columbus, Ohio with a jungle of houseplants, a clowder of cats, schools of fish, a pair of turtles, a lounge of lizards, and an insomnia of housemates. You can learn more about her at www.lucysnyder.com.

JOHN F.D. TAFF is the World Fantasy Award-nominated and multiple Bram Stoker Award®-nominated author of *The End in All Beginnings* and *The Fearing*. His short stories and novellas have appeared in innumerable magazines and anthologies over the last thirty years. Peter Straub once tweeted that he was "mighty cool," which Taff will undoubtedly have engraved on his tombstone. Taff's recent work can be seen in *Dark Stars,* the anthology he edited and contributed to, from Tor/Nightfire. Other work will appear in *Morbidologies, Shadows Over Main Street 3,* and a few anthologies that haven't been announced yet. You can follow Taff on Twitter @ johnfdtaff or visit his much-neglected blog johnfdtaff.com.

JAY WILBURN was a Splatterpunk Award-nominated author. He was very proud of that, but he had so much more to be proud of in his writing career. He was a full-time author, able to take care of his family with his writing, and he took the time to mentor other authors along the way. He was giving, caring and to have met him was a true gift. He will be sorely missed by the horror and writing communities.

ABOUT THE EDITORS

DOUG MURANO is a Bram Stoker Award®-winning, Shirley Jackson Award-winning editor and founder of Bad Hand Books. Visit www.badhandbooks.com for more information.

D. ALEXANDER WARD is an author and anthologist. His most recent novels are *Pound of Flesh* and *Beneath Ash & Bone*.

He edited the Bram Stoker Award®-nominated anthologies *Lost Highways: Dark Fictions From the Road* and *Gutted: Beautiful Horror Stories* (co-edited) as well as *The Seven Deadliest* (co-edited) and *Shadows Over Main Street,* Volumes 1, 2, and 3 (co-edited).

He is an Active Member of the Horror Writers Association and operates Bleeding Edge Books.

He lives near the farm where he grew up and spends his nights penning, collecting, and publishing tales of the dark, strange, and fantastic.

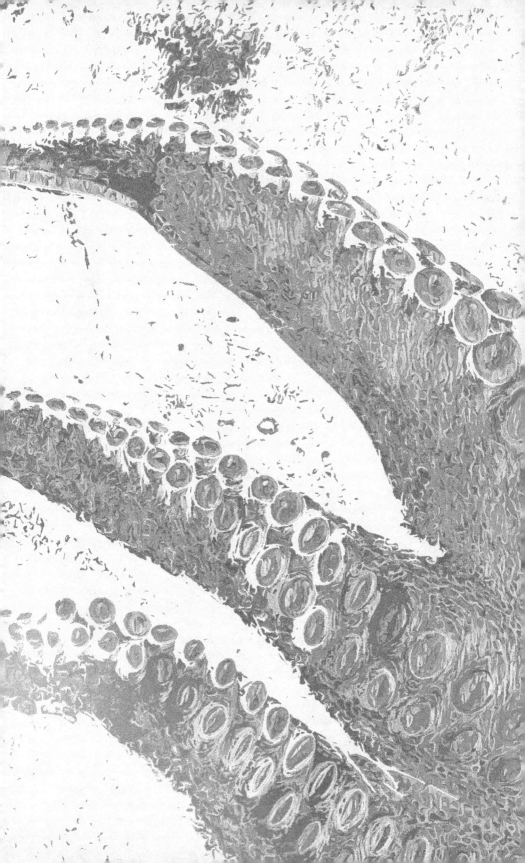

Printed in the USA
CPSIA information can be obtained
at www.ICGtesting.com
JSHW022242070923
47896JS00002B/6